The Three Kings

Also by Alisa Valdes-Rodriguez

◆

The Husband Habit

Dirty Girls on Top

Haters

Make Him Look Good

Playing with Boys

The Dirty Girls Social Club

To Sandra, merry Xmas!

The Three Kings

❧

Alisa
Valdes-Rodriguez

[signature]

St. Martin's Griffin
New York

This is a work of fiction. All of the characters, organizations, and events portrayed in this novel are either products of the author's imagination or are used fictitiously.

This book is dedicated in loving memory to my beautiful, outspoken, recently departed maternal grandmother, Kathleen Elizabeth Conant, who held the New Mexico family together in spite of it all, loved God with all her heart, and made every Christmas special. It is also dedicated to all my New Mexico friends and family, and to the state itself, as it is home to my spirit and forever will be.

Acknowledgments

I wish to acknowledge all of those whose work behind the scenes made this book possible, including but not limited to: my tireless editor, Elizabeth Beier; her inexhaustible assistant, Michelle Richter; artist Mimi Bark, for the cheery cover; designer Kathie Parise, for the snappy, stylish pages; copy editor Julie Gutin; production editor Elizabeth Curione; marketing whiz Joe Goldschein; publicist Nadea Mina; *Latina* magazine for reprinting portions of the book; and last but not least, my devoted readers, whose continued support enables me to do what I love for a living. Thank you all.

The Three Kings

A man in a silver suit and black cowboy hat stands in the bright, high-ceilinged foyer of his modern foothill mansion, molesting his iPhone.

At least that's how it looks to me.

Then again, after spending the past ten months reading *The Rules*, *Love in 90 Days*, and other assorted old and new dating advice tomes for single (or, in my case, bitterly divorced) women, I have begun to cultivate a paranoid view of men as ad hoc rulers of the world who are supposed to be placated and appeased—and, ultimately, trapped—by the likes of me.

Not that I want to date *this* particular man. I don't. He's a client, and his wife is just outside, inspecting the backyard. I am their interior designer. I make the insides of buildings beautiful, while my own innards are a maelstrom of insecurities and disillusionment, romantically speaking.

This man is rich, and his wife is beautiful in the way Rules Girls ought to be beautiful—she is feminine, wears heels, and has long hair. She is mysterious and doesn't talk too much. She laughs at his jokes, but not for too long. She keeps him guessing, and wanting more. In other words, she is the opposite of me. I am trying to be a Rules Girl, but then I see guys like this and I wonder if I'd ever even be happy with one of them. I mean, if you snare a man by lying to him about your essential nature and character, isn't that a disaster waiting to happen? Oh, right, that's what happened in my marriage—only it was Zach who snared me with the illusion that he was, you know, straight.

My client watches me for a moment, with an unclean grin on his face. He once suggested we meet without his wife around, and he winked as he said it. A certain kind of men *all* do this, I am convinced. The powerful kind. For them, women are accessories. I declined, because as a Rules Girl I do not date married men, or cokeheads, or— Well, at this point I don't seem to be dating anybody.

I'm on an online dating site—two, actually, per suggestion of the *Love in 90 Days* lady, and what you get in New Mexico is grim—men who confuse "are" with "our," and who pose in their own bathrooms, taking their own photos with a cheap camera phone, wearing undershirts and with filthy towels all over the floor. They wink at me every day on the site, and every day I delete them all without responding. I'm trying to move on from the painful divorce, but it seems there is no one to move on with. There was one I almost met, but then I Googled him and discovered he belonged to one of those Renaissance clubs where grown men dress up like knights and battle each other at Bataan Park on Saturday afternoons. In his free time, he dressed up like a Stormtrooper and went to *Star Wars* conventions. Scary.

My client. Look at him. Tap, tap, tap. Sniff, sniff, sniff. Touch the nose, look around with paranoid urgency, then back to the phone, tap, tap. Now and then, he snickers wickedly, like something small and slimy off the Cartoon Network. It's like watching a nervous gerbil with a head cold. I try to remember why, exactly, I love my job. Pretty things, as I recall. Right. Pretty things. I have coveted pretty, high-quality things all my life, the result of having been dragged exhausted from the swap meet to the flea market to the thrift store by my miserly mother, in her never-ending quest for inexpensive beauty. He's not a pretty thing himself, this client-o-mine, but he can afford pretty things, and I am the one hired to scour the ends of the earth to find them, buy them, and place them in his home for him.

The rest of the world, the people around him, the house I've worked three months to perfect for him, mean nothing. He's a trader, a wheeler-dealer, a Yosemite Sam lost in a bucking bronco of bucks—or something. Illumination from the enormous modern chandelier makes his puffy white hair glow like some sort of radioactive marshmallow. He is the cowboy Andy Warhol king of the marshmallow men whom The Rules were designed to trap. A real prize, we are told. He chuckles to himself, something helpless and exploitable no doubt caught in his business net and flopping in death throes. Success, American style. Millionaire.

I stare at him and wonder if this is simply what all successful men are like, in the end. Selfish and ugly. I believe so. I wonder, then, why I have wasted the past year trying to get one of them to notice me.

I realize, with a gut-thud of misery, that I will never be able to love any man other than my ex-husband, who left me a year ago saying he was gay. I still cannot believe it; not Zach! He's a grungy kind of tall and (I once believed) thoughtful, gentle white-guy architect with flannel shirts, ratty baseball caps, and a stubbly baby face with soft pink lips and laughing green eyes;

and he came out of the closet almost exactly a year ago, on New Year's Eve, at The Pink Adobe restaurant in Santa Fe.

Why, I wonder, do we women turn ourselves inside out for these beasts? Why do we work so hard to please them when, in the end, they all seem so perfectly pleased to be themselves regardless of what we say or do?

Men. I ask you, who the hell can trust them?

*C*onversation one is with my friend Crystal's husband, Fred. Crystal is a doctor. She is a good doctor, a cardiologist in the land of fry bread, and went to an Ivy League school. Fred never finished college because he figured out you could have a keg party without paying tuition. They're as mismatched as a mare and a pigeon. I have a lot of female friends in this predicament in Albuquerque, because we are Latinas and feel like we should marry Latinos, and then we end up realizing that the ones who finished college all married gringas or moved out of state, and whatever's left is, well, Fred.

Crystal is tall and beautiful. Fred is not. They have two beautiful children who take after their mother. Fred used to have money because he, like his father, worked building houses. I don't mean Fred was a construction worker. I mean he designed and built houses, without a degree, because Fred is smart and funny and charming in spite of being very short and driving a very big truck. Crystal met him in Mexico on vacation and fell in love with him, even though she is ten years older and he uses double negatives.

At any rate, Fred came over, per Crystal's insistence, after Zach moved out, when I had trouble connecting my new home-theater sound system. Fred knows how to do these manly sorts of things, and Crystal had joked that she was going to share her husband with me now that mine was playing patty-cake with the rainbow flag coalition.

So he's at my house, putting things together. We talk a bit, and then he goes home, and fifteen minutes later I have a text message from him, saying: "U lkd hot 2day."

I stared at it for a bit, and texted back: "Did you send this to the wrong person?"

Fred: "Nope."

I wrote nothing back, and ten minutes later I get another one: "ScaredU off?"

My text: "No. Just confused."

Fred's text: "Don'tB UR hot n Im a man. LOL."

My text: "LOL?"

Fred's text: "Ur uptite? want2jump u. just say the wrd i'll cum bk."

At that point, I threatened to forward the messages to Crystal, and Fred called to tell me she'd never believe they were real, because everyone knows what divorced Latina women are like, especially ones who wear low-cut blouses when men come over. I did not bother to tell him the low-cut, colorful blouse was what had been advised to me by The Rules, not something I would have ever actually bought, and that I didn't think of him as a *man*, exactly. He was Fred.

I looked in the mirror next to the front door of my condo, and tried to see what he saw. I didn't see a cheap whore, however. I saw me, five-four, fit at last after a lifetime of being chubby, with a controlled, chin-length layered bob, brown with subtle highlights and sideswept bangs. I saw an efficient, intelligent professional woman with mocha skin, an oval face, and pretty brown eyes that men liked to point out, back when I was fat, right before they said I'd be beautiful if I lost weight. I'd lost the weight over six determined months a few years back. I guessed I was fine now, a size four with toned legs and decent cleavage in spite of all the cardio. I didn't *feel* fine, however. I looked good, in an objective sort of way, but once you've been fat you never really believe the mirror anyway.

My text: "U r a pig."

He let me know he was "just playing," and that he'd never cheat on my friend.

Yeah, right.

I wondered what's worse, a gay ex or a philandering hubby? They both sucked; one literally, of course, and with great sloppy wetness; and one figuratively, via passive-aggressive texting.

I'd call it a draw.

Back to the client, and meandering thoughts.

You don't ever think a man like Zach could ever *be* gay, because he oozes competent log-cabin-bow-legged manliness and never puts his dirty clothes in the hamper. I'm not sure he even knows the word *hamper*. He can't cook, not even a can of soup—in his burly hands, it's a can't of soup. He can barely find the ice function on the fridge door. His hobby is rehabilitating Harley-Davidson bikes while Snow Patrol blares, and it used to be that when I was out of town on business he'd sneak off to Hooters or Twin Peaks or whatever the new boob restaurant was with his buddies, and if I found out, insist it had been "for the wings," which made me wonder if he thought women wore their wings on the front.

Zach talks Thom Hartmann and football with his dude buddies, called dude buddies because they "dude" each other constantly. They all hold their beer bottles between two large fingers, not needing a thumb, and flip it to their lips like flicking dried *mocos* out the window of a moving truck. Zach never throws his head back when he laughs, because he's so in control his laughs never get that big. He'll wear white T-shirts until they're yellow in the pits and won't notice, but also won't notice if you throw them away while he's at work. He wears steel-toed boots and is a structural engineer focused on green building and off-the-grid homes for bearded mountain men, who always end up being his friends and always end up on fishing trips with him, where they all wear hats with hooks in them and talk about the Yankees-versus-Red-Sox thing. You could imagine Zach playing cards in a smoky basement with Seth Rogen, not swooning over Cirque du Soleil with his hands clasped below his chin with Perez effing Hilton. Guys like Zach simply aren't like that. They're not.

Until they are, apparently.

I wonder if my depression is showing, like the exploded hem on the back of these black slacks, which caught on the heel of my pump earlier, as I exited my black Mercedes, and ripped. Please don't be impressed by the car. The trunk is full of weird trash and dry cleaning I keep forgetting to take out. I can only keep up appearances to a certain extent before the sadness of losing Zach weighs me down.

I wonder if anyone can tell my life is fraying, too. I wonder how good it might feel to kick this iPhone man in the nuts, just because he's a man. I wonder why, if God intended all men to suck so badly, he did not make me a lesbian. I shouldn't say this, of course. But still. It would be easier, right? This makes me doubt the existence of a God at all, which, because I'm Catholic, makes me feel dirty and guilty as hell—even though I shouldn't say that word, either. Hell. Fire and brimstone. Lucifer. I married Lucifer, and now he goes by Luci with an *i* that he dots with a hot pink heart.

The iPhone molester man catches me staring and snorts like a walrus bull, like the Old Man with all the sea from which to yank. Yanker. Blech. I look away and force myself not to look back. He is vile, but he pays my bills. Most of my clients, truth be told, are vile pigs. Ah, servitude. And to think I once believed I had escaped it, because I went to college and got a profession and wasn't, God forbid, a bank teller like my mother, who read three novels a week during her off-hours, just for fun. I didn't want to end up like that, underemployed and with an invisible tail tucked between my legs forever and ever, amen.

Oh, and yes, I'll admit that I also felt superior because I had married a gringo from Southern California, instead of shacking up with a life-size homie doll from the South Valley like my cousin Maggie has done repeatedly for the past two decades, since she was eleven years old. Maggie has four kids by four men, none of the dads being around anymore; they're all off somewhere with a 40-ounce, their pants pooling over their homie work boots.

For twelve years, since I went away to college at eighteen, I have toiled under the guilty, ecstatic, college-educated, Starbucksed, Uggs-a-licious illusion of socioeconomic escape. The family has called me a coconut because, being poor and undereducated, they still confuse "poor and uneducated" with "Mexican American," just like Michael Savage. Whoops. Bad thought.

According to The Rules, I'm not to discuss politics or identity on dates. I am supposed to be demure and serene and mysterious. Which is torture.

I have reacted to my family's accusations of sellout-dom by driving back to my downtown loft in my Mercedes and telling myself they, like those who persecuted our Savior, knew not what they did. They have insisted I was cut out for more pedestrian things. I have ignored them.

And yet, here I am, a servant with a tail tucked up just there, in the spaces where no man shall ever be allowed to visit lest the folded pink flesh-terrors therein also turn *him* gay. Me: the celibate twenty-nine-year-old divorcée of the Gay Ex-husband, who, I might add, considers us to still be dear friends because, really, you cannot hate a man for being born gay, though you can hate him for lying.

Zach and I still meet for brunch at least once a month. He invites me, and asks me for dating advice. This makes me pity the entire gay male population of Albuquerque, because no one should follow my advice. But I tell myself Zach needs me, as a friend, and then I suffer through his dating stories over blueberry pancakes at the Flying Star. He tells me terrifying details about his new life that I try unsuccessfully to forget in the ensuing days. For example, I did not even know there were clubs where gay men hung themselves from literal meat hooks on the ceiling.

Zach calls these men "the self-cutters," and he hates them. The self-cutters, however, are drawn to Zach because he seems like a young Ron Howard in Abercrombie clothes.

Zach has a hard time finding men, but not as hard a time as I do, because I, sadly, am still in love with him, and I can't seem to avoid texting or calling the cool men I meet and therefore, according to The Rules (and anecdotal experience), push them all away by being too needy, too easy, too human. I feel sick of myself all the time, failed.

My parents might be right about what I was cut out for, after all.

I am a slave all over. Just like Bryan Ferry sang, I am a slave to love. Perhaps I am still single because I know—and quote—Bryan Ferry songs, and it is the twenty-first century.

The legacies we carry—they cripple us forever.

Massive windows in the living room frame panoramic views of the city of Albuquerque, spread out below and lighting up in the dusk like glittery butter on a piece of hard, dry toast. I stand on the steps between this room and the foyer in my stirrup pants, a long belted black sweater, and chunky red jewelry and wonder why I've been here for an hour when it should have taken ten minutes.

I release my shoulder-length brown hair from the clip on the back of my head, then pin it up again, just to have something to do. In the absence of someone to do, it is always useful to have something to do. This is my new credo, courtesy of The Rules, whose authors insist a "girl" stay busy, busy, busy so she doesn't have time to ponder a life spent alone.

I wish I lived here, in this house. Such a clean, uncluttered space. I could let the worries go in a house like this. The house? She loves me. We've bonded. And now I have to hand her over to *this* dork. Men get all the good stuff.

I wait, and stare out at the world, and try to convince myself the house is in good hands now, even though I can see his hands and they are squishy, soft, and far too white.

The setting sun spills honey over the mesa and valley; it is a stark, enormous desert-and-mountain landscape like a spectacular painting, one of many reasons I returned to this city of my birth once I'd finished design school in Rhode Island.

I'd thought I wanted to get away from New Mexico, like most kids who grow up here. I thought life was better elsewhere because TV shows and movies never used to show people having fun or being glamorous in New Mexico. The media usually ignored New Mexico altogether, or when they did show us, it was on prison-lockdown shows where all the *vatos* look like dudes I went to high school with. Actually, one time, one of them *was* a dude I went to high school with. This is why I left.

No one has yet written a book of rules for dating *vatos*. But if anyone were destined for it, it would be my cousin Maggie. Dating *vatos*, and having their babies, has been her hobby since middle school, and there but for the grace of college is the life I might have led, if I hadn't led this one instead.

I'm not sure I won.

I was eighteen when I went elsewhere, lost weight and corrected my grammar, started having people tell me that with my wide-set eyes and large smile I reminded them of Valerie Bertinelli, before she got fat and thin again.

I began to dress in fancy, expensive pauper layers, like a mannequin in the Urban Outfitters window. Soon enough, however, I realized Albuquerque was a jewel that no one in the rest of the country knew about, and that in the era of Ann Coulter ignorance and lies, it just doesn't make sense to have a name like Christy de la Cruz anywhere but New Mexico if you hope to go at least one day, once in a while, not having to think about the fact that someone around you thinks you're different and mystical and possibly dangerous and absolutely foreign and un-American because of your last name and "fabulous tan."

Here, I'm not special. I'm not a freak. I'm not the token Latina in the room. I'm a person. You don't realize how good this privilege feels until you lose it. I feel badly for those people who never know what it is like to go around simply feeling like a person, no qualifier needed.

I missed my family, too, in spite of having been the fat, tormented geek kid, and in spite of their having wasted no effort in pointing this out to me. I missed my neighborhood. At this time of year, with Christmas days away, all of this comes with the glory that is New Mexico tamales, sandy anise-seed cookies called *biscochitos,* and the scent of piñon smoke in the air. The tamales in Rhode Island sucked, and so did the fact that everyone I met there seemed to think I was an immigrant from a state they thought was another country, if they thought at all.

So here I am, back home, working as an interior designer at the top firm in the state, for rich people who all seem to have come from somewhere else to the oh-so-exotic land of enchantment, and who all have a psychological disorder that ends in the letter D—in this guy's case ADD, OCD, and probably ED. Not sure I need or want confirmation of the latter.

No, wait. Totally sure. I don't.

I'm not that desperate.

Yet.

The man, a trader of some kind, doesn't notice the purpling landscape outside, or the fabulous fading of light and the way the gold just sort of seeps into the ground and the indigo just vibrates up out of it like a bittersweet bruise.

Of course he doesn't. I should be used to it by now. If you're rich enough to afford my services, chances are you don't *care* much about them. Fine design, I have decided, is wasted on the rich. Everything in their world is already beautiful. Why notice new beauty? The closest they come to noticing new beauty is being angry if it isn't there. Usually, they are angry at me. They have no gratitude for beauty.

He doesn't notice the original Ed Moses paintings I've chosen for the foyer walls, either, how their blue, green, and silver-gray streaks mimic the San Francisco skyline reflected on the water. He is originally from that city. I picked them for him. The paintings were Zenlike and brought me instant peace. They are works of brilliance and he doesn't deserve them. I am hit with regret because I don't believe the client is worthy of the artist now. The paintings will be lonely here, unloved and unseen—as will most of what I've done with fabric, color, form, function, and lighting. Ah, well. It is, I remind myself, only a job.

As an artist, you want to be able to make a living, and this is how I make mine. My true love is silk painting—wearable painted silks. Perhaps silk painting will betray me, like Zach did. Perhaps silk painting, too, only loves men, and finds women moody and bloody, risk of stains. This is what Zach told me when he left, stuttering like a cross between a grasshopper and Woody Allen, his hands flying all over the place in frustration. *Women are just, just, just—so moody and bloody.* Both true. Why do I feel ashamed? Surely there are men who like this about us? Just not the buff, charming one I stood on a cliff in the Yucatán with and pledged my undying love for six years ago. Just not that one. That one likes dick. But why stop there? He probably likes Tom and Harry, too. Ah, jest. Ah, humor. Ah, life, how I hate thee. Damn the moon.

He was the first man I kissed. The first everything. The only man I've ever loved.

Fucking ouch.

I think about God, and say a small prayer, even though I know these things don't ever work: *God, if you're out there and you can hear me, it being Christmas and everything, and because you're probably in a good mood for your son's birthday, could you please maybe consider sending me a hot, nice, successful man? Oh, what the heck. If you can send one, why stop there? Send two, or three. The Rules book and the Love in 90 Days book both say a woman should be dating three men at once, in order to practice good distance and confidence skills, and I promise not to sleep with any of them, because Rules Girls don't put out until after three dates, and even though I really do miss sex— Oh, hang on a second . . .*

I feel dirty and guilty all of a sudden, and decide to readdress my prayer to the Virgin of Guadalupe, because she's a woman and she never had sex with a straight man, either, technically, so I figure she'll kind of know what it's like to wonder about it and to have feelings that get you all agitated and squirrely. And I'm not saying God is gay, though it is distinctly not outside of the realm of possibilities. Such thoughts make me a bad Catholic, which is okay, considering that good Catholics were responsible for the Inquisition.

Hello? God? I'm sorry. I think I dialed the wrong number before. I meant to talk to the Virgin of Guadalupe, if she's around. Virgin? Please, please, please send me a hot guy for Christmas. Or two, or three. If you do, I promise you I'll go back to church and everything, I'll stay up for midnight mass this year, and I won't even gag when they put the hideous-tasting paper-bread wafer on my tongue that's supposed to be me eating your son's flesh like some cannibal from Land of the Lost, and I won't try to figure out if the priest is a closet pervert who gets off on looking down women's throats while wearing a skirt. I haven't been with anyone but my gay ex-husband, Virgin of Guadalupe, and just this once, I'd kind of like to know what it's like to have premarital sex with a straight man, or two. You know my cousin Maggie? She's had sex with more than a dozen guys, as you know, and I feel like I have some catching up to do. I know you aren't supposed to approve of any of this, but I suspect you secretly do, and that all that disapproval stuff was made up by men like my grandfather de la Cruz, but if you are a total prude like they say you are, like, I will totally understand if you don't hit me back when your time frees up a little from trying to stop wars and help old ladies in Chimayo win the lottery and all that sort of thing. Okie-dokie, Virgin lady! Uhm, amen? A man? Three men? Cool.

This client has several other homes, all larger and more luxurious than this one, he assures me, in Singapore, San Francisco, and Hong Kong. This one he bought for his new bride, a leggy bottle blonde of questionable—okay, let's be honest: nonexistent—intellect and a European modeling career on the wane; she is at least twenty-five years his junior, born and raised in Albuquerque, and she wanted a "little something" back home to "show her folks how far she came" by marrying a bitter old tycoon with marshmallow hair. Envy marries envy and they live happily envy after.

The woman is at this moment outside in the backyard. I can see her past the dining area, through more enormous windows, in her skinny jeans and sparkly tank top with the fur coat thrown over it. Her artificially puffy mouth is working over a piece of chewing gum as she picks her way alongside the infinity pool, eyeing the B&B Italia Canasta furniture. I've come to think of hers as a Los Angeles face. With New Mexico's emergence as Tamalewood—lots and lots of movies coming here to film thanks to tax incentives—you see more and more Los Angeles faces around town. Taut cheeks, huge fish lips, expressionless foreheads, perpetually surprised eyes. Zach was from Woodland Hills, in the San Fernando Valley of Los Angeles, and his mom had that same face. I remember getting my nails done in Los Angeles one year, when we'd gone to see his folks for Christmas, and the Vietnamese manicurist had stared at me for a while and then told me, "You, you pretty." I'd thanked her, but she continued to express astonishment. "No," she said, "you no understand. You pretty, but not like out-here pretty, you pretty like natural pretty. Very nice, very unusual." I guess that's what being a normal-size woman with her own lips will get you in Los Angeles, which has better tamales than Rhode Island but still ain't home.

I've got a party to go to tonight—a chile roast and *matanza,* actually. While I was married I pretended I didn't know what a *matanza* was. I hate them, because they involve actually catching and killing your dinner, which is smarter than your dog. I'm all for meat, but I don't want to make eye contact with it first. I worry about any person who doesn't hate watching a pig die by sliced jugular, and by "any person" I mean "all the men and most of the women in my family here in Albuquerque and up north." Oh, I'll eat it once it's dead, but I would not kill it myself. Mmm, roast pig. I'm starving. Outta the way, hypocrite comin' through.

I watch the woman and hope she'll take sympathy on me and sign off on the job. The woman's sunglasses are too big and too dark to allow me to guess what sort of expression she wears. I also don't think that telling her I'm hungry would elicit much sympathy, because hungry is her constant state and badge of honor. You can't be that thin otherwise, unless you have AIDS or overactive thyroid issues.

I'm ready to collect my final—and quite significant, thank you—check on this project and go, but they seem crazy enough to, I don't know, maybe be high on cocaine. You can't offend those types, I've learned. The ones on drugs? Forget it. They often pitch tantrums and fits and might decide not to pay you at all, simply for displeasing them.

Rich people suck, but for some reason I'd still like to be one. My family thinks I am one, and I guess by their standards I am. I clear a mid–six figures each year. I own my condo outright, and my car. I also own a vacation home in Vermont. It was Zach's. I got it in the divorce. I should sell it and buy everyone Christmas presents. I have a huge family, and it exhausts me to shop for them because they all want something very expensive from me because they believe I'm loaded. They are jealous of my money and sure I don't deserve it. What they don't understand is that it came from hard work and personal responsibility. They think someone just gave it all to me. They think I'm lucky. That is the main reason I don't spend too much on them. I save my money, because I *earned* it. I paid for college myself. They're no different from me. They could have gotten out, too. But they chose to stay right where they were, and suffer. It's not my fault I have some cash stashed away for a rainy day and they have debt and bad credit.

It's theirs.

The woman finally clacks back into the house in her high-heeled boots, and stops to gaze at the Patrick Martinez street scene painting I placed in the dining area. I chose it because something about her postures and patterns of speech told me that this woman had a less-than-luxurious beginning to her life. Well, that and the fact that she told me she grew up in Española with a single mom on welfare. I recognized in her a kindred spirit of sorts, my having grown up in the South Valley with working-class parents who deserved better than they had but didn't know how to get it. I intuited that she, too, might know what it was like to visit your folks in a neighborhood sprinkled with stray dogs with missing eyeballs, men drinking beer from paper bags, and cars with the birth and death dates of some gangster teen *vato* stenciled in Old English letters in the back windows. Rest in peace, Ricardo, Luis, Cristóbal, etc. Sometimes, they put the guy's photo in the window, too. It's a fashion statement in neighborhoods where getting gunned down by some other illiterate punk is the ultimate in street cred.

She smiles at the painting, and nods, and gives me a thumbs-up from across the cavernous space. Maybe I've misjudged her.

Maybe she has an eye for art after all. The man looks up in time to catch this and says, "Everything good, cupcake?"

"Spectacular," says the woman.

"Wonderful," I say. I'm about to suggest payment, but the man has beat me to the punch. He has already pulled his checkbook, wrapped in some sort of slippery animal skin—likely a *slithering* animal like a snake or an alligator, something dangerous and expensive to kill—from the inside pocket of his suit jacket, with flourish. He is all about money.

I forget, sometimes, having been raised by struggling parents who never had quite enough, that rich people don't *mind* being asked to pay for things. They live for it. The more you charge them, the better they like it. I read in *The New York Times* that Cesar Millan, the Dog Whisperer, charges as much as $100,000 per consultation for rich people's dogs. Oprah Winfrey paid this amount to have him come and give her the same advice she could have gotten on his National Geographic Channel show for free. Be the pack leader, be calm and assertive, dogs are not little people who want to wear clothes.

Rich people don't think anything is any good unless it costs more than what most people make in a year. Thankfully, that is also true of this design project. Three months of work finding comfortable yet modern and colorful pieces for the airy contemporary space, and I've come away a low six figures richer. I wonder where I'll take myself this time. After each job, I like to take a long weekend somewhere exotic. Maybe Bali. Maybe Machu Picchu.

"Thank you," I say to the man and his wife, the aforementioned thoughts all having occurred in a neat, compact matter of nanoseconds. "I hope you enjoy your new home."

I hurry to my two-door Mercedes parked at the curb outside, with a check equal to my father's three years' pay in my Gucci wallet. I am a materialist and a dork. I got the car after the divorce, because continuing to drive the Lexus SUV that I'd intended to fill with Zach's offspring seemed too pathetic.

I jump inside and turn the wheels downhill, to the west, toward the South Valley, where my aunt Tomasa and uncle Felix are in their yard, roasting green chiles next to a long-decrepit trampoline that now serves as a saggy way station for things that should years ago have gone to "the Goodwill"—a broken Strawberry Shortcake roller skate, a decapitated doll, a G.I. Joe doll without legs that, if you think about it, looks a lot like all the neighborhood boys coming back from wars both local and foreign.

The stuff of nightmares.

This detritus used to belong to my cousin Maggie, their daughter. She is thirty-one now. No one in our family is in much of a hurry to get rid of anything, because you just never know when you might need, oh, you know, something like a curling iron without the top clamp, or a ban on women priests.

Maggie had insisted I come to her parents' holiday dinner party because she thinks I need to get out of my funk and stop meeting men "off the *pinche* computer." She assures me "real live men" will be at the party, which only makes me suspect I'll be ducking from a drive-by. The men Maggie likes tend to have their names tattooed on the backs of their necks, in case they forget them, perhaps; they've narrowly missed ending up in Old English letters on the back windows of Chevy Impalas, mostly thanks to the intervention of the penal justice system. The word *penal* makes me laugh, but only because it sounds like *penis* and, let's face it, those things are ridiculous-looking even when you miss them.

I would never make eye contact with them, much less date them. The men Maggie likes, not their penises. This might explain why I went to prom with the only kid fatter and pimplier than me in high school, who is now, from what I understand, a successful character actor in Hollywood, most notably having played a bucktoothed rat in a wizard movie. Come to think of it, no one ever really leaves the South Valley, even when they think they do.

So, no. I will not be falling in love tonight. But I will be eating chile and tortillas, which, as any real Burque woman knows, is almost as good as love. Fresh Hatch green chile, red chile and pork, homemade tortillas, pinto beans, and the company of other human beings, family, home. I'm trying to convince myself that all of this is enough. That I don't need more. That I don't need a man.

So, no, it is not a dinner party in the sense of the word used by my clients, which tends to be all about excellent table settings and bouquets of things that cost a lot of money to ship around the world and put in crystal vases. A dinner party with Tomasa and Felix will take place on plastic folding tables from "El Sam's" (Club) with paper plates and plastic forks. And yet, it is alluring. Seductive. Comforting.

It's something. Home?

It's not much, but it beats staying in and watching, say, Oprah, or *The Dog Whisperer*, or, oh, I don't know, maybe, like— and not that I'm admitting to doing this every night or anything like that—waiting for Zach, the love of my life and my best friend, to come to his senses, get straight, and come home. Hey, I never said I was smart. Or maybe I did. But that was all before I married the gay guy.

Merry Christmas, and all of that, and be merry. And by "merry," of course, I mean *happy*, and by "happy," of course, I mean *gay*.

M aggie and I stand side by side in her mom's cold and barren backyard, which is just an uneven square of dirt delineated by a decrepit chain-link fence. While this sort of yard might get you a hefty fine from the HOA in Tanoan or High Desert, around here it is the style de rigueur, a perfect match to the tone of just about any pit bull or sun-cracked plastic lawn ornament—the preferred one being a Virgin of Guadalupe.

Almost every saggy stucco or adobe house around has a yard like this, with the exception of the one every ten or twelve blocks with a carpet of dead grass that blossoms aggressive and green in the summer because some *pinche* showoff old man who looks like the original conquistadores wants everyone to know he "did real good" working for the gas company or something. He could move to a nicer area, he likes to brag, but he prefers to stay here near the San Jose Parish Catholic church, where he knows who envies him.

Sad to say, my dad, a union carpenter who saved all his money by keeping the heat low and forcing us to live on one big pot of beans a week, has slowly morphed into one of these men, and our two-story stucco house, built foot by foot by my father himself over thirty-five years, now has grass where the dirt used to be and locking gates and a paved driveway. It was well under way when I was a child and got us considered the "rich people" of Barrio East San Jose. Maggie fit in better with this place, which hasn't changed in two decades and looks sort of like a huge dirty-pink butter mint with a tar-pitched roof on top.

We stand beneath an overcast nighttime sky, each of us with a bottle of Tecate slowly congealing in our gloved hands. My gloves are leather, black, and soft as silk, from Coldwater Creek. Maggie's are a cheap knit in hot orange, itchy as a venereal disease, and I'm not even going to guess which dollar store she got them at. Maybe she got them where she gets most of her clothing these days, from Victoria's Secret; she works for the company at their call center in Rio Rancho, so gets discounts on clothes and always has free underwear.

"Love is always around the corner," she says, mysteriously, sucking an ash into her cigarette.

"So is death," say I.

"You're an idiot," she tells me.

"Tell me something I don't already know," I reply.

On the other side of the trash-stitched chain-link fence is a dry arroyo, or irrigation ditch, used by local farmers during the growing season, for alfalfa fields mostly. Albuquerque is technically a city, and in some parts it does, indeed, resemble a city; but in the valley, near the scribble of water known as the Rio Grande, it is downright rural, with working farms and underemployed barrios patchworked side by side. Right now the ditch is being used as a homemade track for some moron's four-wheel ATV adventure, done to the soundtrack of *banda* music.

"Freakin' Mexicans," says Maggie, who, like me, is Mexican American but who, unlike me, seems to think there is some big difference between those of us born *here* and those of us born *there*, other than the fact that the kids born up here do worse in school (but better in gangs) and the kids from down there often manage to have silver teeth by the age of six and excel in school.

I ignore the comment and focus on the gunning of the ATV engine. I try to be mindful about it, because mindfulness is all the rage among my friends who live anywhere other than the South Valley. You know, the whole notion of appreciating the here and now for what it is, not for what we would like it to be. Living fully in the moment, which is great if you are relaxed in yoga class, with enough money in the bank, and really fucking miserable if you've just been hit by a bus and don't have money for the ambulance ride. Moments, it turns out, are as relative as time and space.

I focus on the present moment, and try to be fully here, to find some value in it. The best I can come up with is a half-assed definition of security through tradition, as in: Some things about my old neighborhood never change, and riding motorized vehicles in acequias, with children on the handlebars, is unfortunately one of them. I used to have hope that through my own success I could help elevate this place; lately, however, I pretty much just want to avoid it and let it sink into the abyss of inertia.

It is possible to love and loathe one's natal neighborhood at the same time. I'm living proof of that.

Come to think of it, I'm not sure a girl from the South Valley can ever truly embrace mindfulness. Some things, seriously, you just don't really want to be fully there for. Gunshots, your neighbor's heroin overdose, the half-dead dog in your neighbor's yard, tied to an old pipe on the side of the house with a rope during blizzards.

Only people who grew up basically happy and fulfilled and never went hungry appreciate mindfulness fully. This is why Americans love TV so much; for the rest of us, comfort comes from the escape offered up by mindfulness's opposite: mindlessness.

My great-uncle Ramón, Maggie's paternal grandfather, who was old when we were little girls and is stooped and shrunken as a dried shrimp now (but no less prone to dirty jokes about, say, blondes and baboons) turns the green chile in the outdoor roaster and whistles toothlessly to himself. The dented contraption looks like a big black trash barrel with mesh sides, turned sideways like a spit, and the roasting chile smells acrid and full, something like a cross between popcorn and ganja. Sweeter smoke seeps from the loosely arranged ground nearby, where the now-departed pig slowly cooks in a pit in the earth. I'm starving, and cold, and a bit buzzed, and chugging along toward numb, which makes me realize that mindfulness is also the inverse of alcoholism. I am not inclined to slide into either, and I guess that's a good thing.

Inside the house, just beyond the tattered screen door with a ripped part that serves as a de facto cat door, a dozen or so family members—including my mom and dad—mingle, standing on the shag carpet or sitting on the lopsided thrift-store sofa and mismatched armchair recliners. The older women have short hair, potbellies, skinny legs, and earrings shaped like Christmas ornaments. The really old ones sit around gnashing their gums and pretending they can hear what you've said by smiling and saying, "Oh yeah, right, right, that's a good one, honey."

The young women are beautiful and mostly plump but not yet fat, with shiny dark hair and perfect makeup and jeans with trendy poly-blend teenybopper shirts from one of those stores in the Cottonwood Mall with a name you've never heard of anywhere else because the store is going to be out of business in six months.

The old men are just like the old women, minus the earrings, and sometimes the only way you can tell them apart is by seeing which one is telling the other one to shut her mouth. The ones being rude and bossy are the men. The ones tolerating it like whipped dogs are the women.

The middle-aged men come in two types; there are the ones who work regular jobs, for the electric company or something, and they wear jeans with starched button-down shirts and nice shoes, maybe cowboy boots; they always drive big trucks. Then there are the other ones, who drive whatever car the woman they're mooching off at the moment has let them borrow for the night with the request they not spill beer all over the seats again. They dress just like the young men even though they are in their fifties or sixties already, which is to say they have hugely baggy black jeans on, belted somewhere in the middle of their asses so that you can see their plaid underwear, massive clumpy shoes that are called work boots in spite of no work ever having been done in them, and big T-shirts with various slogans on the front; this is all worn with gold chains around the neck and crisp new baseball caps that sit just on the top of the head and not pulled down over the ears. Often, they leave the tags on the caps, because they saw this in a rap video once and therefore it, like talking smack about "bitches and hos," must be cool.

Sprinkled around for good measure are a few of the Chicano intellectual types who've gone to UNM and studied with Tobias Duran and have come back to the 'hood to educate the rest of us on the colonialist and imperialist reasons we dress so badly, and how if only we'd reconnect with our indigenous roots we'd have something more interesting to talk about at these things than gossiping about who got knocked up, out, or down and who thinks she's "all bad now" because she dared to get a scholarship to, I don't know, Brown University, maybe, which isn't even called Brown for "*la raza* or notheen." For what it's worth, these MEChA types generally live in Nob Hill or High Desert, and have lots of bumper stickers on their Subarus.

I can't hear what everyone is saying in there, but I'm pretty sure it's more or less what they were saying when Maggie and I came out here. They're watching the Lobos and talking about whatever it is they talk about. Work, finding work, hating work, gossip about those relatives not lucky enough to be here, Wal-Mart sales if you're older and didn't go to college, forty reasons to boycott Wal-Mart for *la causa* if you're younger and did. It's cold as a *bruja*'s *chichi* out here, but Maggie, having sold her soul to the Marlboro Devil in sixth grade, has to smoke every twenty-three seconds to stay alive, and I like talking to her more than I like talking about Wal-Mart or work, so here I am.

"You found you a man yet?" Maggie asks this point-blank in a bored way that might make someone unfamiliar with my situation—Great-Uncle Ramon and his faulty hearing aid, for instance—assume I had been divorced and on the prowl for, say, a decade. Maggie adds a blown curl of tobacco smoke by way of wary punctuation, and raises one of her painted-on reform-school eyebrows in a doubting, cynical manner, as if she already knows the answer because, let's face it, she always does.

"Nope. No man."

"Guess that's why my lights go out all the time. You and all your personal toys every night."

"Ha-ha," I say, without amusement, even though there is some sad, vibrating grain of truth to her accusation. "Maybe you should try paying your bill before you get the red tag on the door."

"That's what men are for," she says. "And if you had you one, you wouldn't need all them—" She stops here and makes a humiliating buzzing noise.

I grimace. There's nothing else to do, really. I should never have told her about that store, Self Serve, on Central, which was introduced to me by a Betsey Johnson devotee, a lawyer woman I know from MANA, the Latina organization I belong to that mentors bright girls who want to go to college. I told Maggie about the sex-toy shop—tastefully designed for women and not sleazy at all—in the spirit of sisterly sharing, and have suffered her judgment nonstop ever since.

"I know how you educated women are with your plastics and plug-ins," she says, when I fail to respond to her last overture.

"Right, and homegirls don't use them?"

"We don't *need* them, because men aren't afraid of us emasculating them with our big salaries and fancy cars."

Maggie makes a snip-snip motion with her fingers, but something in her eyes tells me that she does, actually, understand my lot in life, and she has compassion for me.

She likes to rag on me about my education, but it is mostly said as a joke because I think deep down inside she wishes she'd gotten the hell out of here, too.

"You have the men, I have the money," I tell her.

"It'd be fuckin' nice to have *both*," she muses.

"Hell yeah," say I.

"But that's not how this whole system is set up, cousin," she says. "Seems to me the whole thing is designed to reward the women who need keeping, with love, and to punish the ones who don't need men by scaring the men away."

"Have you been reading *The Rules*?" I ask.

Maggie shakes her head and takes a long draw on her cigarette. "What the fuck are The Rules?" she asks.

"Nothing," I say with a shrug. "You know them already."

A s kids, Maggie was by far the smarter of the two of us, even
though her beauty masked this fact for many people. She learned
to read earlier and aced school without even trying—until she
got pregnant at her *quinceañera* and dropped out.

She tells me now, "Men follow us homegirls around like *per-
ritos*. They're falling out of trees."

"And penitentiaries, apparently." I point with my chin across
the arroyo, where a few homie-type dudes are out walking their
pit bulls, sliding their eyes up and down Maggie's body, which is
always on display for men.

"Dude, furlough sex is the best," Maggie says with a painful,
joking gleam in her eye. "A little hair-pulling, a few bites. Just
how you big shots like it."

"You're lame," I say.

"Takes one to know one," she fires back, mature as ever. She
sticks out her tongue at me and I feel obligated to do so back,
though I do it without much sincerity.

For a moment, we are kids again, and life is good, and men
don't fucking matter, and we're filled with hope in spite of all
the obvious reasons for despair.

Mindfulness.

I watch Maggie for a moment, and try to remember a time when I didn't feel inferior to her in some way. Nope. Can't find a spot anywhere throughout all of time as I have known it. No amount of money, no college degree, changes this. Our self-image is burned onto our brains and hearts like branding by the time we are ten years old.

She is slightly chubby now, but still absolutely gorgeous, with full curves that belie her having had four kids, and wears very tight dark jeans with thigh-high black stiletto boots and a black biker jacket. Her face is heart-shaped, with a full mouth and intense, large, bright, upturned cat eyes. She has three pounds of eyeliner on, and sparkly purple shadow that in spite of being slathered on with a putty knife still manages to make her deep brown eyes pop. Her dark hair is worn long, in looping wavy curls that scream "tiger stripes" or "strip club"—hair that takes far too much work, I think. She has lips you might think were fake if you didn't know her since she was two, which I have. She was a pretty baby. She's a pretty thirty-one-year-old. She has always been pretty, in a solid and tough, "will kick your ass, can dance hip-hop and old school in the driveway with the car stereo on, loves Gs with bald heads and knife scars, 'round the way girl" kind of way.

"So, no man then, damn," says Maggie, bringing the conversation back around to my single state.

"I've been trying, but the men on Match are losers."

"Yeah, right," she deadpans. "You mean you still need time to cry over some spilled homo *leche*. You coulda had you a ring by now if you played it right."

Leche, as in milk, as in the Mexican slang for . . . man juice.

"It's hard, okay?" I fight the urge to cry and feel sorry for myself. "I screw it up every time. There, I said it. I get clingy and stupid. I think it's all because of Zach. I still love him."

"*Tonta,*" she says, smacking me softly upside the head. "What are we going to do with you?"

"I don't know. I'm trying to learn new ways of doing the dating thing, from these books. It's hard, though. I need to find men to practice on. That's what my therapist says. I have to practice being aloof but alluring, disinterested yet interesting. Do you know how hard it is to do that? It's like a big charade."

She takes a long draw on her cancer stick and does her best to look like a gangster from a 1920s film, plotting someone's doom. "That *fuckin' joto,*" she says of my ex-husband, using a Spanish slur for "gay," blowing smoke, her eyes narrowed to slits and mean as those of a beaten fighting dog. "I should get Cesar to knock him around."

"Who's Cesar?"

She perks right up at this question. "Oh, didn't I tell you? He's my new man." She quivers a little as she says this, the way a dog might wiggle at the word "walk," which is her usual accompaniment to the words "my new man."

Maggie changes men the way most women change tampons. They never leave her, she leaves them. There are still men from ten years ago that beg Maggie to take them back. She is a man magnet.

"What's he do?" I ask.

"Me," she says with a nonchalant shrug. "And good, too."
She laughs to herself.

"Besides that."

"He's got him a job, okay?" she says, defensively. "Why you
always gotta ask what a person does instead of who a person is?"

This says a lot. I'm not sure I'm ready to listen, however.

"Okay, who is Cesar? Please tell me." I sound as sincere as a
kid asking to be grounded.

"He's hot and tough as shit," she says with a look of victory.

"Ah. That sounds more like *what* he is, actually."

She ignores me. "I can get Cesar to fuck the *joto* up," she says.
"He's down for whatever. I say jump, Cesar jumps. I say hump,
Cesar humps."

"Sounds like a show poodle."

She raises a corner of her mouth to acknowledge my lame
joke, and says, "Get him to fuck Zach up, man. Kick his *joto* ass."

"Zach would probably like the attention," I suggest dismally.
"A little spanking goes a long way in Zach's world nowadays."

Maggie laughs. "No, seriously girl. Cesar would do anything
for me, he's so sweet. He used to be a Blood, but he got out and
now he's religious, Pentecostal. He's good to my kids."

I resist the urge to compare and contrast gang membership
with joining a Pentecostal church, and let her keep talking. I do
wonder—when the *Love in 90 Days* lady says to be open to different sorts of men, if she means reformed gangsters.

"I can ask homeboy to fuck *joto* up." She smashes an orange-gloved fist into her other hand and I have flashbacks of being pinned down and pummeled when I disagreed with her. I shudder, then I shiver.

"That's very Christian of you," I say sarcastically. Then I remember that Rules Girls are never supposed to be sarcastic. Sarcasm is my calling card. Men supposedly hate sarcastic women, which must be why Elaine was always single on *Seinfeld*.

"Hey, I'm not the Christian, he is."

"Thus, him going out to bust heads on your heathen behalf."

"Bust some *faggot* head—yeah, girl." She is furious with me for not standing up for myself better, and her wounded eyes show it.

"Please don't call him that. It disgusts me when you do that."

"*Joto*? That's what he is, *que no*? *Pato joto* faggot."

"Don't," I say, louder and more firmly. "It's not his *choice*. He was *born* gay, okay? Ten percent of all people are. There are gay animals in the world at the same rate, too. There's a documented case of gay male penguins at this zoo—"

She interrupts me. "Spare me the faggot pigeon story."

"Penguins."

"Whatever. I don't care."

I consider the penguins, and realize that there is no better bird to hold up as an example of gay wildlife. Tuxedos, spiky hair—they look to be on the way to the symphony after popping in at the Whole Foods for a nice Pinot Noir.

"I bet their nest is very tidy and fashionable, with tiny IKEA linens," I say.

Maggie stares at me blankly, and I suddenly miss my friends from outside the barrio. They would appreciate the joke, sarcasm and all.

I hate being a Rules Girl. I suck at it.

"He just needs someone to fuck him up," she says of Zach.

"No, he doesn't. He's had a hard life hiding it from everyone and living a lie. Hate him for lying, but not for being gay. We don't like when people use slurs on us, and we shouldn't use them on other people."

"Fine, then, Cesar will break the cocksucker's kneecaps for lying his *joto* ass off."

"Eew," I say, but my widened eyes betray my interest in the idea. I might like to do it myself, with a metal baseball bat. I know, it's not healthy. But neither is anything about me anymore.

"*Órale.* Let's see him go down on some dude, with broken kneecaps," says Maggie. It's not funny, but it makes me smile nonetheless. I think I'm getting mean. Sometimes, as the South Valley taught me well, mean is the only solution.

I bet Cesar the Lovemuffin would agree, if Jesus let him.

Jesus is big in the barrio. Everyone here knows just what he'd say or do, and it almost always coincides with their own personal opinions.

We stand in silence for a moment, laughing with our eyes and watching Uncle Ramon take a pinch of snuff out of the back pocket of his stained plaid pants—pants he's been wetting and wearing since I was born—and stuff it between his lower lip and gum, in the place where teeth must have once been. I do not recall ever having seen him with teeth, though I do remember him always spitting to the side. He reminds me of a mule, with a small body and a normal-size head, like some weary but tough beast of burden with big old hairy ears.

Maggie drops her cigarette butt into the powdery pink dust, and crushes it under her sexy boot, freeing up my nose to finally take in the biting chile smell; it is definitive of New Mexico in the fall and winter—hot, smoky, spicy, and green. Home.

Maggie bends over at the waist now, to shake out her long hair with her hands. She has done this since middle school, back when everyone wanted big, permed hair. Lots of girls around here still do, sadly. Back then, we read in *Seventeen* magazine that this was the key to fluffy hair, the upside-down head wag and scalp massage. We used to lie on Maggie's bed and read those magazines cover to cover, following the advice on every single page. I can't believe she still does the hair thing. Maggie hasn't evolved much, come to think of it, since we were thirteen, other than to become a mother and, unbelievably, nearly a grandmother. Yep. Her oldest child, Claudia, is fifteen and expecting any day now; her babydaddy is in his twenties and goes by the name Rascal.

And I take advice from these people *why?*

Maggie straightens up again, wild and rosy-cheeked, and says, "*Pato joto pinche* gringo faggot motherfucker. Don't nobody mess with my Christy." Her wicked eyes smile at me because she uses these gay slurs to taunt me now, not because she necessarily agrees with them, though she probably does. Politics are not Maggie's forte.

"That's enough," I say, defending the honor of a man I hate.

She looks at me as though I were strange, and I feel small and insecure. She's my same height, five-six, but in her heels towers over me. Two years older than me, Maggie was always much cooler.

When she started wearing makeup, I wanted to start wearing makeup. When she fell in love with New Kids on the Block and covered her walls with their posters, I naturally had to do the same. I wonder when, if ever, I started to realize following Maggie's advice wasn't always the sound choice.

Oddly, I realize that I have never come to this conclusion.

I still value her opinion more than that of my closest friends from my other life as a middle-class professional woman, and particularly more than Crystal's opinion, because Crystal married Fred and Fred's a fucking cheat.

The Rules never talks about how most married men cheat. Oh, no. It talks about how great it is to be married, and why we should do personality overhauls and get nose jobs, just so we can have that supreme honor.

I hate The Rules, and yet I cannot deny that they work.

Maggie rolls her eyes. "Well, anyways, guess who's back in the neighborhood and asking about you?"

I feel my heart rate increase ever so slightly, and run through the list of possibilities. It could be any number of girls with tattoos and baby-doll shoes who were in the *chola* gang and used to beat me senseless for the crime of getting good grades, wearing preppy clothes, and therefore "acting white" on those days when Maggie was making out with a boy and therefore wasn't around to defend me on the walk home from school.

Or it could be any of the boys who used to pelt me with stones and oink at me when I walked by (and worse) for being the fattest girl in school. Or it could be Keith Garcia, the only boy who ever talked to me, and that probably only because he was one of the few kids fatter and pimplier than I was, with high-water pants whose flood level was higher than mine, and he was also in gifted and honors classes. I think I mentioned him earlier. Like me, he was a much-tormented "geek," and, like me, he is now successful, insofar as one can be successful doing voice-overs for rats. Coincidence? I think not. Geekdom's where it's at.

I settle on Keith Garcia.

"Keith?" I ask, hopefully.

Maggie's face twists in annoyance. "Girl, you shoulda got over that lard-ass *pocho* a long-ass time ago. That dude? Psh. Nah. Guess again."

"I loved him," I remind her. "He was kind to me."

"Control freak in Urkel clothes."

"He knew what he liked."

"He's a wife beater now, I hear."

What? The only nice kid in my entire West Mesa High School class is now a wife beater?

Maggie says, "Forget Keith. Guess again."

"Keith is a wife beater? But he was a sensitive thespian."

"Y *qué*? Sensitive thespians can't beat their wives?"

"Not as a rule, no."

"Okay, well, what about Phil Spectator?"

"Spector?"

"Whatever. Phil Speculum," she says, and does her fingers duck-bill style, like the gynecological tool.

"He's not an actor," I say. "He's a record producer. With really, really bad hair."

"Okay, then what about *este* whatshisname, Charlie Sheen?"

"Slightly better hair."

"No, I mean the domestic violence."

"He's a wife beater? I thought his only crime was bad acting."

"Aww, snap!" Maggie holds up for a high five, and I reluctantly deliver.

It wasn't that funny, really, but I take what I can get. At least she occasionally appreciates sarcasm.

After months of rejection from men, Maggie's approval feels like sunshine.

I say, "Keith was way hotter than Charlie Sheen."

"Then explain me that Gary Busey," she says, disagreeing with my assessment of Keith as hot via a disgusted facial expression.

"I can't 'explain you' anything about Gary Busey. 'Explain me'? Who are you, Desi Arnaz? You grew up on *this* side of the border, right?"

She ignores this. "Or that Christian Slater. He's a wife-beating thespian, *verdad que sí*?"

"I have no idea."

"He is! I read it. I'm telling you!"

I tell Maggie, "I forget I'm dealing with the woman who can quote the last fifty-two issues of the *National Enquirer*."

"*Entertainment Weekly* and *People*, loca. I don't slum it with no *National Enquirer*. You still don't think much of me, do you, you and your fancy degree?"

"I have seen you buy the *National Enquirer*. You can't lie to me. You forget that I actually know you."

"Once. One time. I admit. It had Brad Pitt on the cover."

"Yes, I believe it did."

"You have to buy everything with Brad on the cover, of course. But the point is, that Keith thespian fucker wasn't no good and I knew that, and we don't need to be pining after him all these years later."

"Fine. We won't."

"So, guess again. Who's back in town?"

"I don't know. I give up."

Maggie waits with a stupid grin on her face. I blink at her to let her know I'm not in the mood to play "guess the *vato*." Finally, I tell her to forget it, because I don't care. It works.

"Fine. I'll tell you then, if you're gonna be all like that."

"I *am* 'all like that,'" I mumble.

"Yeah, how could we forget, Little Miss Mercedes-Benz."

"I like my car," I protest.

"Yeah, but you shouldn't show it off to men, honey. They have egos like eggshells."

Maggie flashes me a grin and bounces on her toes a little with the excitement of what's about to come out of her mouth.

"Okay," she says with a big grin that is shockingly white, considering her eating and smoking habits. "It's Balthazar."

"Who?" I know exactly who she is talking about, but pretend not to because I don't like remembering him.

"Balthazar Reyes. From down your street."

My nose accordions at the forced memories of Balthazar Reyes. He was a tall, buff, handsome, and mean-as-hell kid who used to tease me mercilessly, starting in second grade and lasting until ninth grade, when he mysteriously disappeared just in time to miss out on my miraculous discovery of running, sensible eating, and apricot facial scrub. I was in love with him; he detested me. I thought of him as the sun and the moon; he considered me worm and snot.

"The bully?"

"He ain't like that no more, girl. He's a teacher now, here in the Valley. Just moved back. He teaches art or some shit."

"Oh, great," I say. "The Neanderthal is teaching art. Just the kind of guy vulnerable creative kids need."

"He's cool now."

"He made my life hell."

She shoots me a dirty look. "Just forget that already. What's wrong with you? He's fine *now*. He's all mellow *now*. He's your type *now*."

I shrug. "It's hard to forget the guy who held your head under a running faucet just because he didn't like how your pants rubbed together at the thigh."

"So *school* his ass," says Maggie. "I mean, you're all skinny and pretty and rich now, and it's your turn to flaunt that shit in his face."

"And you want me to do this *why?*"

"Because life is all about revenge," she says.

"Gandhi, right?" I say. "Or is that Martin Luther King, Jr.? No, wait. Jesus. It was Jesus Christ."

Maggie twists her face at me, in approval and annoyance. "Bitch, that's your problem right *there*," she says. "You should never quote the dumb fuckers who get their asses assassinated. History belongs to the killers."

"This is where you're wrong," I tell her. "No one remembers the killers' names. The peacemakers live on forever."

"No, honey. It's the pacemakers that keep on ticking. The peacemakers get themselves shot. It's basic Darwinian principle. There is no peaceful species on this earth."

Maggie shakes her head at me. "To hell with nonviolence. You deserve to knock Bully Balthazar's inner child down a block or two, Christy. That's all I'm saying. When you see this man, he will be filled with remorse and he will fall to his knees and beg forgiveness. I *live* for that shit, man."

"Sounds positively horrible."

"No, girl, it's good to see men crying on their knees."

"Uhm, no. I don't think so. That's not what it says in *The Rules*."

"Fuck *The Rules*, then."

I sigh. "Maggie. It's not going to happen, because I'm not going to see him. Send him my regards, though. Tell him Christy says 'Merry Christmas, asshole.'"

"Except that he's here," says Maggie, pointing to the window. "I invited him."

"What?" I ask, my moody blood running cold as a winter Tecate.

"Yeah, girl." Her eyes are positively wicked with anticipation. "I invited him and told him some hot girls would be here. That's him, right there, in the cap. With the other two guys." She points to the window.

I follow the line indicated by her finger. Since I last looked in the window, a bunch of new people have come, including a trio of men who look like they've just stepped out of central casting for "yuppy men of multicultural backgrounds." They are chummy with each other, dressed like professional men in their off-hours, and all quite good-looking in that singles-bar-in-the-nice-part-of-town way that scares me to my marrow. If you're me, you avoid groups of men like this in clubs, because they invariably don't return your smile or, worse, say something rude or, even worse, hit on your friends and don't notice you're there.

"I'm going home," I tell Maggie.

"Not if you want to live," she replies, and her claw locks onto my arm. Even through my leather jacket and her orange gloves, I can feel her acrylic nails ready to cut me. I stay put and look in the window some more, at an advantage because, it being dark out here, I can see them but they likely cannot see me. They're hot. Every single one of them. I'm doomed.

"See, *prima?*" says Maggie. "And you thought I didn't know your type."

I now recognize the man in the army green baseball cap as my childhood tormentor. He is the darkest of the three men, and has stunning light brown eyes with long, dark lashes, as before.

He smiles and I see those straight, perfectly white teeth that used to make my heart race. He has no sharp teeth, like other people do, just these great big squares, all perfectly in line with each other. When he smiles you can see his back teeth, too, his smile being large and contagious. His nose is wide, almost African-looking, and his cheekbones are exquisitely sculpted in line with his strong, masculine jaw, dotted at the moment with a most attractive sprinkle of stubble. He seems not to have aged at all, in looks, though there is something a little more patient about his face.

He is of medium height and build, not all that tall but incredibly strong without being bulky. His neck is strong. His shoulders are wide and solid. You feel like he could pick up anything that was in your way, including a car or a gang of Minutemen.

He's very confident and solicitous in his carriage, and he appears to be really listening to what one of the others is saying.

In other words, he looks like Balthazar, but he's nicer than Balthazar ever was. It's like an episode of *The Twilight Zone*. He wears a pair of faded black jeans, a bit on the baggy side, with a white button-down shirt that sits open at the top to reveal a set of colorful beads around his strong neck.

"He still looks good," says Maggie.

"Unfortunately," I reply.

"Hey, don't do that," she tells me.

"Do what?"

"Hunch over like that. Get all insecure. You're better than that. You're as good as him—better, in fact."

"Whatever," I say—and then I remember that Rules Girls always say nice things about themselves, to themselves, even when they don't mean it. No one lies like a Rules Girl.

"You're right," I tell Maggie, straightening out my shoulders. "He'd be lucky to have me."

"That's more like it," she tells me.

The other two men look sort of alike, but completely distinct at the same time. One is fair-skinned, with large hazel eyes and short dark blond hair that is sticking up stylishly all over his head in clumps. He's got a delicate sort of face that is still manly, in the vein of Maggie's beloved Brad Pitt, but with a bit more Latino *sabor*.

"Bet I know which one you like," I say.

"The William Levy clone?" she shrugs. "I got Cesar at home. I'm not prowling."

"Right. Cesar. Why isn't he here?"

"Working."

"Doing what?"

"He works as a cashier at the 7-Eleven, okay?" she says, defensively. "I know that's not good enough for *some* bitches, but it's good enough for me."

"I didn't say anything."

"You didn't have to."

I feel terrible to realize she thinks of me as a snob, and even worse when I realize that she's right. I mentally change the subject, and look at the William Levy lookalike again. He wears a white oxford-type shirt, wide open at the collar and with a suit vest in gray over it, with matching slacks, definitely the best dressed of the bunch. His lips are pink and pouty, and he looks like the kind of guy who is often on the verge of laughing.

The third young man is tall, brown, with upturned, Asiatic eyes. He wears a full suit and tie, and has a stern, serious look to him, with glasses. He has dark black hair and eyes to match, with eyebrows I think of as being common among Mexican men, sort of diamond-shaped. His chin is not as strong as the others', but his gaze is more profound and interesting somehow, and his body stronger than it might at first look, like he might be a bodybuilder underneath the fancy threads, and very graceful.

Maggie grabs my arm and starts to lead me toward the house. "And you know what? It's cold out here. I'm going in. You better come with me, or else Uncle Ramon is going to tell you the one about the three Swedish exchange students and the horny gorilla."

"I hate you," I tell her.

"I love you, too," she says. "And like I always tell my kids, you're going to thank me for this someday."

Suddenly, I remember the prayer I sent to the Virgin of Guadalupe earlier today. Three men.

It worked?

No way.

La Virgen heard my prayer and sent me three men, two weeks before Christmas. A chill runs up my spine, and I say a small, silent thank-you to that amazing creature, the patron saint of my people and the barrio. Then I realize I should say it out loud.

"Thank you, Virgin," I say.

Maggie stares at me in shock, offended to her core. "Who you calling a virgin, whore?"

"Not you, don't worry," I say.

"*Pues*, I knew you were a realist."

And on we walk.

I smile defensively as soon as the screen door smacks into the lopsided frame, and try to look like I'm just standing here in the too-warm family room, having the time of my old life, like any other family *matanza* that just, you know, happens to include three very attractive men who happen to show up in my life precisely the day I pray for them, one of whom was the bane of my early existence.

I liken the effort to look normal under these circumstances to trying to have a good relaxed belly laugh while death stands by in his black robe, watching you with his scythe tucked up in his armpit, rubbing his skeletal fingers together in anticipation.

The trio of good-looking men are off to my right, in a corner near the big-screen TV, sitting on some folding chairs with a group of three older men that (horrifyingly) includes my *father*, talking sports from what I can tell. "What is the deal with the Broncos?" That's all I hear before tuning them out.

I don't look at them long enough to find out what the deal is with the Denver football franchise, not because I don't care (I happen to love the Broncos, because around here it is either them or the Cowboys, and Zach liked the Cowboys) but rather because I don't want my eyes connecting with *his*.

I turn to look the other way, to the left, doing my best to be a Rules Girl, too good for them all, yet happy and having the time of my life. I look toward the kitchen and pretend to be Cassandra, my diamond name.

Let me explain.

Love in 90 Days says that if you are naturally insecure as your real self, you ought to create a stage name for moments like this, where you feel and act like someone better than you. Cassandra is confident and sexy and knows that men love her. I channel her now, and yet Christy keeps banging on the door of my soul, reminding me that I am fat, stupid, a failure at love, unable to keep a man. Cassandra tries to ignore her, but pretty soon, as is usually the case, they meld into an even more insecure version of Christy. I know I am a grown woman who wears a size four quite nicely now, but I still feel like a little girl whose nickname given to her by her own priest was "Butterball."

My mother is busily, frowningly scrubbing something at the sink in a way that makes her upper arms quiver. Then again, a brisk breeze makes her upper arms quiver these days. She used to be the hottest girl in town. Age, like divorce and online dating, blows.

The kitchen is visible through a sort of cut-out window to the family room. When she spots me standing there looking like a woman on her way to the electric chair, she shoots a nervous look at the young men, drops the wooden spoon she's been scraping with, and scurries over, short as a hobbit and dressed in elastic-waist denim pants and a red sweater with a sparkly reindeer on it.

Her haste tells me she is in on this, somehow. When she starts to arrange my hair for me, I'm convinced. There is a pin on her sweater that, when you press Rudolph's nose, plays "Jingle Bells" in a small, scary little tinkling piano sound. She got it at the bank where she works as a teller, and it is the sort of gift that makes her proud of her job.

I press it just to give Cassandra something to do other than give in to Christy's pessimism, it being the emotion felt by no Rules Girl anywhere, ever.

Rules Girls like Cassandra are perky as an Osmond on Prozac. I hate Cassandra, and she hates me back.

Así no, hija," my mother chastises me and my hair under her breath. I half expect her to slick her hands with spit the way she did when I was a kid. Unforgettable smell of hell, that.

"Stop it, please," I tell her, though I stop short of saying I don't take hair advice from women who dye their own hair an unnatural shade of reddish yellow. To save money, my mother also *cuts* her own hair with a Flowbee she bought on TV back in the nineties, which explains why she looks like Joan of Arc crossed with Charytín Goyco.

"But you're all *windblown.*"

"It makes me sexy," I deadpan.

"*Ay, no,*" scolds my mother. "Sexy, no. Messy, yes; sexy, no." She tucks an errant lock of hair behind my ear. "*Así,* that's nice. You look nice and decent now."

"Oh, good," I say. "Wouldn't want anyone to know the real me."

"*Cállate la boquita,*" says my mother, but she has a twinkle in her eye. "Always so negative."

"It's *sarcasm.* That's not the same as negative."

Mom clicks her tongue at me in disapproval, as does Cassandra, my inner Rules Girl. Mom plays the role of good and decent mother, but the truth is she and I share a bawdy sense of humor and a cynical outlook on the world. She was just raised to be nicer than I was, and guiltier. I think she's proud of my obnoxious streak.

"Aunt Guadalupe," Maggie says to my mother with a secretive glance at the young men again (which tells me they've been plotting about all this), "I'm just about to get another drink in the kitchen, can I get you something?"

Of course, I think. Maggie is always the more dutiful *hispana* daughter in these situations. I never offer to get things for old people, just like I rarely give my parents money and never assume my place at these gatherings is in the kitchen. I'm all wrong.

It isn't that I wouldn't *like* to help old people, it's just that I forget to remember to do it. It isn't that I can't be perky and positive and confident, it's that I have so much practice being dark and cynical, thanks to college and all my smartypants friends, that it's hard to stop.

Maggie is one of five kids, and the only girl, and the oldest; she spent her early childhood serving her brothers, and her late childhood becoming an underage mom; being of service is natural for her when she's not trolling for new men, smoking cigarettes, or, apparently, setting me up with men who will undoubtedly, once they get to know me, reject me, just like the others.

"*Dame un* Coke, Magdalena honey." My mother pats Maggie on the arm and gives her a grateful look that makes me jealous.

"*Y el jefe?*" asks Maggie, indicating my father with a nod of her head in his direction. I hate when people call Mexican husbands *el jefe*, because it means "boss" and, trust me, they don't need any encouragement to go there. It dawns on me that traditional Mexican women follow The Rules to a T—and most of them are miserable.

Mom rolls her eyes at the mention of her husband, which, I think, should not be the right reaction to a spouse. "What else? Get him another beer, *querida. Tú sabes.*"

"I'll help," I say, suddenly aware of Balthazar's eyes on me. You could pour acid directly on my skin and it wouldn't burn more than his gaze of doom. I smile at Maggie and try to look like I'm incredibly jubilant.

Truth is, I want to be anywhere but here.

"No, you wait here," says Maggie. "I'll get you another beer, too."

"I don't want another beer. I want to die," I tell her softly, without changing my facial expression.

"I'll help you with that later," she says with a grin as she waltzes off to the kitchen, which is crowded with women in various states of making stuff. I stay with my mom in the family room, mostly filled with men and children.

"I'm glad you wore black," my mom tells me. "Black is so figure-flattering, but don't sit on the sofa here, okay? Dog hair." She lowers her voice to a whisper. "They never heard of a vacuum? A lint roller? You can get you a good one at the dollar store for ninety-nine cents. But my sister, pssh. She's always been *asquerosa*."

"Okay." I take off the leather jacket because I'm starting to sweat. I drape it over my arm. Mom looks me over and switches to home-shopping mode.

"That is gorgeous, just gorgeous. The empire waist, that's a perfect look that is perfectly slimming, and the necklace is absolutely divine."

"Thanks, I think."

"You need to freshen your lips," she says, dropping the "up" as usual.

"Mom, stop it."

"*'Jita*, there's men here, *single* men, young single men with *good jobs*," she hisses under her breath as she continues to smile in a fake way and fiddle with my neckline. "Maggie told us one of them came here to see you."

"I'm not in the mood," I say.

Good jobs? Like I don't do fine on my own?

No matter how well a Latina does at her job, there is always going to be someone in her family under the delusion that she will starve without an idiot man to pay her bills.

It's the rule.

Mom stares me down.

"You have to stop waiting for that man to come back," she tells me. "He's not coming back, and good riddance, you don't want the AIDS."

"Zach, mom. His name is Zach. You can still call him by his name. You don't have to call him 'that man.' And I don't have 'the' AIDS, and neither does he. Trust me, I tested. And tested."

Mom looks around, paranoid. "Don't say that so loud," she says. "You don't want people treating you like no leper."

"Mom."

"I don't want to say his name. It leaves a bad taste." As usual, she has dropped the "in my mouth." My mother is forever dropping something in her speech.

"Okay."

"You have to move on, Christina."

"I know that, mom."

"You have to get out there again."

"I've been trying. It just isn't working out."

"Oh, this is terrible. I hate to see you like this." Her eyes well with tears. "You used to be so vivacious and full of life."

I resist the urge to tell her those two descriptions mean the same thing, and fall into the time-honored pattern of her guilting me into consoling her for my bad behavior.

"I'm sorry, Mom. But I don't mind being single. I really don't. I like it." This, of course, is a lie. No one enjoys being single unless they are autistic, and even then only sometimes.

"Nonsense."

"You never tried it, remember?" I say to my mother, who married at eighteen and has been with my father ever since. "It's actually quite enjoyable." Another lie.

Maggie returns, with a can of Coke for my mom and a beer that I didn't want for me. She loops her arm through mine, just on top of my jacket.

"I said I didn't want this," I tell her.

She glowers at me. "Sorry, I checked the icebox, but they don't got no wheatgrass juice or soy milk. No Kambucha down this way. You're shit out of luck, Christy. It's beer or Coke, take it or leave it."

I take the beer, but only because she's shoving it violently in

my face now, and I set it on a milk crate by the door that is serving as a table. "Kombucha. You're funny," I tell her, sarcastically—
and surprised she's heard of it. "Hilarious."

"That's some nasty shit, by the way," she tells me.

"Concur," say I.

"Let's go give this cold one to your dad," she suggests. "He
looks thirsty."

"No, let's not. Let's you go give it to him and me go home." I
struggle to get free of her grip, and she tightens it.

"No can do," says Maggie.

My mother threads her arm around my free one, and they
nod at each other the way two cops might on a top-secret case.
I am officially in a human straightjacket prison lock, being carted
across the room like a woman en route to the gallows. I trip along
in my pumps, and arrange my face in as relaxed a smile as I can
muster, given the crazed pounding of my heart and the anxiety
hormones flooding my body.

It's like when I was fourteen and Maggie took me to Cliff's
Amusement Park, and I didn't want to go on the rickety roller
coaster but she made me, and I threw up all over her as the mountains turned pink at sunset. Lovely.

You think she'd remember a thing like that.

I'm tempted to repeat it, just because, but I actually really like
this shirt, and I suspect Rules Girls don't throw up for the hell of
it—at least not while anyone's looking.

Hello," Maggie chirps to the men, waving. "How are you gentlemen this evening?"

My mother whispers something to my dad, and he goes away with her after excusing himself. The other two old men, distant cousins of my mom's and Maggie's mom's, stay seated with the young ones, and so begin the hellos and greetings. To my horror, Maggie introduces me as "Christy, my rich and single coconut— I mean *cousin*—and famous interior designer, blah blah blah, she makes me sick."

Balthazar stares at me with a secretive, confused smile, a little nervous maybe, as though he's trying to figure out whether I remember that he used to throw stink bugs at me in the summer at the community center pool, when he wasn't trying to dunk and drown me in the green chlorinated pee-water.

"Christy, you remember Balthazar, from school and down your street?"

I smile through my horror. "Yeah. Hey."

"How're you doing?" he says, his face registering alarm, and maybe confusion.

"Better than when you tried to drown me," I say, to my surprise, as I shake his extended hand. I'm sure Cassandra would never talk to a man like this, but I don't care. Christy's in charge at the moment.

"*Órale*," says one of the old men to the other, under his breath. They exchange a bewildered, trapped look.

"When I *what?*" Balthazar asks, seemingly truly perplexed.

"Tried to drown me under the faucet outside your house, when I rode my bike past, summer of 1988."

"I don't remember that," he says. Then his face brightens and he corrects himself. His look of confusion has shifted to reveal his impressed faux surprise. "No, wait, yes I do! *You're* the *fat* girl?"

He stares at me in disbelief.

"She *was* the fat girl," corrects Maggie.

"I prefer to think I was the smart girl, or the nice girl, or just plain old Christy," I say. "But, yes, to you I suppose I was merely the fat girl."

Balthazar looks me up and down now, hungry and lustful and approving, and I want to kick him in the nuts. Cassandra wants to date him. Fuck Cassandra.

Y ou look great!" He beams at me. "I mean, wow, what a transformation! You should be in a magazine or something."

"Definitely not fat anymore," says one of the other men, I don't know which because I'm busy giving Balthazar the death stare.

"You made my life hell," I blurt, with the zingy non sequitur "I don't want to be in any magazine" following not because it is necessarily true, but simply because I don't know what else to say.

Balthazar's beaming fades a little now, though I wouldn't go so far as to say he looks wounded. "I bet I did," he says. "You know, sorry about that. I was a stupid punk."

Maggie barrels forward, pretending I haven't been rude. Through the introductions and hand shaking and general fake merriment, I find out that the other two young guys with him are Balthazar's cousins, from his dad's side. He tells us that the men's names are Melchior and Caspar, and I think he's joking.

"Ha-ha. Very cute. I get it. Like the three kings," I say sarcastically, wanting desperately to get out of this house and situation. "That's very Christmasy. Thank God no one is really named Melchior, though, right? Can you imagine? 'Hey, Melchior, Caspar, dinner's ready!' Wow. That would suck. What are your real names?"

The guys look confused.

"Those *are* our real names," says Caspar. "Our moms were all pregnant with us more or less around the same time, and our dads—they're all brothers, from Santa Fe originally—got to talking about it, and they thought it would be funny to name us all after the three kings, given that our last names are all Reyes, and how our moms are all different races. Zar's mom is from the Dominican Republic and black, my mom's Italian, and Melchy's mom is Chinese."

"Chinese American," corrects Melchior.

"Whatever, dude," says Caspar. "My mom's Italian American, but we just say Italian."

"It's inaccurate. My Chinese American family's been here since the early 1800s; I think we can stop calling ourselves Chinese now."

"Melchy, do you ever shut up?" asks Caspar.

"Occasionally," answers Balthazar, for his cousin. "When he's got food in his mouth."

"Oh," I say, completely embarrassed now. "Sorry. I didn't mean to be offensive."

"She totally can't help it," says Maggie. "She replaced a fat body with a fat mouth."

The men all laugh at me now, and Cassandra is dismayed to see it took exactly two minutes for them to catch on to how pathetic I am.

Shut up," I tell her.

"See what I mean?" she asks them.

"Yep. I can see that," says Caspar as he stares intently into my eyes in a most disconcerting way. He is too hot for words, although if you were to use words they'd be *intense, steady, seductive, warm.*

Melchior chimes in. "It takes a lot more than that to offend us. We're pretty tough." He flexes a biceps as if on cue, and it is so round and so significant that it threatens to burst the cloth of his very fine shirt.

Maggie smiles at me, and nudges me toward these men at the very same time she pretends to get a text message on her phone.

"Oh, would you look at that," she says in very-bad-actor mode, with a phony roll of the eyes. "My kids. I have to take this. I'll be back in a bit. Here, Christy, why don't you take a seat?"

She shoves a chair beneath me before I have time to protest, and off she goes.

"Maggie!" I call out after her, furious. She smiles sweetly at me and bats her lashes. I get up and follow her halfway across the room as the men watch in amusement.

"What are you doing?" she hisses. "You need to stay over there and be charming."

"I can't be charming."

"That's true," she says, thoughtfully rubbing her chin. "I should have remembered that. Then you should at least try not to be really *rude*."

"Why are you doing this?"

"Hello? Revenge is a dish best served cold. James Earl Ray, Pontius Pilate, and Nathuram Godse."

"Excuse me?" I ask.

"Those," she says, tapping her smart phone's Google application in a patronizing way, "are the names of the people who killed Martin Luther King, Jesus, and Gandhi. You, my dear, were wrong. People do remember. It's on the Internet now. Nobody can forget."

I glance back and find all three of the Reyes cousins staring at me at once. They smile in a way that makes me think they must have just been talking about me.

"Oh, God," I say.

"You're good," Maggie tells me. "Go murder him with your beauty. They totally all want you, and it was priceless to see Balthazar's face when he realized who you were."

"I thought you said he was asking about me."

"I can lie sometimes, for a good cause."

You see? She is totally a Rules Girl. Maybe that's my problem. I'm not good at lying.

"I still hate you."

Maggie blows me a kiss and starts to walk away, backward. "I'll be back in a couple of minutes. I just wanted to give you time to get to know them."

"You promise you'll come back?" I ask, agonized, hurrying after her again, sneaking another look at the cousins. They are very cute, every single one of them. And single. Every single single one of them. And I hate them all because of what Balthazar did to me. And what Zach did to me. And what Fred does to Crystal. And on and on.

"Scout's honor," she tells me.

"You got thrown out of Girl Scouts for smoking," I remind her.

"True. But that wasn't my choice. I was still a good Scout. They were blinded by antitobacco prejudice."

She turns away from me now with a dramatic swish.

I return to my seat in the circle of men, feeling totally out of place and uncomfortable. I smile awkwardly as I sit, making sure my legs are together and ladylike. Wouldn't want to turn them all gay, all at once, with, say, a giant gaping camel toe, now would we? Why do I feel so sweaty and damp?

"So," I say with a stupid clap of my hands that I'm sure would horrify the authors of *The Rules*. "Where were we?"

"You were making fun of our names," says Balthazar.

"No, I *think* I was talking about how rotten you were to me when we were kids."

"I'm sorry about that." Balthazar affects a pout.

"Yeah, but would you be sorry if I were still fat? I don't think so."

"Of course I would." He looks wounded and sincere, but still manly enough to burp softly into his own hand.

"Listen, Christy. I *was* rotten to you when we were kids, and I know that. I'm sorry about that. I want to get that out in the open so that there's no wondering if I remember it or any of that, because I do. I remember how awful I was, and it was stupid, and I was just this stupid kid. I was going through a lot of things back then, I don't really want to get into that or use it as an excuse, but there you have it. Basically, I took it out on the only victims I could find, people like you. It was bad. I thought it would make me feel better about myself and it never did, and, yes, I've been to therapy."

Silence. The two old men, who take "therapy" to be a code for "batshit crazy," excuse themselves now and shamble away, leaving us young people to talk amongst ourselves about things decent people don't discuss in public, like how one used to be fat, or how one has been to the loony-people doctor.

Therapists are off-limits in Barrio East San Jose, as are gays, lesbians, whole grains, organic produce, and sex toys.

That went over well," I joke, sarcastically of course, because I don't know what else to do. I look at Balthazar and say, "I see your social skills are still in tip-top shape."

He looks deflated, and sorrowful, and frustrated, but I refuse to be fooled or to feel badly for him. He was awful to me. I must not forget it.

"They probably needed a bathroom break," suggests Caspar helpfully. "Prostates are all worn down, like sucked mints."

"Thanks for that mental image," I tell him, and he cracks a grin. I like Caspar. I bet Caspar was never mean to people as a kid.

"I like her," he tells Melchior, about me. "She's funny, and she's standing up to Zar. Zar was a dick to me, too, when we were kids. I was skinny and tiny."

"Definitely two points in her favor that she's dissing you, bro," says Melchior.

"Considering what a rotten bastard I was to her, you might kick it up to three points," says Balthazar with miserable self-pity. I'm not falling for it.

"How generous." I smile in as pretty and sarcastic a fashion as I can at Balthazar.

"No question, I was bad."

My smile falls a little. "You mean that?"

"Yes, I mean it. I've grown up a lot since then."

"Not me," I joke. "But I think that's apparent to anyone who knows me. I am habitually immature."

The men laugh. They find me charming. People are always fascinated by the fat people who manage not to be fat anymore, as though it took superhuman power, which it doesn't. It takes saying no to the Ding Dongs and the Ho Hos. That's all. Either that, or they're drunk.

"So, what are you up to these days?" he asks. "We should change the subject, considering how I'm trying to make up to you and all."

"Hopeless endeavor," I correct him. "I'm not in a forgiving mood."

"But it's almost Christmas," says Caspar.

"Whatever," I say.

"Perhaps it's hopeless to make up with you," says Balthazar, and then, picking up on my defensive use of big words and still itching to one-up me, adds, "But I shan't lose faith in the reformative powers of sincere remorse."

"When did you get wordy?" I ask. "You used to be more like, I don't know—"

"Retarded?" offers Caspar.

"Mentally challenged," corrects Melchior.

"He was a little slow," I admit, relishing the chance to strike back even though, to my recollection, he hadn't been stupid at all; he qualified for gifted in elementary but stopped taking those classes for some reason around fifth grade.

"I think we've talked about me and my obvious stupidity enough," says Balthazar. "Let's hear about Christy and her wonderful life now."

"Right," I say sarcastically. "Because now that I've lost some weight life must naturally be better. American mythology."

"Hey, I'm not stuffing your head in the sink, am I?" retorts Balthazar, but he quickly backpedals when no one laughs. "Bad taste, my bad. Sorry."

"What my foot-in-mouth cousin is trying to say," interjects Caspar, "is that we'd all like to hear less about him and more about you now. Tell us about yourself."

The cousins seem to wait for me to say something interesting. I am struck dumb, however, because while it is easy enough for me to talk about my work and design concepts, or even music and art and anything else that interests me, it has always been difficult for me to talk about myself.

But, I think, I've been through harder things lately. What the hell, I'm even a little interesting. Cassandra stands up in my brain and stretches her arms over her head before checking our cleavage, and sticking our chest out. It's her turn now.

Thank you, beer.

"I'm an interior designer," I say. "I live downtown."

"Maggie already told us that part," says Caspar. "Tell us something new."

"My husband is gay."

They all react as though they've been hit with a stun gun.

"Alrighty, then," says Caspar. "I'd file that under 'too much information.'"

"How are you married to a gay man?" asks Melchior. "Is it for citizenship or some other convenience? Are you gay, as well? Keeping up appearances? That puts us in morally ambiguous and, frankly, disillusioning territory."

"We divorced."

"But you called him your husband." Melchior stares intensely at me and seems upset by the change in information.

"My mistake."

"And you're holding your hands in a condescending manner," he says. "When you steeple your fingers like that, it is a subconscious dismissal of the intelligence of everyone else in your group."

I look at my steepled hands, the fingertips of the left touching the fingertips of the right. I separate them and place them behind my back.

"He's a dick," says Balthazar of Melchior. "He's always pointing out some random crap like that. Just ignore him."

I smile and blink rapidly, sarcastic being my general defensive attitude. "Builds character."

"Where did you go to school?" Caspar asks. He is squirrel-like, in a good way, very bright-eyed and seems utterly interested in what I have to say. Melchior also seems interested, but perhaps a little moody and withdrawn now that I've already managed to confuse him, whereas Zar just seems amused and annoyed by me.

"I was an interior design major at the Rhode Island School of Design."

"Wow," says Balthazar. "I remember you were pretty good at art."

"Still am," I boast.

"I bet," he says, unruffled by my attempt to annoy him.

"That's awesome," says Caspar. If he had a big bushy tail, he'd be shaking it with energy and excitement. I like him. He seems fun.

"I teach art now," says Balthazar. "At Dominguez Charter School for the Arts."

I can tell Balthazar wants me to be impressed, so I smile sweetly, then ignore him.

How about you guys?" I say to the others. "What do you all do for a living, or for fun, or whatever?"

The cousins look one to the other, waiting for one of them to take the initiative to go first.

"Well," says Melchior importantly, "I'm a primate biologist. I teach at UNM, and I specialize in chimpanzees."

"He wants to learn their language," adds Caspar.

"So he can tell them all about how interesting he is," jokes Balthazar.

"I founded the Placitas Chimpanzee Rescue Project," he says, as though I should have heard of it, which I haven't.

"Oh?" I ask emptily.

Caspar catches this instantly. "They've got a couple dozen chimpanzees out there and Melchior is studying their language."

"What he *thinks* is their language," clarifies Balthazar.

"They *talk*, bro," says Melchior frostily. "Just cool it."

Balthazar looks doubtful but tactfully keeps his mouth shut this time.

"That's super interesting," I say to Melchior. "I love chimps. They're so cute."

"Do you *know* any chimpanzees?" he asks me coldly, deadly serious; if I'm not mistaken, he is angry. If he had hackles, like a dog, they'd be raised.

"Well, no. But I guess I should say I feel like I could love them if I got to know them."

"And please don't call them 'chimps,' they find it degrading."

I laugh, until I realize Melchior probably isn't joking. Balthazar is laughing with me, and sympathizing with me through his gaze.

"You 'love' chimps," Melchior says bitterly, as though I have deeply offended him.

"She loves the *idea* of chimps, dumbass," says Caspar. "Don't give her a hard time. My God. Normal people aren't well-versed in chimpanzeeness. You need to get out more often—and by 'out' I don't mean 'with chimps.'"

Melchior makes a conciliatory face, which impresses me. Most men would have flipped straight into defensive, blaming mode. "I wasn't trying to hassle the beautiful lady," says Melchior. "I was merely trying to ascertain whether she actually loved any specific chimpanzees. Apologies."

"How this conversation has already turned to bestiality, I have no idea," quips Balthazar before chugging down what's left of his beer. He always was funny. It's just that I was usually the butt of his jokes.

He's funny now.

But I'm a Rules Girl. Because dumb as it sounds, I want him to like me.

I will smile demurely, but I will not laugh.

Men love that shit.

"Where did you study chimpanzees?" I ask Melchior, trying to make amends now, though I'm not sure why. Mostly because he seems like he might be a serial killer now, though a hand-some, half–Chinese American one. Chinese are never serial kill-ers, are they? But the Chinese Americans? Hmm. Must Google that one.

"Harvard," says Melchior.

"Nice!" I say.

"It was. Especially since I grew up in a landlocked state and Harvard is, as we know, in Cambridge, near the sea. Chimps love the water."

"Where are you from originally?" I ask, wondering if he con-siders himself a chimp from this last statement.

"Santa Fe."

"Wow," I say.

"Trust me, it's not worthy of a 'wow,'" says Balthazar.

"Says the man from Albu-crappy?" spits Melchior.

"Touché," says Balthazar.

"It's a fine place to grow up, though, right? Santa Fe. We liked it, right Melchy?" says Caspar, who is really starting to grow on me for his ability to be upbeat.

"I liked it fine." He addresses me as though he were at a lec-tern and I were a graduate student. "But I'm happy to be here in Albuquerque now. It's a great place to be for what I do. I direct one of the largest chimpanzee research programs on earth."

"Yes, you mentioned that." I try not to look worried for him.

Melchior smiles in an awkward way, and turns to Caspar. "Your turn."

"Me? Why me?"

"Because I picked you, fool."

I sort of like Melchior, too, I decide, even though he is a potential humorless serial killer and a pompous ass, because like most American women weaned on Barbies and Easy-Bake ovens, I have a need to please unpleasable men. He takes control and seems to know exactly what he wants, and he is clearly a geek. I am a sucker for smart, slightly cruel, awkward men, which might explain the whole marrying-a-gay-architect thing, and might even explain why I was in love with Balthazar way back when. Geeks know what they want in life, and they usually have passion for it.

"Okay, well, you know my name is Caspar. Notice how it's actually pronounced casPAR, with the accent on the last syllable? But everyone always says it CASper, like the friendly ghost."

"Nice. Haven't heard that one before," grumbles Balthazar, who is funny and yet at great risk, for a moment, of returning to his nasty former self.

So why does it turn me on?

Grr. I hate being female.

Caspar continues his introduction. I learn that he is a talent agent with the Carter Willis agency in Los Angeles, one of the top three such agencies in the world, and that they've stationed him in New Mexico because of the thriving film industry here. He says it with so much humility that I actually ask him to repeat himself to make sure I heard him right. He represents celebrities, he tells me, though he doesn't want to share with me who they are—which tells me they are probably famous. Otherwise, why wouldn't he tell me? Caspar says he lives in Santa Fe, a city he says is far too heavy on single men and madly lacking in single women. The more he talks, the more I like him.

"He's totally putting on a show right now," says Balthazar. "It's sort of nauseating."

"Dude," returns Caspar, clearly irritated and finally seeming to lose just a bit of his calculated patience. "What the hell is that supposed to mean?"

"Just what I said. You're as good an actor as any of your clients."

Caspar smiles uncomfortably at me. "I think he's had a few too many brewskis," he says. "Once a bully, always a bully."

Okay, your turn, then," I tell Balthazar. "Fill me in on the part of your life since eighth grade."

He smiles and says, kindly and succinctly, "I left here, and went back to Texas to my dad's for high school. Then I went to art school in Boston. Taught art in New Hampshire and Maine, now I'm back teaching here."

"Oh?" I ask, surprised and intrigued. "Where did you study art?"

"Mass Art."

"Good school. I didn't realize you were an artist. Maybe a graffiti thug, but not an artist."

"Well, I guess it wasn't at the top of the list of things we talked about." He grins with shame and grownup confidence. "Plus, I pretty much hid it because it was considered very gay around here. Er, no offense, or— God, sorry."

"It's okay," I say. "I hate my gay ex. Say what you like."

"He's a sculptor," says Caspar. "And very good."

"Her gay ex is a sculptor, too?" asks Melchior.

"No, douchebag. Our cousin Balthazar is a sculptor."

"Thanks, *primo*," says Balthazar.

"Nothing to thank me for, dude. It's true. You are a sculptor. You're a dick, too, but you're a dick who can sculpt."

Balthazar shrugs off the compliment and tells me, "I came back to teach art in the South Valley, because this is where my heart is."

I'm about to find this endearing against my will, when I am rescued by Maggie's return, with her own chair and another beer for me.

"What did I miss?" she asks, all jiggles and freshly sprayed perfume.

"Their life stories," I tell her.

"And were they good?"

"Mine was," jokes Caspar. "I don't know about these guys."

Maggie laughs too hard, and I can smell acrid smoke staleness rising off her lips. "You know, I was thinking just now, that if you're all single—you are, right?"

The cousins nod.

"Well, then," says Maggie, and I brace myself because I do not like the way she looks right now, like she's up to no good. "Do I have a pretty cousin here, or what?"

"Stop it," I demand, but it's too late. The cousins are all staring at me and agreeing because, really, what the hell kind of choice do they have. Back me into a corner with a pit bull and I'll sing any song you ask.

"Then here's the plan," says Maggie, rubbing her hands together like death hovering over the Koresh farm as the FBI burst through the windows.

I want to go home.

Good," Maggie continues. "Then here's what I think we should do. How long are you guys around? I mean, in town?"

"They all live here, more or less," I tell her.

"Even better! Okay. Here's the deal. Christy's ex-husband turned out *joto*."

"We heard," says Balthazar.

I interrupt, in horror. "Maggie! Cut it out!"

"No, no," says Melchior, who appears to still be terribly confused by the ordeal with Zach. "Let Maggie finish. This is getting interesting." He sits forward in his chair, elbows digging into his strong thighs.

"And this beautiful woman just sits around hoping he'll come home again, reading useless dating books, meeting strange men from online dating sites, and alienating all other manner of men—and it's absurd."

"Shut up," I mutter.

"So what do you say we all make a pact that each of you takes her on three dates, and we'll see who wins?"

"Nice," I say, sarcastically. "Because I'm a mail-order bride and can be given away to the highest bidder."

"Shut up," Maggie says. "It's just for fun. Like a contest." She turns to the guys now. "They have to be good freakin' dates, okay? Because at the end of the three weeks, during which time you will each have taken my lovely cousin on three dates, she's going to pick one of you to keep dating. But only one."

"What is this, some bad reality TV show?" I ask.

"Smashing," says Balthazar, his voice dripping with sarcasm.

"I think it's a good idea," says Caspar. I wonder if he ever disagrees with anyone.

"Works for me," says Melchior. "But I need to know that we men have the option to opt out if, after the three weeks and three dates each, we decide that your cousin isn't right for us, should she decide we are right for her."

"Hey!" I protest. "I thought I was supposed to be the prize cow, not you."

"Fair enough," Maggie tells Melchior. "But I can promise you there's nothing disappointing about Christy. She's an amazing catch. She just happens to have married a fag who ruined her life."

"Not appropriate terminology," says Balthazar. "Slurs are not cool."

"Right?" I ask him, surprised to agree with him on anything.

"She's single and wasting away," says Maggie.

This makes me furious. "Dating hasn't been at the top of my agenda. I'm not sure anyone here got the memo, but women can actually support themselves and live happy lives without men nowadays."

"Okay, pipe down there, Rosie the Riveter," says Maggie as she leans forward and sticks her arm into the center of our circle. "Let's all put our hands in that we're going to do this thing, and that you men are going to show my cousin the time of her life."

latonic," I blurt, and realize, yeah, I'm a wee bit tipsy.

"What?" asks Balthazar.

"Platonically."

"Earthquakes?" asks Caspar—who is cute, but I am now thinking might not be the brightest of the Reyes trio.

"That's plate tectonics, you moron," Melchior corrects Caspar.

"*Platonic* means 'just as friends,'" explains Maggie. She looks at me in a defensive way. "I know you think us GED grads from the South Valley don't know words like that, but some of us do."

"Yes, the same ones who know the name of the man who killed Gandhi."

"What?" asks Melchior, confused once more, naturally.

"Never mind," I tell him.

"Explain the platonic thing," says Balthazar, to me.

I sigh and roll my eyes at him in a condescending manner that feels incredibly much too good. I say, "I'll do this, but we have to keep it strictly platonic through all these dates."

"Great idea," says Melchior.

"I agree," says Caspar.

Balthazar seems to be thinking about it, and nods his head in agreement. "Good thinking, Christy, because I absolutely do not relish the idea of putting my tongue anywhere Melchy's tongue has been."

"Just mine?" asks Melchior in disbelief. "What about Caspar? You like sticking it where Caspar's stuck his filthy slug?"

"Don't call them that," mocks Balthazar, echoing Melchior's earlier defense of chimpanzees. "Slugs are very sensitive. They are easily wounded by salty words."

I will not laugh. Or even crack a smile. I will not find him charming. He is evil, incarnate.

And I still love him.

No, dude, that's not what he's saying," says Caspar. "None of us want to stick anything where any of the others stuck it."

"This is starting to make me very uncomfortable," I say.

"Me, too," says Maggie. "So let's stop talking about Christy like she's a methadone clinic, and just agree on the terms real quick, and move on. Three weeks, three dates each, and Maggie picks the winner at the end. I mean, unless you guys aren't competitive. Cuz that's what this is, a competition to see who has the mad date skills among the Reyes cousins."

"We are competitive," says Caspar. "Always have been. The problem is, I always win. So it's not exactly fair."

"That's bullcrap," says Balthazar.

"You both lack proper etiquette to make a lady feel special," says Melchior. "I've no doubt that in such a contest, I would be victorious."

Maggie laughs out loud, thrilled with her evil plan.

"Can I withdraw, please?" I ask, weakly. Everyone ignores me.

Maggie says, "Just remember, nothing normal, and nothing ordinary. I'm getting the full report back on these dates, and they better be interesting, or you'll be disqualified."

"Define 'interesting,'" says Balthazar.

"Okay," Maggie says thoughtfully. "But it's easier to define 'not interesting.' Like you can't take her to dinner and a movie. That's totally boring and predictable."

"Nothing passé," says Caspar, and I like him again because he has used a word that is surprisingly large for what I'd begun to think of him.

"Yeah, what he said," says Maggie, pretending to be stupid again.

"How about Burritos Alinstante?" asks Balthazar. "What if I take her to the BAI drive-through?"

Maggie stares at him, dumbfounded, and I giggle.

"I think he's joking," I say.

"I should hope *so*," says Maggie.

"Probably not, girls. He's all about the quickie," says Caspar.

"So no drive-through," says Balthazar with the sort of sarcastic, annoying facial expression you might have if someone who knew nothing about astrophysics were, say, explaining astrophysics to you and you were an astrophysicist. "I got it. Got it."

Maggie puts her hand in first, and I wait until the cousins all have theirs in before reluctantly and somewhat giddily adding my own. I'm vaguely aware of my mother staring at me from the kitchen, her eyes alight with pleasure. I should send *her* on these dates, I think.

"Okay," says Maggie. "Let's do Rock, Paper, Scissors to see who gets the honor of taking Christy out first."

All I can think of now is an episode of *SpongeBob SquarePants* I once saw when I was watching Maggie's kids for her while she went dancing at Graham Central Station with another one of her men.

In the episode, SpongeBob and his mentally challenged best friend, Patrick the Starfish, play Rock, Paper, Scissors, but it is no fun because Patrick always does paper. When SpongeBob asks him why, Patrick says it is because he's sure that this way a magic pencil will fall from above and draw all his dreams come true. SpongeBob, the upbeat realist, suggests to Patrick that this sort of fantasy might be unwise to entertain, and disappointing. Patrick frowns, and suddenly there it is, the magic pencil, falling from above, ready to draw their dreams to life. Except that when it draws another SpongeBob, that one is evil. I'm not sure what the parallel is, except to say that I'm sorry I wished for three gorgeous men falling all over me, because when I did it, I was SpongeBob DoubtfulPants, not Patrick the idiot optimist.

I know better than to do something this brand of stupid.

And yet, here I am, watching the Reyes cousins rock and scissor and paper their excellent, manly hands, vying to whisk me off to the land of dreams where, as my experience has proved, men and love only lead to pain and disappointment.

Secretly, I pray for Balthazar.

Melchior wins, and I already feel like I need a big magical pink eraser.

Days later, and I stand helplessly in my underwear in my master bedroom, which is separated from the main living area of the loft by a stand-alone wall made of recycled Bustelo coffee cans. The wall is prettier than it sounds, constructed by an artist, and the cans make the shape of the Virgin of Guadalupe, all reds and yellows and blacks. I thought it was clever. Zach hated it. He hated anything that was too "Mexican," other than me. Maybe "hate" is too strong a word for a guy who never expressed feelings other than, you know, the occasional crotch itch, until he came out.

I stare at the clothes I've laid out on the large, low Japanese modern platform bed where, I swear to you, Zach used to make love to me as though he actually *liked* women. His was a ravenous lovemaking, grunty and full of dirty talk and faux-strangling "me—Tarzan, you—Jane" styling. Tell me, can a man who is a closet homosexual do that? I mean, without winning as Oscar? Come on. It just doesn't add up.

I sigh, and try to work up the energy to get dressed for the date. Right. The first date, with Melchior the half-Chinese chimp man and potential serial killer.

Two days have passed since the *matanza*, and I've been guilted into following through with this thing by Maggie, who keeps calling and telling me how bad it will make her look to my mother if she fails in this task that, true to my instincts, my mom did in fact set her up to do.

Apparently, some members of my family have even begun to wager on the situation, betting on which man I'll pick or whether I'll just end up alone. I suspect they've grown too lazy to drive out to the Route 66 Casino for shrimp buffet night. My family members are always telling me how short they are on money, always asking me to help out, but they always seem to find enough money to go gambling. This is one of the many reasons I don't give them a dime anymore. They bet on everything, including my love life. Nice to know they're there for me when I need them, rooting for me.

I've picked dark jeans and a black long-sleeved T-shirt from Banana Republic for the date, because Melchior told me to wear something comfortable that I could "shimmy up a pine tree in," which has me profoundly worried. Pine trees are sharp affairs, bark and needle alike, with not much welcome to shimmying. I've just relayed this information to Maggie, who is on the other end of the phone line.

"Pine tree?" asks Maggie. "What the *cojones* is he planning?"

"Maybe we'll be foraging for pine cones at sunset, like brown bears."

"Maybe he thinks he's so well endowed, he's like a pine tree, and you'll shimmy up his hot shaft."

"You're not helping," I tell her, because this makes me think of cat dick.

Cats' penises are apparently barbed like medieval weaponry and hurt like hell, which is why the in-heat lady cats are always wailing like banshees during their copulation. Seriously, for most of the females on earth, it just ain't worth it.

"I already *so* don't want to do this, and you're only underscoring that sentiment for me. I think I'll bag out."

"Whatever. No, you won't. You haven't been on a proper date in ten years."

"Right. And tonight will change nothing."

She ignores this. "What kind of shoes are you wearing?"

"Jogging shoes. Rykäs. Purple stripes."

"Oooh. Sexy," she mocks me. "Make sure you stuff the back of your bra, too, so it looks like you have a hump. Dork."

Shut up, Maggie. Melchior said I might want comfortable footwear."

"Call him Mel. Melchior sounds like a ghoul."

"I tried," I tell her, hiding my surprise at her use of the word *ghoul*. "He insists on Melchior."

"Why?"

"He said Mel reminded him of a guy who'd own a greasy diner."

"Seventies sitcom. He's dating himself."

"No, sadly, he's dating *me*—and it's all your fault."

"And your hair?" she asks, except that I don't get a chance to answer (but would have said "in a ponytail" if I had) because she's suddenly shouting over the noise of television at her kids to stop beating the crap out of each other. Four kids, four dads. And I'm taking her advice *why?*

"Sorry," she says once she returns to the phone. "It's chaos over here. You should be grateful you're about to start a super-fun thing with a bunch of hot guys."

"Right. Because look where it might lead someday. Instead of the peace and serenity of my own loft apartment, where I can do whatever I want whenever I want, I could, if I play my cards just right, someday be screaming at my kids."

"Ha!" she cries, sincerely. "True. I hadn't thought of that."

Well, right, she never thought of that, or birth control, or her future. Sometimes smart people can be incredibly stupid. Thus, everyone who had potential and wasted it.

We talk a little more, then I end the conversation because the door buzzer goes off like a dying crow. I grab my Coach hand-bag off the dresser and head to the living area of the loft. It has soaring ceilings with exposed ducts and feels sterile and cold in the dead of winter, like now. I hurry to the speaker box by the front door and press the TALK button.

"Hello?" I sing, though I am pretty sure I know who's there.

"It's Melchior," he says in a voice that is richer and deeper than I recall. I have to stop myself from laughing at how utterly creepy that name sounds with that voice. *It's Melchior, I've come to suck your blood. And darken your mood. Bwa-ha-ha-ha-ha!*

"I'll be right down."

I do one last makeup check in the mirror next to the door, wrap myself in my puffy black Banana Republic parka, and realize how nice it feels to actually be going *out* with a man, and thinking about how I look. I haven't dated since college. Dates once you're married don't count, because you usually end up fighting about something and going to bed without sex.

That, to me, is the definition of marriage—which makes me wonder why so many women seem to be in such a rush to marry me off again, including, apparently, myself.

At least let me have a little fun first.

I walk to the elevator with a spring in my step, and even hum on the way down (five floors) because no one else is in here with me and I look pretty cute in the mirrored walls.

When I burst forth from the front door to my building, Melchior beams at me like I'm the cleverest girl in the world. He is as handsome as he was before, like a taller Wilmer Valderrama type.

"Hey. You look nice," he says. "I like you in jeans, and you have the little ponytail going. Very nice. How are you?"

I shiver in the cold and shut the door behind me, then fold my arms across myself. I greet him with a handshake, which he awkwardly returns, and thank him for the compliment. He looks nice, too, big and brown and hulking and strong, in his dark blue jeans and white sneakers and beige and white Columbia ski jacket. I know better than to compliment him yet, though.

Okay, okay, okay. Not a good example.

But still, I believe there is something to the idea of making a man work for your attention, not because I'm old-fashioned, but because I think all humans ascribe higher value to things that are harder to get. That's why dirt is free and gold is expensive. I am gold, I tell myself.

"Shall we?" Melchior smiles and gestures away from the door.

We start toward the curb. It being a Saturday early afternoon in downtown Albuquerque (which is dead on weekends before eight P.M.), there are few cars on the street. He heads right toward his car—or what I *think* is his car. It doesn't look like any car I've ever seen, unless you count the absurd vehicle in the film *Back to the Future,* or the thing they drive in that show my parents watch about storm chasers. I gasp. Melchior apparently drives a time machine made of old swamp coolers and chicken wire.

"It's homemade," he tells me, knowing from experience with other women, perhaps, that the car is the reason my jaw hangs slack and my feet have stopped moving.

"You *built* your own *car?*" In spite of my promise to myself to have a mediocre time, I'm already smiling ear to ear. This is just too weird.

"With an engineer friend of mine from NMSU. It's all solar." He eyes the overcast sky. "The battery should be good for the rest of the evening. Don't worry."

"*Should* be?"

"Will be. No worries. You game?" he asks. He walks toward the car. "It won't bite. Not unless you ask it, nicely."

"I'm the same way," I joke. Just can't contain the sarcasm. Oh, well.

"*So*," he says approvingly, with a wink I don't think I should like. "My kinda girl."

He goes to the passenger side of the car and opens my door by wiggling and fiddling with things. As I start to slide myself into the cab, he asks me what I think of Becky. He then tells me "Becky" is his car's name.

"I don't know yet," I lie, because it wouldn't be nice to tell him I've never been taken out in a car that looks like it was stapled together from fallen space junk.

Melchior smiles broadly at this, and I am sure he's misunderstood my reticence, taking it for admiration. Men, I've found, are quite good at that sort of thing.

He jogs around the front of the car and lowers himself into the driver's seat with something similar to grace. He smells good in that first-date kind of way, like cologne and toothpaste.

"Little Miss Chrissy. How are you?" he asks, as he fiddles with a few awkward knobs. Something beneath us shudders to life.

"Okay. But it's Christy."

"Christy! Sorry. I'm good at science, but terrible with names. Oh, and that noise is just the engine. Don't panic."

"I figured."

"I know it's sort of a shock to most people," he says, indicating the car with his hands and eyes. "Most women think it's disgusting. But here's what I tell them."

"Them? Are there many?"

"Huh?"

"Women. You said 'here's what I tell them,' implying there was a 'them' out there."

"Over the years, you know. I've had a few dates. Usually just first dates."

"No seconds?"

He shrugs. "Sometimes seconds, but most women I've met around here seem to want a guy with a fancy car."

"*This* is fancy," I say sarcastically, "in it's own Cracker Jack box, special sort of way."

Melchior laughs at the bad joke this time as he pulls the car away from the curb. "In its own geeky way," he says. "It does not leave a carbon footprint, which is pretty much all I care about."

"Admirable," I say, honestly. I think of my marshmallow-headed client in High Desert, and his collection of Hummers. I'm not sure he'd know what a carbon footprint *was*. If he did, he'd want a giant Gucci loafer for it, and perhaps a pinky-toe ring.

"Here's the thing," says Melchior confidently once we're humming down the boulevard. "Once you've gotten to know chimpanzees the way I have, and you've seen what humans are doing to the planet, you can't bear the thought of doing anything else to damage their habitat."

"Makes sense." I like the way he drives, very laid-back and confident. Maggie swears that you can tell how a man will be in bed by the way he drives.

"I should stop lecturing you. I'm prone to it. Sorry." He flashes me a grin. "Professor's downfall."

"No apologies. It's interesting, what you said."

"I should be focused on our big date here."

"No worries. So, hey. What do you have planned for us, anyway?"

Melchior smiles. "Ah! You'll see."

"Gotta give me more than that."

"No, no. I want it to be a surprise."

"I hate surprises." I do a little childish pouty thing with my mouth, and realize this is a face I only make in the presence of men.

It is stupid.

I need to stop it.

It's like I allow myself to regress to a dependent, childlike state when they're around. It's what I was raised for, I understand, but it isn't what I have to perpetuate. I clear my face, and sit up straight and strong.

"Okay, so now we know you hate surprises. What else don't you like?" He steers the contraption through downtown, and as I suspected the homeless men out walking around, and the women on their way from the bus stop to their jobs dancing on poles, stop to stare. He doesn't seem to notice.

"What *don't* I like?" I repeat. "Is that what you asked?"

"Yeah. I figure we should get right to the point. People waste all their time on first dates talking about what they *like*, when it's the stuff people don't like that makes or breaks the deal, seems to me. I mean, pretty much everyone likes miso soup, or pretty sunsets. Everyone likes dessert. Everyone likes sex. Why even talk about it? Me? I want to know what you hate. Show me a man's loathings, and you show me his personality."

"Wow." I consider this question as he drives. "I don't like dirty dishes," I offer.

He grins at me. "That's the best you can come up with? With this big, corrupt world, the best you can do is dirty dishes? Must live a sheltered life, Christy."

"I don't know. I just don't like them. You know how there's always someone and you go over to their house, and they let their dishes pile up for, like, days? I hate that."

"Ugh. People *do* that?"

"You never saw that before?"

"Nope," he says. "But in your defense, I'll say I don't do a lot of socializing with people."

"Except for first dates, with no seconds," I tease.

"Now that you've told me about the crimes people commit against dishes, I think it's probably a good thing I don't have second dates, don't you? People are slobs."

"And chimpanzees," I ask, "are . . . clean?"

He acts like he hasn't heard me.

"Now *me*, here's what I can't stand," he says. "Women who sweat self-tanner at the gym."

"Pardon?"

"I go to Midtown Sports and Wellness, and there are these gringa girls there— well, really just one. She wears white T-shirts, and when she sweats, it is all brown because of all the self-tanner she must have in her skin."

I laugh out loud because I also go to that gym and have seen the very woman he's talking about. I tell him so.

"No *way!*" he cries. "How come I never see you there?"

"I don't know. Probably because I don't look like this when I go. I'm usually very schlubby."

Come to think of it, he does look rather familiar to me. Yep. I've seen him. In a tank top and sweatpants. I've lusted after him, actually. I'm not proud of this.

He purses his lips at me as though this were impossible. "Oh, I think I'd notice you if I'd seen you."

I'm still laughing a little. "It is pretty gross. She's the one in the super-short shorts, right?"

He laughs now. "Yep. Not a good look on *anyone*."

"Not even Bruce Jenner?"

He laughs, then takes a deep breath and blows it out. "Yeah. Oh, and I hate when people don't pick up after their dogs on the hiking trails. I also hate country music and trans fat."

"You say those last two like they go together."

He laughs again. "Yeah, well, they pretty much do. Trans fat shouldn't be legal. It's like eating motor oil, which should also be illegal."

"Don't hold back," I say. "Let me know how you feel about stuff."

He grins at me again. "I hate truck stop bathrooms. And fake nails on women."

"But they're okay on men?"

"All fake nails," he says, deadly serious and missing the joke. "And I hate the way indigenous people in Mexico get to be Mexicans here but indigenous Americans are not Americans but *Native* Americans."

"That's sort of random."

"Oh!" he cries, as though I interrupted his train of thought, or maybe like he hasn't heard me at all. "I also hate car alarms that go off when no one has gone near them, and peanut butter that comes all swirled together in the jar with jelly. Dude, let me pick my own jelly, okay? *Thank* you. Swimmer's ear. Hate that. People who do Sean Connery imitations. Hate that, too, because no one ever really does it very well, and Sean Connery just isn't interesting enough to deserve imitation. Snoop Dogg's hair. Hate that. Cornrows in general, I hate, especially if they smell like pot."

"I don't know if it's fair to judge cornrows if you don't have black hair," I suggest.

"Actually, I hate pretty much everything about Snoop Dogg. His clothes, his arms, the way he slouches, the fact that he went on *The Martha Stewart Show.* I mean, seriously, what is Snoop Dogg *doing* on that show? Martha went to prison, and now she's got that dude for a guest?"

"Martha got street cred now," I suggest. "Martha's gangsta."

"I don't know. And Bill Gates. Serious hate. I'm not sure why I hate Bill Gates, you know? I just do. And splinters that go under your fingernail. And cats. Everything about cats."

"I hear they have barbed penises," I offer, thinking from the lack of response to anything else I've said that Melchior is not really listening to me anyway.

He looks at me briefly now, but doesn't respond beyond opening and closing his mouth a couple of times. He's speechless.

I can't blame him. I'm a bit rusty.

The speechlessness is brief.

Melchior drones on: "Gas barbecue grills. Hate them. I mean, if you're going to cook with gas, just do it inside, right? Of course, I hate war and climate change, and imperialism, and human-centric thinking, and the word *buggy*. I have just never liked that word. *Buggy*. Ugh. I'm not sure why."

"Interesting."

He takes another deep breath, and I brace for another list.

"But enough about me," he says, mercifully. "Where did you grow up?"

"Uhm, here. In the South Valley. My parents live on the same block as Zar's mom."

"Oh, right. Dolores. Good people."

"So," he says. "We came down from Santa Fe a lot for the holidays when I was a kid. I'm surprised I never saw you."

"I'm sure you did. I was the fat girl. Remember?"

"Oh, right. Hard to imagine. You have pictures?"

"Uhm, no. I don't really carry around pictures of when I was a fat girl."

"You should. You could flash them at random and be all, like, hey, look what I did. I used to be fat and now I'm beautiful."

"No, thanks. I mean, thanks for the compliment. But no, no photos."

"If I had lost a lot of weight, or done something else that was really hard, I'd carry pictures around just to brag to random people, you know? In fact, I do. Here. Take a look."

He opens a thing that is most analogous to a glove box, and produces a photo album. He hands it to me. I open it, and find a carefully scrapbooked collection of photos of chimpanzees in various states of chimpness. Melchior appears in some of them, holding the chimps, being held by the chimps, feeding a baby chimp with a bottle, etc. I am relieved there are no photos of Melchior making love to a chimp, though of course there is always time to really get to know him.

Then again, I could use that time to do something useful and womanly, like learn to sew.

These are nice," I say of the photos, mostly because I'm not really sure what else to say.

"That's my family. I mean, I have a real human family up in Santa Fe and in Española, but these guys, they're my heart." He stops to beat on his chest with a fist. "I love them. They are my world. I started studying biology in college, I don't think I told you, but I went to Harvard, and I thought I wanted to be pre-med, and I had this chance to do an exchange in Africa for a semester, in the Congo, and it wasn't the safest place in the world or anything like that, but it was my first exposure to the incredible world of chimpanzees. I was twenty, and I was sold. Forget medical school, I told myself, from now on, it's going to be all about them chimpanzees. . . ."

He goes on like this for several more minutes, telling me all about his favorite professors at Harvard, and finding sixteen other reasons to mention Harvard, and how he wished Jane Goodall were younger and hotter, because she was just the kind of woman he'd like to marry, and where he went to graduate school—which is Harvard, don't you know. He is very cheerful and interesting, and clearly loves what he does, and Harvard, and isn't shy about talking.

"So after Harvard one thing led to another," he sums up, as he pulls into a parking lot in the warehouse district near American Home furniture store in the center of the city, "and before you knew it, I ended up being one of the main guys doing chimpanzee research in the world."

"It's important to love what you do," I say helpfully. "I love what I do, too."

Melchior's brow furrows. "You know, it's more than love with me. I love what I do, but it's bigger than that. The work I do, it has a higher purpose. It is truly a calling."

"I'll just call you the Chimp Whisperer."

He winces. "I think I told you, they *hate* to be called chimps.

I know it sounds crazy, but they really don't like it. Chimpanzee society is incredibly formal, and they don't understand nicknames."

"Oh. I didn't realize it was formal to fling one's own feces. I suppose it depends on what part of Europe you vacation in, though."

He shoots me a whithering stare.

I shrug. "At least that's what I've heard."

"But enough about that." He smiles at me again. "We're here," he says pleasantly. He points to a sign on the side of the warehouse. It reads STONE AGE ROCK GYM.

"Rock climbing?" I ask, as we disembark from the vehicle.

"Indoor. I love it," he says as he jogs around to my side and we begin to walk toward the front door together.

"I've never done it," I say, fear gripping me.

"I have been climbing for ten years. I took it up at Harvard. It helps with the work I do."

"I bet."

He looks intently at me for a moment, then says, "Chimpanzees split from human evolution about six million years ago, so relatively speaking, we're still quite closely related—but they definitely have the climbing advantage. I've tried to talk these people here into letting me bring some of my animals here for a climb, but the management won't allow it."

He pauses to open the door, and walks in ahead of me.

For some men, six million years apparently isn't quite enough time to have evolved some manners.

I head inside and find a bright, cavernous warehouse several stories high, with every inch of space occupied by colorful hand and foot grips. The floor is one big soft pad. Good. At least I won't die today.

Loud rock music blasts, and several very fit young, hip, and outdoorsy–type people climb around like spiders on leashes. I follow Melchior to the front desk, where he suggests we pay fifty-fifty for our session and makes sure I get rental shoes and a belt that looks like it might serve a double purpose at an S and M shop.

We take a seat on a bench, stash our street shoes and coats in cubbies, and put our shoes and belts on. Melchior continues to tell me about his animals. About how unfair the world is to chimpanzees, who laugh and have empathy and can learn the names and meanings of the numbers 1 through 9. They are altruistic by nature, he tells me, and far more humane than human beings.

"Really," I say. Truly, I find the whole thing interesting, but I'm also a bit worried about my apparatus, and by the fact that he doesn't seem to notice I'm struggling with it.

"Okay!" he perks up, bounding to his feet. "Who's ready to climb?"

Finally, he notices that I've botched the belt thingy, and he helps me. With his jacket removed and just a tight long-sleeved T-shirt on him, I can see that my suspicions about his well-muscled body were indeed correct. This is a man who works out. A lot.

He is stunning, far more buff than Zach, and taller, too. He's like the Rock, if the Rock dug monkeys.

"There," he says with a sweet grin, adjusting a strap on me, and patting me on the hip when he's done, in a way that sends butterflies through my torso. It has been a long, long time since a man touched me there. Or anywhere, for that matter.

"That should do it. You ready?" he asks.

I smile, and nod, and realize that, strangely, Maggie might have done a good thing here. Maybe I am ready to get out there and date again. This might be fun.

Then again, it was fun having my wisdom teeth removed. It all depends on your attitude, and the drugs you have readily available.

Lessons from a South Valley native.

Days later, and Maggie's mouth is open as she listens to the recap of my date with Melchior. We sit in puffy velvet armchairs near the fireplace, in a corner at Satellite Coffee across from the University of New Mexico, drinking cafés con leche.

Hers has a gallon of whipped cream on top; mine is nonfat. She munches a massive chocolate chip cookie, too. I have a handful of roasted almonds. She wears a mysterious thing that looks like jean overalls, but is red, shiny, and skintight. I wear soft heather gray pants, a matching turtleneck, and a long zippered hoodie sweater. I am Mister Rogers; she is RuPaul on a bender.

Maggie agreed to meet me here on the condition that I pay

for it, because she insists she is not stupid enough to pay four bucks for a cup of coffee—but if I am, she is more than happy to drink it. She had me buy cookies for her kids, too, which is fine. Not that they need any more junk food, but whatever. Those kids are not my problem. If I let them be my problem, my life will be mired in regrets and miseries I'd rather avoid. I'll do it right when I have kids of my own. Until then, they sink or swim on their own. It sounds cold, but it is survival.

She has brought a catalog from the community college, which she hopes to start next month, in computer programming or nursing, she can't decide. She wants me to help her pick out classes. I tell her that her real talent is and has always been story-telling. She should be a writer.

She doesn't want to hear this.

"I need *money*, Christy," she tells me. "Writing is a stupid way to make a living."

"There are people who do it," I object.

"Whatever."

"Then be a nurse," I suggest without much feeling. My heart aches because I want her to escape her world so desperately, I want to help her, but I don't know what I can do to convince her that the only real way out is to do what you love.

"Why are you looking at me like I'm a stray dog?" she asks.

"Because. Forget CNM," I tell her, gesturing to the big adobe buildings across Central Avenue. "Go to UNM, get a four-year degree. The associate's won't help much. It probably won't help at all. There is no bigger scam than the associate's degree."

Maggie looks wounded. I have never seen that look on her face. She is usually so tough and in control.

I feel something strange in my chest, and realize it is guilt. As quickly as it comes, I send it away. Guilt is the domain of the weak. I am strong. That's how I got out, and it's going to have to be her way, too.

Outside, it is snowing and cars inch along Central Avenue with their headlights on.

"I'll do these credits and transfer them," she says. "I can't afford no UNM right now anyway, not with Christmas presents and all that. Unless they let me pay in free panties, I'm out of luck." She drops her pen and buries her face in her hands for a moment, in despair. "Shit, girl, life was easier when Cesar was selling drugs."

I look at her with wide eyes to tell her to shut up, and then give a paranoid look at all the college students and others seated nearby. All I need is to have her get me hauled in to confess about Cesar's drug and gang activity.

"You can't talk like that around here," I whisper.

"Whatever," says Maggie. "Like they don't all buy them." She stares at my ears and neck, makes a wry face, and says, "Nice bling. New?"

"Yeah."

"Must be nice."

"Maggie, please. Let's not get into this again, okay?"

"It's just, your mom and dad, they need help with the mort-gage sometimes, and you don't ever step up. But you got all that bling. I don't get it."

"Personal responsibility," I tell her.

"They're your parents, Christy."

"And I love them, which is why I think they need to learn to stop gambling and take some responsibility."

"Fine," she sighs, annoyed with me. "Tell me about the date."

She takes a sparkly pink notebook, the kind a girl would use, out of her plastic fringy handbag, and picks up the pen again.

"What is that for?" I ask.

"I'm taking notes. I'm keeping track of the game."

"Game?"

"That's what this is. Let me live vicariously through you," says Maggie. "I want every detail. If you won't help a *prima* out, at least I can come for the ride."

"See?" I tell her. "That, what you're doing right now, that's what writers do! You're a natural-born writer. If you'd just do that, you'd be fine."

"Just shut up and talk, *cabrona*," she says, blushing. "You're so stupid."

So I tell Maggie about the rock-climbing lesson—where all I could do was worry about how huge my ass looked to Melchior as I scrambled for footholds and he stood beneath me holding on to the rope that, if he let go, suspended me above certain doom.

"I'm sure your ass was fine. I mean, *what* ass? You practically don't even have one anymore. You whittled it down to a a white-girl ass."

"I don't even know why I cared, honestly," I lie. "I wasn't that into him."

"He's not that bad, is he? He's totally hot, Christy. *Qué te pasa?*"

"I know. He looked great climbing, too. Very muscular, and after a while he seemed to loosen up a little and cheered up and stopped talking about his chimpanzees, for about ten minutes. It was a nice ten minutes."

"That's totally sweet, by the way," she says. "Him talking about his animal friends."

"Yeah, when it's not creepy."

"How is it creepy that he loves animals and the planet, *pocha?*" Maggie gives me a dirty look. "Creepy is when the dude is talking about how he killed his dog for not fighting well enough."

"I see your point. But— It's one thing to love animals, but he's obsessed with chimpanzees. I mean, *obsessed.*"

"So? He worships them. He's sheltered, and smart, and hot, and he's got that Aztec-*chino* vibe going. He's got a good job with a pension. It makes you want to save him, doesn't it?"

"I don't know. Maybe."

"What else happened?"

I tell her about how after an hour of climbing I was starting to get blisters, so he helped me get the awkward harness off and his hands lingered on my hips again and our eyes connected and, I tell her, "we had a moment."

"Hot," says Maggie.

"It actually sort of was. He was very muscular and sweaty."

"Hot."

"I think he smells good. We definitely have good chemistry, from a pure pheromone point of view."

"So that's good, right?"

"Anyway. I don't know. I miss Zach."

"Shut up. *Tonta*."

"I do. I'm sorry. I just don't believe any of this."

"Shut *up*."

"Anyway, I could never sleep with a guy like Melchior. I'd just keep thinking of his monkeys, like their ghosts would be right there in the room with us."

Maggie laughs out loud and tells me I'm crazy. I tell her about how we got back into Becky and drove to the foothills, to a pretty isolated spot. Melchior had some frozen food in this compartment in the back of Becky, and he pitched a tent, tucked me into a folding chair with a puffy blanket and a book about chimpanzees, and built a fire and cooked me dinner in the mountains.

"There's a refrigerator in Becky?" asks Maggie, dumbfounded.

"More like a morgue. It's like a drawer that slides out."

Maggie looks at me with a disgusted face and just blinks for a minute.

"Welcome to my world," I tell her. "Run while you can."

"What did he make?" she asks, finally.

"He made buffalo steak and corn on the cob."

Maggie stares in disbelief. "He served you some prairie cow nonsense that ain't anybody eaten for four hundred years?"

"Yes, and he had a sermon about how cows are ruining the

natural habitat of the West and how we should replace them with buffalo, which are native to the land and good for it, and how their meat is healthier, and how cows contribute to global warming with their farts."

"He talked farts over buffalo dinner?"

"Indeed."

"And you didn't leave right there?"

"How was I supposed to do that? Hike?"

"Was it good? The buffalo?"

"It was very good. It was actually good, yes."

"Did you freeze your *nalgas* off?"

"It was surprisingly warm in the tent, and he said that was the point, that he wanted me to see that people need very little energy to be comfortable."

Maggie looks doubtful now. "I give him extra credit for coming up with an original date," she says. "But if some *loco* tried to take my ass on a bufffalo steak picnic in December, I'd have to hurt him."

"Once we had some wine in us, he started talking about his ex-wife, and then it got sort of interesting."

Maggie wipes a bit of whipped cream from her upper lip. "Melchior was *married*?"

I nod. "I know. I had a hard time picturing it myself."

"Y?" she asks. "What happened?"

"She came out of the closet."

Maggie's mouth hangs open in astonishment. "No!"

"Yup. She's a personal trainer at the very gym I go to."

"No!"

"She ran off with another personal trainer."

"*Pues, mira!* You have a lot in common, you and El Chimp Whisperer."

I wince. "I know. I'd rather we didn't have that in common."

"Be happy about that. It's good. You can commiserate."

"I am happy, sort of. And surprised. And I don't want to get my hopes up, Maggie. I can't go through any more pain with men. I just can't."

"Any nookie?"

I balk. "What? No! I am following the rules you laid out."

"I just figured, the tent, the fire, the dark, it's cold, you had some wine. You can't always control yourself."

"I can. *You* can't maybe, but I can."

"You suck." She sips her drink with laughing eyes. "I missed you."

"I'm right here, dummy."

"No, I *missed* you. When you were married to the fag, you stopped hanging out."

I make a face to let her know I still don't approve of this obnoxious slur. "I know. Sorry. Zach. He wasn't comfortable . . ."

"With girls and spics, I know," she says abruptly, stating the obvious and until now unspoken truth that Zach just wasn't all that down with the barrio or my family. Forget chile. Ketchup made Zach sweat.

"So, who's next on the list?" she asks.

"The friendly ghost."

"Oh! Caspar. We like him. He is *fine*, girl."

"You just think that cuz he's *guedito*," I say. "You should examine that. A little self-loathing, care of Univision, has sunk in, methinks."

"No. He's just fine. That's all. Zach was white as shit, and I never thought he was fine."

"Shit's brown," I remind her.

She laughs. "*Órale*. You are so literal, *'hita*. Sometimes I think you're all Rain Man or something."

Maggie shakes her head and looks around at the self-important-college-student types clogging the café.

"You know, I always wondered how a smart and pretty girl like you ended up with such a sad personal life. You're just plain cynical. That's why."

"Maybe so," I say again. "But if that's the case, I like being mean."

"I like you mean, too." She looks at her cheap Timex. "I have to get to work. Doing overtime to get the kids some nice things."

"Okay."

Maggie gathers her plastic Target purse and the keys to her ancient dented Impala and scoops the community college catalog up as though it were made of gold, a wistful look in her eye.

"Just try to be nice to the ghost," she goads me. "I want a full report back."

"Honestly, Maggie, I don't think I can go through with this whole thing," I tell her.

She shrugs. "It's up to you. I'm just trying to help you out. Talk to you later."

I watch her start to go with a terrible guilt, because she has to work so hard for every scrap life gives her, and I have just netted a windfall that could tide me over until next spring if I want. I could help her, but in the end what good would it do? She'd spend what I gave her, and end up right back where she was.

I remind myself about personal responsibility, the main reason I don't give my family my money: We all have to live with the decisions we've made. Maggie, unfortunately, made the wrong ones, and it's up to her to get herself out.

Speaking of getting herself out, why is she standing there in the doorway, mouth hanging open, waving me over?

$\mathcal{I}$ go to the door, where Maggie is now jumping and flapping like a half-dead bird.

"What the hell is wrong with you?" I ask.

Maggie cannot speak. She can only point outside, to the sidewalk, where a man is standing and making out with what appears to be a very busty blond college student in a pair of tight pink sweatpants that read FIRM across the ass.

"Zach?" I say, softly but no less miserable for it.

"Girl, what the *fuck?*" asks Maggie.

"Maybe she's a drag queen," I offer weakly, the tears forming in my eyes.

The kiss ends, and Zach, wearing his mountain man parka and hiking boots, pats the girl on the butt, and pretends he's going to bite her neck. Then they start to walk away, toward the east.

"Get your stuff," says Maggie.

"What?" I ask, as I am numb and cannot breathe right. I feel dizzy and sick.

"Your overpriced purse and whatever, your overpriced coffee. Go get them."

I stand, dazed, so Maggie huffily goes and gets my things for me, shoves them at me, and opens the door. A cold, snowy wind blasts in.

"Where are you going?" I ask her.

"We," says Maggie dramatically, "are going to go ask Mr. Fag there a question or two."

I feel like we are Lucy and Ethel, and Ricky is up ahead with his hand on some backup dancer's hind side. We give chase, through the snow, and catch up to them at the stoplight by the Frontier Restaurant. I look at the place. It is a giant yellow barn of a thing, and I feel like the pig being led to *matanza*.

"Hello, Zach," says Maggie, just as my supposedly gay ex-husband locks lips with a woman nearly young enough to be my daughter, and certainly white enough to join the Aryan Nation as its prized pinup girl.

Zach looks up and sees her, his face registers recognition, and his eyes quickly scan the scene looking for the thing he dreads most. Me.

"Hello," I say as his eyes find mine.

"Christy!" he says, stunned. He drops the blonde's hand, and the girl stares balefully at him. She hangs on his shoulder and cocks her head to the side at me.

"Hi," I tell her. I jut my hand into the space between us. "I'm Zach's ex-wife. The one he told he was gay in order to divorce."

The blonde looks confused. Zach laughs uncomfortably. Maggie cracks her knuckles and stares him down.

"Okay, okay, look," says Zach, shrugging the girl off him again. "I can explain."

And he does. Standing there in the darkening snow, my ex-husband tells me that he was inspired by a novel he read, in which the protagonist, unable to face the prospect of enmity with his wife if he asks her for the divorce he's been wanting, tells her he's gay in the hopes of getting a divorce while still remaining friends.

"So you see, Christy, it's actually because I love you so much that I didn't want to lose you."

Maggie pulls back like she's going to knock his teeth out, and he flinches. Maggie seems to enjoy this.

"So what was the real reason you wanted out?" I ask.

"I don't know," he says, though clearly he does know. "I guess I just didn't think we were compatible."

At this news, the blonde gloms onto his beefy shoulder again.

"You wanted bigger boobs," I say, remembering how he'd suggested I get implants once, and how he used to always go to the strip clubs and Hooters.

Zach shakes his head no, but it is without sincerity and his eyes flicker, for the tiniest of moments but long enough for me to see, on his date's ample, gravity-defying rack.

Maggie pulls me away from him now. "Get me away from this man before I kill him," she says.

I stumble numbly, blindly along at her side, and try to feel something. Anything.

Fail.

"Do you believe me now?" she asks, tears choking her own words.

"What do you mean?"

"You need to get out there, Christy. You need to give real men a chance. You were always too good for that spindly little asshole."

I look up at her now, snowflakes in my eyelashes, and say, "You know what, Maggie? You really should be a writer. You just described him exactly. He *is* a spindly little asshole."

"Fine," she says, impatiently. "I'll study writing, if you promise me you'll go on the rest of those dates, and please stop following the advice in those fucking books written by anorexic white women who hate their noses."

I mope for a few days, set fire to photos of Zach, make a voodoo doll of him and stick pins in the crotch, and then, before I know it, date number two comes around.

Caspar picks me up, and he's brought a gift for my mother—which is odd and endearing at the same time. It's a new set of scrapbooking papers from Michael's, from the Crafty Chica line; she'd been mooning over her sister's copy at the *matanza*, but I am stunned that anyone—much less a man—noticed.

"She's going to love it," I tell him. "I'll just leave it with the doorman and be right back." I duck in, and return promptly.

We're standing on the same sidewalk outside my loft, albeit on a busy weekday mid-morning, on our way to grab coffee before whatever date it is he has planned.

It is a cold, bright, sunny day, with zero wind, and I feel oddly liberated that Zach is not actually gay, and as though I can actually move on with my life now, trusting my instincts after all. My instincts about Caspar?

Mexcellent.

Caspar is truly "fine," just as Maggie said. He's completely out of my league, and every time he smiles at me I do a quick double take to make sure he's not actually looking at someone else. I never get men like this. I rather wish Zach would happen along again, so that he could see me with this man.

Caspar is what you might call a pretty boy, very different from Zach. He's tall, slender yet strong, and dressed in jeans that look very expensive and tasteful without trying too hard and a white button-down shirt with a black bomber jacket over it. It's odd, because I have inadvertently worn a very similar outfit, jeans with a white cashmere turtleneck and a black leather jacket over it. His hair is stylishly messy, though it certainly looks intentional. He smells faintly of expensive cologne, and he's got a sparkly Rolex on his wrist.

"That was very nice," I say, of the scrapbooking kit.

"Hope it doesn't seem like I'm trying too hard," Caspar says as we easily begin walking down the street, I assume to his car. "I just really like what I know of you so far, and your family is great."

Caspar's shiny black BMW is a million miles removed from

the freakish contraption Melchior drove, and it's a lot like my own black Mercedes. We have similar tastes, obviously. He's got the top-of-the-line model, too, a large sedan with a clean beige interior that smells brand-new. He starts the engine and it barely makes a sound. The stereo plays gently, something jazzy and unobtrusive.

"You don't have a name for it, do you?" I ask him, still smarting from the last date.

"For the car?" he asks. "You mean, like cousin Melchy with La Becky?"

My eyes widen at his instant understanding of the subtext of my comment. He grins.

"You gotta be patient with Melchy, Christy—do you prefer Christy, or Christina? I heard your mom call you Christina, and I don't want to screw it up."

"Christy is fine." I relax into my seat, amazed at how different two cousins can be. One kept forgetting my name; the other remembers both ways people call me.

"Either way, the name suits you," he tells me. "Christy is incredibly cute, and Christina is a beautiful name. You are both cute and beautiful, so there you go."

"Thanks." I hate myself for blushing.

"It's true." He pulls into traffic, and is a very good, confident driver. "Not many women are both. You have your beautiful women, like Gisele Bündchen. And you have your cute women, like Rachael Ray. Every now and then, you get the women who are both, like Scarlett Johansson or Natalie Portman. Or," he says, tilting his head a little bit toward me without taking his eyes off the road, "you."

"I don't think I belong in the same category as those women."

"I do." He says this matter-of-factly.

"Well, you're wrong."

I smile to myself. Yeah, I think, in Cassandra mode. Maybe I am.

Look, I don't want to sound like a bragger, because that's idiotic, but I've met all the women I just listed. I know what they look like in person, and I know what they look like without makeup. You are every bit as cute and beautiful as Natalie or Scarlett."

"Whatever."

"Hey," he says cheerfully. "Listen to me for a second. I went to a Hispanic women's empowerment event not too long ago, because one of my clients was giving the keynote, and I heard someone say something very interesting. They said Latinas are not very good at taking compliments. They said you guys are always deflecting them. They did a whole workshop on how women need to learn how to hear a compliment and just say thank you. Accept it. Stop selling yourself short. Your subconscious hears it, whatever your response is, and believes it. So if you're always downplaying your greatness, you become, in a way, your own worst enemy."

"I take compliments very nicely in my job," I say, annoyed that he's right.

"That's different. Lots of women are confident about their work, but lousy at taking personal compliments. So you're cute and you're beautiful, accept it. And I am enjoying getting to know you."

I hesitate before saying, "Thank you," and realize afterward that it feels very good.

Zach, before he became "gay," had a habit of pinching whatever fat he could find on my arms and telling me how cute it was to find a woman my age with so much baby fat. Now that I think about this, it wasn't such a nice thing to do, though at the time I rather agreed with him.

I smile because, really, I *can* do better than the ex. I can. There *are* better men out there.

"That's what I like to see," he says as he catches my grin.

Caspar turns his car onto the freeway headed north, and explains that the coffee will be drive-through Starbucks because we are going to a party at a house in Santa Fe. He apologizes for the long drive, but says that when he heard about the party, he didn't think he could deny me the fun of going.

"It is always amusing to watch rappers make asses out of themselves, but I figure it will be even more fun if you're there to laugh with me."

He refuses to tell me whose party it is, but does it in such a nice and pleasing way that I feel no urge to push. Rather, I just sit back in the luxury of my seat and enjoy being driven somewhere mysterious by a man who has, so far, made me feel very good about myself, just by being around him.

"Can I ask you something?" I say.

"Sure." He smiles at me.

"The poor people in your family up in Santa Fe—do they always ask you for money?"

Caspar's eyes open wide and he nods. "All the time."

"Same with mine," I say.

"Do you give it to them?" he asks.

"I used to," I say. "But I don' think it ever actually changes or helps anything."

"Agreed," he tells me. "People need to learn to take care of themselves."

Too good, I think, to be true.

We get to Santa Fe, a brown adobe city nestled at the foot of the majestic dark purple Sangre de Cristo Mountains which are, at this time of year, lightly powdered with snow. We keep driving north.

The large adobe house is just outside of the city, on the road to Las Vegas, New Mexico, up a twisty mountain path, in a juniper and piñon forest. Caspar drives deftly through the challenging snow along the bumpy dirt road and through the gates of what appears to be a massive ranch or hacienda.

We come forward a bit and find a valet stand, with two freezing-cold men in red coats waiting. Caspar realizes we have no choice but to use valet service. He says it feels lazy to him to do this, but "when in Rome or Santa Fe, do as the locals." He is so down-to-earth, and yet obviously also so successful, that it brings me comfort. Maybe there are thoughtful people left in the upper class. Maybe my aspirations of wealth are not shallow.

The rapper whose house this is has left a couple of very hot tall black women in ski bunny outfits, models most likely, stationed near the valet stand, to direct us up the hill to the house. I roll my eyes at Caspar, and he gently rolls his back.

"New money," he says softly as we hike toward the very obviously blinged-out house at the top of the hill.

"Do you come from money?" I ask. He laughs.

"I grew up comfortable. Sure. You could say that. I don't like to brag about it, especially around my cousins, because they both struggled as kids. I mean, Melchy does all right now, but Balthazar— You know, he was raised pretty poor and he's still really struggling. I have huge admiration for people who come out of difficult circumstances, and go on to succeed." He eyes me in a way that lets me know he means me. "But Balthazar, I doubt he could support a family, you know? It's sad. But, yeah, I'm comfortable. No doubt."

This should not make me unspeakably happy, but it does anyway.

If I were to ever marry Caspar—and not that I think I would, but you never know—his parents would not need help with the mortgage because they took out a bad loan on a refi and are stuck with an interest rate they didn't bother to read about.

I love my parents, but they can be just plain stupid.

I'm dying to ask Caspar what "comfortable" means, and what his parents did (or do) for a living, but now is not the right time. We are on the large wraparound porch, with the view of the entire city and valley, and it is being monitored by a couple of burly thugs with sunglasses. I get nervous at the sight of them, but they instantly recognize Caspar and break into big grins. They do fancy handshakes with him, hug him in that manly back-slapping way, and open the red velvet rope to let us into the entryway of the enormous house. The door is very tall, maybe fifteen feet high. I can hear loud hip-hop music and laughter.

"Remember," Caspar whispers as we step into the house, which already smells like pot and expensive perfume. "It's a circus and none of them realize they're performers in the freak show. I wanted to show you what sins Dirty South can wreak upon Southwestern charm."

There is a large sunken living room, which with the right furnishings could be exquisite because of the grand views of nature outside the large windows. As it is, however, it looks to have been decorated by someone channeling Scarface—very gaudy gilded furniture that is inappropriate for any home, but wildly so for a modern adobe masterpiece like this. Dripping with gold, and sitting like Jaba the Hut in the center of the leather sofa, is a young, obese man I recognize as the rap star Switchblade Mouff. He is fat as a dumpling, and wears a hockey jersey with jeans, a million fat gold chains, and massive dark glasses. He is surrounded by girls very much like the ones who waited back at the valet kiosk, and they appear to be helping him with a marijuana cigarette the size of Delaware. At the sight of Caspar, his face lights up. He flashes a mouth (or should I say "mouff"?) full of gold and diamond-encrusted teeth, the looks of which instantly make me want to brush my own.

Caspar and Switchblade hug each other, and the rapper introduces him to the assembled girls and fans as "my agent." Caspar does a little small talk, and then takes me by the arm to lead me around the house. Switchblade is so high he doesn't seem to care where we go. There are, surprisingly, a lot of famous people here. Five movie stars, and at least six other music stars. I knew New Mexico was starting to attract celebrities, because of our growing film industry, but I am frankly surprised to see so many of them here. To round out the crowd, there are a bunch of the types of people you'd expect to find with stars—handlers, groupies, parents, friends, even some small children running around in the ganja haze, playing with toy guns.

Merry Christmas, bang bang you're dead.

I realize from the way Caspar introduces me to people that he thinks I might be impressed by the celebrity factor. He clearly doesn't understand that I deal with these types of people all the time in my work. I mean, New Mexico's rich elites are a little different from Southern California celebrities for sure, but the software giants and weapons makers who hire me have every bit as much money as these people and, I think unkindly, better taste.

"Interesting," Caspar tells me.

"What is?" I do my best to look demure and not stare, just like The Rules book says to.

"You. You're not impressed by any of this."

"Should I be?"

"No. Not at all." He grins. "I'm glad you're not. It's nice. With my cousins, you know, especially with Zar, there's the wow factor with the whole celeb thing. It's tiresome."

We sit near a massive kiva fireplace that rages at one end of a great room overlooking a giant ridge and river below, and soon a girl in short-shorts (December? Hello?) brings us champagne on a silver tray. We take the flutes and Caspar makes a toast.

"To me hopefully doing better on my date than Melchior."

"A girl never tells." I clink my glass with his. He watches me in amusement as he takes a sip. It is very hard, but I try to seem disinterested yet polite, in the interest of making him crazy for me.

"Let me guess," Caspar says. "You have celebrity clients."

"Something like that." I try to smile mysteriously, and, by Jove, I think it works, because Caspar's eyes widen and he looks a bit caught off guard.

Caspar takes out his iPhone and asks if he can see any of my work online. I have a portfolio on my Web site, but feel awkward about it.

"Is this a test?" I ask him.

"No, I just— I'm curious now. You've got me wondering."

I direct him to my site, and to the portfolio.

"Hot," he says of the photo of me in all black that graces the home page. I catch myself about to blow it off, or about to confess to the picture having been airbrushed to make me look thinner and with whiter teeth, but Cassandra stops me.

"Thank you," I say, looking him directly in the eye. "I like that top a lot. The photos came out well, I thought."

"She learns quickly, too," he says, tapping my temple affectionately. "Nothing like a smart, pretty girl."

Caspar continues to look through all the pages in my portfolio with his jaw dropped open.

"You didn't tell me you were brilliant," he says.

"You didn't tell me you represented Switchblade Mouff," I counter.

This makes Caspar laugh out loud. "Yeah, okay," he says.

"Except that for *you*, your work is something to brag about. You are incredibly talented. And for me, I don't think there's anything all that dignified about saying you rep someone named Switchblade Mouff."

"Except that he's really famous and very rich."

Caspar shrugs. "He's a dipshit kid from the Bronx who got lucky, and I got luckier." He stares at the images of a house I did last year. "But this, this! You got it."

"Yeah?"

"Yeah. You got talent, girl. I'm not used to dating amazing women. This is going to be fun."

Why is he staring at me? I wonder, suddenly.

Oh, that's right. He's staring at Cassandra. She better not let me blow it.

I look around at all the models and perfect-looking women, and give him a doubting face.

"They look great. It's true. But most of them don't go much deeper than that. Most of them just want to be around me or other agents because we can introduce them to famous people, or they think I can get them in a movie or something."

"Oh, come on, the entertainment business is big enough that there must be a lot of interesting women around. And Santa Fe, too? I mean, you've got the artists and the writers. Maybe you just run around in the wrong crowds."

He glances around and shrugs in defeat with a chuckle. "Gee, you think?"

We both laugh out loud at this, because he really doesn't fit in here any better than I do.

This is when he tells me that he did not bring me to this party to meet Switchblade, or any of the other celebrities, but to get my opinion on a young man who is going to perform for the party in a little while.

"He's Switchblade's find," Caspar tells me. "He wants me to sign the kid. I heard a demo, but Switch told me to really appreciate him I had to hear him live. I wanted to see what you thought."

"Another rapper?"

Caspar laughs. "No, babe, that's the thing. This guy? He's supposed to sing like an Andrea Bocelli from the hood."

We keep talking and Caspar tells me that Switchblade has been looking for someone to do interiors for his new Malibu beach house. "I'd like to go show him your stuff right now."

"No," I say, as Cassandra, demure and confidently touching his arm. "Please, don't."

"What? Why not?"

"I don't know how to say this, Caspar, but I'm sort of choosy about my clients. And I'm pretty booked up right now, well into next year."

A Rules Girl always seems independent, busy, and confident. She doesn't need a man's help.

Caspar looks very impressed now. "You're *rejecting* Switchblade?"

"Don't think of it like that." I look around at the room, which is very tacky. "It's just that I think a client and a designer need to be in sync with their ideas, or it ends up being a long drawn-out fight, and the client comes away disappointed."

"You've never seen his house, though."

"Is this his house, too?"

"Yeah." Caspar looks about him as though he understands, finally, my point. "You think he's got bad taste?"

I smile and blink sweetly, a Rules Girl through and through. "I think he has great taste in agents."

Caspar blushes a little, and beams a smile at me. "Well, you should know, a lot of it is an act. I think he'd really dig a nice, tasteful villa. He just hasn't ever been exposed to that kind of thing."

"Thanks, Caspar, but I'm cool. I've got jobs lined up for all next year. I'm booked."

Caspar downs the last of his champagne, and gives me a look of confused admiration.

"Wow," he says.

"Wow what?"

"I have never in all my life met anyone like you. A girl from the South Valley, who through talent and hard work has risen to the top. Impressive."

With a tingle, I realize I've never met anyone like him, either.

"I hope this doesn't sound obnoxious," he says, "but from a purely objective standpoint, I think of all the Reyes cousins I am the best match for you."

"You think?"

"Melchy, well, let's get real here. He smells like monkey scat, for one."

I laugh. It is unkind, but funny, and I appreciate his use of an obscure word.

"And Zar's just flat broke."

"Which isn't a big deal," I say, because it is the right thing to say.

"I'm sure you do well on your own," says Caspar. "That's not what I mean. It drives me nuts when the old ladies in our culture always say you young professionals have to marry rich men. It's stupid. What I mean is, you know, you need someone at your own level, who isn't going to be threatened by what you have."

"You think Balthazar would be threatened?" I ask.

Caspar leans back, totally at ease in this house, and in this life, and says, "No offense, but Zar is a little provincial. I don't want to color how you feel about it, but, you know, I'm just being honest here."

"I appreciate that," I·tell him.

"Hey, it's my nature."

Maggie has met me at the Midtown Sports and Wellness for my usual morning workout. She has the mornings off now, and is working nights at the call center. She doesn't usually exercise, being prone, as we know, to cigarettes and beer, but I've convinced her to come just to people watch; and because I'm starting a new job in Corrales after the holidays, and am preparing for it, I don't have a lot of time to be hanging out in cafés. Whenever possible anymore, I try to get together with my friends and family to do something other than eat, which is all anyone ever seems to be able to think to do.

Maggie wears tight gray sweats, the thick kind we wore back in high school. They look like they could have been issued by a women's prison. I wear my usual baggy yoga pants and sports bra with a tank top over it. I'm on the elliptical trainer on the top floor, in the cardio room, with the windows that look out over the parking lot. The ellipticals are in the second of three rows of machines facing the windows and the large TVs screwed into the wall above them. I have never liked watching TV while working out, preferring my iPod and jamming out to Latin dance music, whether it's rap, reggaeton, or salsa and merengue.

Maggie sits on the seat of a stationary bike next to me, staring in disbelief at the man who comes in shorts, black socks, and dress shoes to walk on the treadmill each morning, and the other guy, on the stair stepper with a towel completely over his head.

"Do you have to be some kind of crazy to join this place?" she asks me.

"Yes," I say, realizing that I'll never completely give up sarcasm because, let's face it, it's just too much fun. "That, and narcissistic."

Maggie herself gave up on the whole sweat thing about five minutes into it, forty minutes ago. I've just barely broken a sweat, since I am used to doing 1.5 hours of cardio a day, plus half an hour of weights and abs afterward.

"So this kid, he could sing?" she asks me, her eyes still in stern judgment of the knee-sock man.

I try to find a way to explain to her the completely un-expected and magical experience of listening to eleven-year-old Jacob Lewis sing that night, in the courtyard of Switchblade Mouff's house. The sky was dark, the lights of the city a couple dozen miles off at least, and there he was, this absolutely stun-ningly beautiful African American kid with the face of an angel and little round glasses on his nose, standing on the tiny stage and singing an aria from a Bizet opera. Even the most hardened thug among the group could not help growing teary-eyed as he went on to sing in his incredible tenor an arrangement of well-known classical pieces.

"It was the last thing I expected," I tell Maggie.

"That's what I wanted." She nods approvingly. "That's a good-ass date."

"Yes," I say, as I ramp up the tension a bit, enjoying the burn in my quadriceps.

"So what happened next?"

I tell Maggie about how all the industry people, music and film, crowded around the kid, and about how Caspar got roped in by Switchblade to push them back. I tell her about how Caspar talked to Jacob's parents and signed the kid to a contract on the spot.

"He was amazing with Jacob," I tell her, panting just a little. "He was soft-spoken and sensitive, and made him feel safe. He told the family about how he usually takes fifteen percent but that for such a brilliant young man he'd cut back to ten. He made them feel comfortable and trusted, and you could just tell he was sincere and real. You know? You could tell the kid was overwhelmed. He goes to this arts school in New York, and Switchblade is his uncle, but like through marriage or something. They were out here for the holidays."

At this moment, the crazy self-tanning white woman I have told Maggie about—and whom Melchior had noticed before— appears, in her usual pink short-shorts riding deep into the crack in her ass. She's got to be about forty-five but is in relatively good shape from running. She has dried-out blond hair, and likes to stand with her feet planted very wide. Every man in the gym stares at her because of this, but not necessarily because she is attractive. Rather, it is because she is obviously horny and in love with herself. She is not, however, in as good a shape as she thinks she is, and appears to be some kind of nymphomaniac exhibitionist.

Maggie stares is horror at the woman we've come to call Miss Streaky Cheeks, because, just as I've told Maggie, there are stripes down her legs where she has sweat the self-tanner away. Her white T-shirt is also blotched with brown sweat from the same thing.

Maggie mouths "What the fuck?" to me, and I try very hard not to laugh. Miss Streaky Cheeks wears headphones and likely can't hear it when Maggie says, out loud, "Ain't it funny how badly they want our skin tone, and how much they like our food, but how rarely they seem to like us?"

"Maggie, please," I say. This is not the time or place to start a fight, I think. In fact, there is never a time or place to start a physical altercation, if you are a grown woman with children, but that doesn't stop Maggie. "Disgusting," she says.

"ack to the singer," I say. Maggie peels her eyes from Miss Streaky Cheeks.

"I bet she smells like herpes," she tells me.

"Ick. Please, let's talk about my date again. Before you get me thrown out of this place."

"What is Caspar going to do with the kid?" she asks, with a sigh meant to convey her weariness with white people, gyms, and all the other stuff I've adopted in my life.

"He's not sure. We talked about it a lot, about how the industry might treat a kid of color singing opera, but the thing is, this kid was fantastic, Maggie! He was—I don't know. He had a maturity to him. He has potential to be like Andrea Bocelli or Plácido Domingo or something. Or like a male whatshername."

"Who?"

"Famous black woman who sang opera."

"The closest I ever got to opera was watching the movie about Mozart," she says.

"Jessye Norman," I blurt. "That's her name. He's like the male version of her, only he's still a little kid."

"Sounds like you had a much better time with Caspar than you did with the other one."

"Melchior."

"Weird-ass name."

"I know. Suits the man."

"No, now come on. You never know, Christy. Take your time and get to know these guys. You really don't know what's what until you've had at least three dates."

"I know that Caspar is a really cool guy."

"That's what you think right now."

"He just is, Maggie. You know. When you know, you know. He's nice, and kind to children, and he's really, really good-looking. You have to admit."

"What does he have planned for your next date?" she asks.

"I don't know. I don't care. I really want to see him again. I did The Rules, and they totally worked. He's texted me three times today, but I haven't written back. I'll wait until tomorrow and then tell him I've been really busy."

I smile and Maggie smiles back, and tells me she's happy for me and my newfound ability to make men beg.

I tell her about how Jacob came to sit with us for a long time after the performance, and how he told us his dream of getting hooked up with the Disney Channel and maybe having his own show.

"Caspar was real gentle with him, and told him that the big musical stars out of Disney tend to be girls, but that he would try to do what he could to change that, though he couldn't make promises. He was so direct with Jacob, but so loving, too. He was a compassionate agent, Maggie! I didn't think that existed."

The timer buzzes, and the hour of cardio on the trainer is over. I get off it, and tell Maggie I have to do the treadmill for another thirty minutes.

"You're a masochist," she tells me.

I snap my sweat towel at her, and she snaps hers back at me, and we both look at Streaky Cheeks and burst out laughing. Yep. Things are pretty much back to where they were in tenth grade. Except with a bit of hope, thanks to Cassandra, on my romantic horizon.

By the time my first date with Balthazar rolls around, I dread it. To my great surprise, I haven't been able to stop thinking about Caspar, and so I naturally have very little interest in starting something new with someone new, who is actually someone old who I have disliked for a very, very long time. But a Rules Girl and a Diamond Girl both date three men at once, and they don't get serious with any of them.

And so the day comes, because if you just keep breathing days have a tendency to do that, and before I know it, Balthazar has pulled up to the curb outside my loft, in his run-down old Ford pickup truck. I watch him from my living room window, wait for the door buzzer, and stall a little so that it doesn't seem like I've been sitting here for an hour, waiting for a date I don't particularly want to go on. I tell myself that this is just another opportunity to practice The Rules, but in reality I feel sick foreboding because of how this man used to treat me. It is nearly impossible to forget a thing like that.

I find him downstairs in faded Levis and a plain white hoody sweatshirt that looks new. He wears cowboy boots, which I find surprising. In junior high school he made fun of such footwear.

"Hi," I say, coldly, but with my best Rules Girl smile.

"Yo," says Balthazar, his shoulders shrugged up around his ears. He tries to look nice and harmless, but I'm not buying it. He looks embarrassed to be here, too, and seems to have a hard time looking me in the eye. I flinch, expecting something cruel to come out of his mouth.

"You look nice," he says.

I suppose it is mostly true. There is no greater inspiration to look your best than revenge, sadly. I'm wearing my most expensive, most flattering jeans, with pink Uggs and a form-fitting sweater and short black jacket.

"You have always looked great," I tell him with a bright smile. "Now is no exception."

He indeed looks very handsome, with his short dreads and his nerd glasses. His arms are big, stronger than I originally thought they would be. I can see big-gun biceps beneath the sweatshirt.

We walk toward the red truck. A *Sanford and Son* truck. It is high, old, and sort of crappy, truth be told. A man's truck, if that man were, say, a sharecropper who held his pants up with a piece of rope. It would go with the boots nicely if we lived in, say, Anton Chico, circa 1921. But we are in downtown Albuquerque, where most people at least try to be hip. I am cool, however, and mention none of this, because Rules Girls don't judge, or they don't do so out loud, anyway. At least he hasn't hung fake metal testicles on the back of it like some of the men around this state.

Balthazar helps me into the cab, which is about six miles off the ground and smells of resin, gasoline, and wool, and even shuts the door for me. He's acting like a gentleman, and I'm acting like a lady. We're both being lovely people, though I suspect we're just going through the motions here, and I wonder why either of us bothers.

He hoists himself into the driver's seat and fires up the engine with a great blast of revving. He's a revver. I should have known. The bullies are always a little show-offish.

"Nice *truck*." It comes out mean, like maybe I'd told Hitler "nice moustache." I meant for it to sound like a sincere compliment.

"Not a truck girl, I bet. What do you drive, Christy? A Lexus? Range Rover?"

"Mercedes," I say sweetly.

He chuckles, revs again, and pulls the truck noisily down the street. The laughing undoes me, and I push Cassandra out of the damn way to get a swing in.

"Nice to know more than a decade can pass and you're still laughing at me," I say.

"Look," he says after a big, patient sigh. "I told you I'm really sorry for middle school, and I meant it. If this is torture for you, we totally don't have to do it. We hated each other then, and . . ."

I interrupt him, my voice cracking with emotion that catches me off guard. "You hated *me*. I never hated you. I was nothing but nice to you. I always saw the best in you. I, I was practically in love with you. *Was*, okay? Don't get any ideas."

He tilts his head in thought. "Really?"

"Oh, like you didn't know it. Come on."

"I didn't. I was oblivious to a lot of things, Christy. Not that it matters now, but I should tell you my mom, she was going through some heavy shit back then, doing some bad stuff, and pulling us kids into it. I didn't know better. I was around all these dealers and pimps and people like that, and I just did what they did. I know better now, and I'm really, really sorry. But if you can, and I know this is hard, but if you can, try, for a little while, just try to see the kid I was, and try to understand that for me, there was no other way then. I was blind."

I sit silently, hit by the realization that he was truly just a child when these ugly things happened. He's a man now.

"Okay," I say. "I'm sorry. I'll let it go."

Balthazar looks over at me, and his eyes look a little extra wet, like he's fighting back tears. "We were from another country; I was born in the Dominican Republic. Bet you didn't know that, right?"

"I didn't."

"My dad knocked my mom up when he went there on vacation, and after I was born she came out here to be with him, but they didn't get along. My mom, she's had a lot of sad things happen to her, Christy. I love her to death, don't get me wrong, but sometimes girls, when they suffer a certain kind of abuse, they carry that with them for the rest of their lives. They never get over it, they keep repeating it. My dad, well, he saw that, and he loved her but he knew he had to get away from it. It's— It's a sad, long story that has nothing to do with you, but I feel like it might help you to see where I was coming from, if you knew the kind of home I grew up in."

"I'm very sorry, Balthazar. I didn't know."

"She worked for an escort service."

"I'm sorry."

He shrugs. "It was hard, to be a teenaged boy, interested in girls for the first time, with an artistic streak, and to be in this whole pimp and drug world. She got my brother hooked on crack, you know."

"Gosh, I'm so sorry. That's awful."

"It doesn't excuse what I did. I know that, and I own what I did. I just want you to understand, Christy, that I'm not that same boy I used to be. I've grown up, and with a lot of hard work, I like to think I'm a better person now. I'd like you to give me that chance, to prove it to you. But I know that what I did was terrible and painful for you. We don't have to do this. I understand if you despise me for how I acted. I can take you back home. Is that what you want?"

I think about it, and shake my head. "No," I say, trying to think of what a Rules Girl might say in this situation. I take an extra moment to gather my thoughts, something I do not normally do, and say, "I am grateful you felt comfortable opening up to me, and I am pleased that you've been able to pull yourself out of your circumstances. I'm proud of you."

Balthazar's face, braced for a blow, softens in surprise and he shoots a sideways glance at me, with a wry little smile.

"Wow," he says as the smile grows into a big grin. "I'd say we've both grown up a lot, girl!"

He drives on, the smile slowly fading. "You like pupusas?" he asks.

"They're okay." The truth is, I detest pupusas because they are deep-fried, and laden with calories that would take my career from me if I consumed them. Pupusas leave oil slicks on your fingers and lips.

"Be honest." He looks over at me.

"I'm being honest," I lie. "Whatever you like is fine with me."

"Too fattening?" he asks. "I'm just guessing here, from the look on your face."

"Okay, yes, you caught me. I'm not big on pupusas."

"No worries. I'm flexible. New plans. Pupusas not happening. Got it."

He turns the car down some side streets, heading toward the part of the far south and west valley where a lot of recently arrived immigrants live. My grandfather's brother, the loan shark, lives in the area, and I rarely visit him here because it's a bit on the dangerous side.

Balthazar brings the truck to a stop in front of a small Mexican seafood restaurant whose sign has been hand-painted on the side of the cobalt blue building—which is a residential house. To my surprise, the window displays an A rating from the state health department. I would have taken it for a D based upon the two rottweilers in the side yard, but hey, you just never know.

"Best ceviche in town," he says. "I think ceviche is carb-free. Right?"

"Uhm, probably. Sure."

"What? You want to go somewhere else?" he asks in a slightly teasing tone.

"No," I lie. "It's just, Maggie. She said these dates had to be out of the ordinary. And this," I shrug in that way of people who don't want to be offensive but do it anyway, "well, it's pretty ordinary."

Balthazar smiles at me at last, but it is a wicked sort of smile. "I heard her," he says. "But here's my question: Out of the ordinary for *whom?* This place is certainly humble, but I'm guessing it's far from ordinary for, well, let's just say for a lot of fancy professional-type people who live downtown."

I sit there in the cab, looking at him as he grins at me like a cat caught with a dead mouse. "I don't understand," I say.

"When's the last time you had dinner in the deep barrio?" he asks.

"Other than last night at my mom's?" I reply, obnoxiously.

"Your mom's is hardly the deep barrio, and you know it."

"Yes, it is."

"Christy, your parents live in a middle-class area that just happens to be populated by brown people. That doesn't make it the barrio."

I can't think of anything to say.

"So, what is it? How long since you went to a place like this, in the heart of the ghetto, run by immigrants?"

"There's a Vietnamese place by the fairgrounds where my ex and I used to go," I offer. "We heard gunshots there once."

"The *Mexican* barrio, Christy. When's the last time you set foot in one?"

"I don't know. I can't remember."

His grin bursts into a full smile and he laughs heartily. "Exactly!" He points a finger at me now. "So *this* is your out-of-the-ordinary date. I bet my cousins took you to some real elegant nonsense and you'd seen it all before."

I glance out the window again, and see three men with cowboy hats going into the restaurant. They wear gaudy jewelry.

He's right. I realize it, and admit it, and he is happy at last, because he seems to think he's caught me in some kind of weird lie, which he hasn't.

Except he has.

I follow Balthazar into the restaurant, and he greets the hostess in his perfect, sing-songy Spanish. My Spanish is pretty weak, so I just do the usual thing and smile and stand back. I feel like everyone in the place is staring at us. We take a table by a window, and it hits me how wonderful the place smells. Lime, chiles, pork, seafood, corn masa. The server is charming, and the tables and menus are spotless. I am ashamed to find this information surprising.

We place our orders, and try to talk, but find that there isn't much to say. At least I can't focus, because I'm too worried a cockroach will show up.

"So, what did you and Caspar talk about on your date?" he asks me.

"Oh, you know. Just stuff."

Balthazar shrugs. "I just never have found Caspar to be a stimulating conversationalist, and I was curious."

I think for a moment, and say, "He asked me questions." It is also an accusation, meant to point out that Balthazar has *not* asked me any questions.

"I just asked you what you and Caspar talked about," he says, instantly comprehending the slight in my comment.

"Yeah. True."

"So, what did he ask you?"

"He asked me what I disliked, and later he asked what frightened me."

"And you said—?" He leans forward on his elbows, interested to hear the answer.

"I don't remember."

Balthazar laughs.

"What scares *you?*" I ask him, because it would be bad to admit to the things that scare me—getting fat again, being single forever, never having children, growing old alone.

"Clowns. And needles," he says.

"That explains why you were never a junkie in the circus," I say.

He laughs. "I guess. Hate those things." He pantomimes giving himself a shot. "I am man enough to admit that I actually faint at the sight of 'em. Ever since I was a little kid. Vaccinations? Forget it. I'd literally pass out and fall on the floor. Me and needles? Nuh uh, nope. No way."

"Interesting."

"So what scares you, Christy? Besides the barrio, I mean?"

"That's not true," I protest.

He leans back smugly, his eyes now trained on the front door. "We'll see," he says. "We'll see."

The front door opens, and I watch in horrified fascination as an entire quinceañera party walks through the door. The girl whose party it is wears a tacky white wedding dress with a plastic tiara. Her girlfriends wear sherbet orange dresses that match the belts worn by the boys over their cheap tuxedo pants. The boys have all topped themselves with white cowboy hats. They all speak Spanish.

"Unbelievable," I say, snidely, to Balthazar. "A Mexican Memphis. That's what this neighborhood has turned into."

As a Mexican American I am used to tacitly and sometimes openly mocking the country people who are newly arrived from Mexico, for their taste and sensibilities. Balthazar does not meet my bemused comments with something snarky, as is usually the case, however. Rather, he studies my face with a sort of sadness, and says nothing.

The food comes, and we start to eat. Balthazar's eye keeps wandering to the kids from the quinceañera party, until he's unable to contain himself. He opens the messenger bag and pulls out a very expensive camera, and says to me, "Excuse me for a second."

I watch as he crosses the restaurant to where the kids are. He kneels down so that he is eye to eye with them where they sit, and chats with them a bit. I see them listening, suspiciously at first, but gradually with trust. Soon, he is up and snapping photos of them. They mug for the camera at first, but he says something to them and they stop. They act as though he weren't there. He hovers for about five minutes, snapping shot after shot, and coming to life in a way I have never seen. He is light on his feet, animated, intense, and—dare I say it?—beautiful to behold.

There is a possessed look to artists when they are absorbed in their work, a look I have always found irresistible.

He has it.

When he comes back, he looks joyous.

"What was that all about?" I ask.

"Here," he says. "Move over."

He scoots into the booth seat next to me this time, and starts to show me the shots he's gotten. Many are exquisite—so much so that they literally make me gasp.

He has shot in black and white, and he's found things in these kids I did not see at all. One shot is of the girl, sipping her drink through a straw and staring off into space, philosophically. He has captured confusion, sadness, worry, and a weary desperation in her gaze.

I realize, with great shame, that I had been so busy looking at the dress that I hadn't bothered to see this girl's eyes. She has a soul.

"I thought you were a sculptor," I say.

Balthazar shrugs. "I've had to learn to do a few different things to support myself. I've done a lot of wedding photography."

I remember Caspar telling me that of the three cousins Balthazar has the least money. That could be another reason he brought me here instead of planning something more showy and elaborate. He probably could not afford anything else.

"You take great photos," I say. "You've got a great eye."

"'Great' is an overused superlative," he answers with a

friendly wink. "Tina Modotti was a great photographer. I'm good but not great. I have a great eye, but my pictures are merely good."

He is not boasting. He's just being truthful, and I have to say I agree. "True," I say. "These are good. But in your case, these really are very good."

"I suppose I should just say thank you because that's what people are expected to do in these situations," he mumbles. "I've never liked social conventions for this very reason. They hamper truth."

He clicks to another shot, this one of the boys in the group, all bunched together looking at a Nintendo DS held by the one in the middle. The kid playing the game appears to have just screwed up, because agony registers on each and every face—agony, and brotherhood—but, I realize with a jolt, no envy. The word *community* comes to mind.

"That's a nearly great one," I say.

He examines my face again, and says, point-blank: "If I didn't know better, Christy, I'd say you look surprised by the way I've seen these kids."

I look right back, and say, "You're right. And I'm sorry about that."

Balthazar puts his hand gently on my back, and rubs the space between my shoulder blades.

"*Alma*," he says, his eyes narrowing at me.

"Soul?" I ask.

"You've got a good spirit," he tells me, with a quick smile, before darting back to his side of the table. "You just have to make peace with where you're from."

"Excuse me?" I say, balking and offended. "I know where I'm from."

Balthazar just smiles at me, serenely.

"So, now, Christy de la Cruz, famous designer," he says, safely on the other side, with the echo of his hand still burning through my shirt in tiny shivers. "Tell me about interior design. What has it done for you? But more importantly, what has it done for the world?"

Maggie and I speed-walk around the hard dirt track at the middle school near her house, after dinner. Well, we try to speed-walk; Maggie shuffles and tries not to keep grabbing for the cigarettes in her purse.

She's brought her male pit bull by way of compromise with Cesar, who is home with the kids playing a board game. Jenga, she told me. This surprised me, because I figured they'd just sit around giving the kids beer. Turns out they always have game night on Wednesdays, and this is no exception.

I think of them all gathered around the table, in their decrepit cookie-cutter tract home with the predictable bad lighting and mass-produced framed prints from Hobby Lobby and fake plants and Jesus place mats. Happy. I wonder if the couple whose home I just finished will ever have game night with their kids in it. Nah. I can't see it. What I do see? Parties full of self-important people who steal off to the bathroom to snort coke. Kids who are tended to by a nanny who they will end up accidentally calling mommy in front of their real mom, who will be high on prescription meds and driven to attempt suicide.

"You like game night?" I ask.

Maggie's face lights up. "*Love* game night. The little ones are starting to like chess, if you can believe it. You should come over next week and join us."

"Maybe."

"What, we're too low-class for you?" she jokes, but not really. "Cesar's super-smart, girl. I'm serious."

"That's not it at all," I say. I think about how it used to be that I thought I would never want my life that predictable and hearth-centric, but lately I crave exactly this sort of stability. Maybe I'm just getting old. Older. There is only so much going out you can do before it starts to feel like a chore. There is something comforting in the idea of a home and family. What I do not think I want, however, is a pit bull. It keeps stopping to crap, which is astonishing to me, because it has gone four times and has not run out yet.

"Again? *Caramba*, Maggie. Where does he keep it all?"

Maggie shugs. "One of life's great mysteries." She dutifully bends over, bags the excrement with the ease I might exhibit in choosing a croissant at the corner French bakery, and carries it to the trash can with no trace of disgust on her face.

I balk. "What if there was a hole in the bag? You didn't even check. What if it gets all over your hand?"

She shrugs again, placid, unshockable. "Hand sanitizer in the car. Water fountain over there. It's like I tell the kids, what don't kill you in the germ world makes you stronger. Antibodies."

She smiles because she sees the horror on my face. At least she has this over me. In this, Maggie has won. Motherhood hardens you, I realize. In popular culture, mothers are always portrayed as soft warm places for everyone else to land, but in reality they are made of stone.

"Do you think I'm a snob who's unable to see soulfulness in the barrio?" I ask her as we round the corner on lap nine.

"Of course," she says, without hesitation.

"Glad you had to think long and hard about that one. Thanks."

"It wasn't a very challenging question," she says. "What's next? Is Brad Pitt hot?"

He's getting old, you know, Brad Pitt." I stare at Maggie and wait for a reaction.

"Hotness of his magnificent magnitude knows no age."

"Robert Redford," I say. "People used to say that about him, but he looks like Orville Redenbacher now."

"Still hot."

"If you like old men, maybe."

"See?" she says, turning her upper body toward me and raising her brows, but still speed-walking like a goofball. "Snob."

"Uhm, no. Honest. There is a difference."

"It's not a secret, Christy. Everyone knows that you went elitist on us a long-ass time ago. I'm pretty sure it's when we all went to see *Jerry Maguire* in eleventh grade and you decided you were gonna model yourself on that horrible woman with the lips." She scrunches her lips up in a cloyingly annoying way.

"Renée Zellweger?"

"*Esa*. You were all Zellweger. With your bleach-blond updos and your cardigans and little gold jewelry."

"You? *Are insane.*"

"Please, you started to dress like her, and act like her, and you know you thought you'd grow up and marry some cheesy-ass agent who sprouted a conscience and had a breakdown because of it."

We both look at each other as we realize what she's just said.

"I don't mean Caspar," she says. "Except that maybe it all makes sense now. He reminds me of Tom Cruise a little bit, in that good-looking white-boy way."

"Caspar's not a sports agent. And he's half Mexican."

"Same difference."

"That saying makes no sense. 'Same difference.' You cannot have a same difference. You have same, and you have different."

"Whatever." She rolls her eyes. "You grew up to be as skinny as that woman with the lips, and you still dress like her, and now you're falling for an agent. Reality is stranger than movies."

I frown and glare at her. "I can't believe you'd say any of this about me."

"I can't believe you don't see it."

ou call me elitist? What, just because I left Barrio San Jose and got an education and a real career? You think I'm acting like Renée Zellweger because of that?"

I regret the words almost as soon as they come out. I can feel Maggie tense up next to me.

"A real career, huh?" Her mouth purses and her nostrils flare. She increases the pace.

"I'm sorry," I say stupidly, trailing after her. "I didn't mean it."

"Sure you did," she says. "And that's the whole point. You think you're better than I am because you're richer than I am."

"I do not think I'm better than you," I protest.

"And because you're still single and skinny, and I'm just an uneducated housewife and part-time phone service person, right? You act like I just sit around all day, Christy! But moms at home, believe it or not, we work. We don't get paid for it, but we work. I do budgets, I do schedules, I cook. I'm an executive assistant, a chef, a counselor, a coach, a seamstress, a teacher, and a goddamned maid, and I don't get a dime for any of it, and you know what? That's fine with me. Because unlike some people, I actually like the people I hang out with all day. I like my life. You might not like my life but I do, and that's all that matters to me. Okay?"

"Maggie. Please don't do this."

But I know it is too late. She's wound up, and ready to blast off.

Maggie has tears in her eyes now. She stops walking and grabs me by the shoulder. She turns me toward her and looks me directly in the eye. "Stop it. Just stop it. I'm not saying it bugs me that you think you're superior, Christy, because it doesn't. It never has. I'm able to be happy without your approval, just like I'm able to define success on my own terms. But I'm sick of how you act. I really am."

I am struck mute by this outburst.

"I love you, and I always have," she continues. "I always will, too." Maggie smiles at me. "And I'm not trying to be judgmental, okay? But I think you have to understand that I know how you feel about me, and about us, your family, and this place. You were clear about it in high school, all you wanted was to get out of here, and you did, you got out, and you followed your white dream—"

"It's 'white' to want an education and a good job, Maggie? Think about what you're saying."

"You know what I mean."

"No, I don't. I don't know what you mean. I know a lot of people confuse poverty with ethnicity, but I didn't think you'd do it, not to me."

"Christy, you're the whitest Chicana I know."

"Mexican American. And I'm not white."

"You act white."

"Because I don't use double negatives? Is that selling out my people now?"

"And you know what? We have all watched you and it's pretty obvious that you don't have a lot of friends, or relationships that last. You have a lot of nice stuff, and we admire you for it, but we don't know if all that stuff has made you happy. That's all I'm saying."

My eyes well with tears now, too, but I still can't think of anything to say. She's right, of course. She's right about me. I'm not happy. I don't have close friends. I can't find love. But I did just deposit a check in my purse worth triple my dad's annual salary, from just one job that took a couple of months; this year alone I'll clear nearly twenty times my dad's income.

"There are happy rich people," I say, weakly. "I don't think misery and wealth necessarily go together."

Maggie takes my hands in hers. "I know, honey," she says. "But—and this is just a community college psychology class speaking, okay? I'm no Doctor Phil. I'm just Maggie from the barrio."

"We didn't grow up in the barrio. That's what Balthazar said."

"I don't care what he says. Just listen a second, okay? Can I finish a sentence here?"

I nod.

She continues. "There are studies out there that show that the people who are the least happy and the least well-adjusted in America are the people at the economic extremes. The really rich and the really poor."

"Well, I'm not really rich." I think of my last few clients, and how miserable they were in spite of all I'd done for them, and realize that to Maggie I am no different from them.

Maggie laughs. "Maybe not compared to Bill Gates. But you're doing pretty good compared to all of us *campesinos* out here. And that makes you fucked in the head compared to us, too, coconut."

ou think being good at what I do has made me snobby and unhappy and white?" I narrow my eyes at her and wipe a tear away.

Maggie tilts her head to one side as though not entirely in agreement with me. "I think you've put a lot of importance in how things look, and not a lot of importance in how things are or should be."

Maggie lets go of my hands, and turns back toward the track. She begins to walk, and whistles for her dog, which is off watering some weeds with his never-ending stream of urine.

"We should get going," she calls to me over her shoulder. Then, in a teasing and sarcastic voice she adds, "It's nearly dark. And I know how you white people say it is around here after dark. Too dark out here. Not fit for civilized people, right?"

ate two with Melchior comes around, with one week to go until Christmas. I hope that I haven't offended Melchior by calling him to offer to drive myself to his ChimpWorld for our date this morning, but honestly, I can't bear the thought of riding in Becky again, much less all the way to Placitas, listening to depressing anger-rock.

I've stopped at my parents' house to see if they need anything beforehand, probably passively hoping they'll give me a reason not to go on the date. My mother is working on a tablecloth as a Christmas gift for one of my estranged cousins in Estancia, and when I ask her for an opinion on the fact that I am going to spend the day with chimpanzees, she smiles at me.

"Enjoy it," she suggests. "That's what I'd do. But I got married right out of high school. You, you have so many opportunities to do interesting things. I don't know what you're frowning about all the time."

I sit on a folding chair in the corner of the sewing room and tell her the truth, that I thought I was falling for Caspar, but that Balthazar and Maggie have made me feel badly about how well I've done in life.

"They say I'm a snob, mom. Do you think that's true?"

My mother frowns at me over her reading glasses in a way that tells me she has likely had this exact conversation with people about me, behind my back. "Maggie said that?"

"Yes."

"I'd expect it from Balthazar, but not from Maggie."

"Why from Balthazar?"

"He always felt threatened by you, Christina. He had that immigrant mentality, and you were an American."

"What?"

"Think about it. You were the artist he wanted to be. You had the nice, stable family he wished he had. You were more American than they were, and you know that's a big issue in the barrio, who's American and who isn't. That's why he pushed you around."

"It's because I was fat, mom. Which, now that you mention it, kind of goes with being American for a lot of people."

"Nah," she says. "It's crabs in a barrel."

"What do you mean?"

"You never heard that saying?" she asks.

"No."

"When you catch crabs and put them all in a bucket, the ones on the top try to escape. None of the crabs want to be there, but the way the ones on the bottom think they're going to get out is by pulling the one that's almost made it out back down."

I think about this image.

"But Maggie," my mother continues, "I am surprised she'd fall for that, too."

"I see your point, Mom, but I have to tell you, I wonder if they're right about me. Maybe I am stuck up."

My mother goes back to her sewing with a melancholy look on her face. The light comes through the window. In the diffused winter sunlight, she seems to glow, gorgeously.

"There's nothing wrong with seeking beauty," she says. "It's what I do here, in my own work. I like beautiful things, too. But maybe the problem is that in this country, they teach us that to be truly beautiful, things have to be perfect."

"What do you mean?"

"Well, I find beauty in inexpensive things. I know they're inexpensive. You probably don't realize that I know they are, but

I do. I know what I am. Where I am. How little I have. But that has never stopped me from finding beauty in spite of it all, and you know what, Christina?"

I wait for her to answer.

"Sometimes, and I'm not sure of this, you know, because I've never been like you or the people you work for and hang around, but I think that when you have to work extra hard to find a beautiful thing, like when I go to the swap meet or the thrift store, and I have to go through hours of ugly stuff just to find that one little beautiful thing that is hidden there with all the trashy stuff, then the excitement and the way I feel about it, the appreciation I have for it, it's so much bigger."

I nod, because even though my mother never voiced this to me, I have always known it is how she operates.

We've never talked openly about it.

Then again, there's a lot we don't talk openly about.

You know what?" I ask her.

Now she waits for me to finish my thought.

"Growing up watching you hunt for beautiful things, mom, it made me love beauty. It made me want to be a designer."

She smiles. "I'm glad."

"But I think I'm starting to understand something about the world of high-end design that I didn't understand at first."

"What's that, sweetheart?" Her face betrays a faint smile, as though she has been waiting a long time for whatever I'm about to say. As if she were not surprised by it in the least.

"I don't know how to express this, really, but I'll try," I say. "It's like the yin and yang symbol, you know what that is?"

"The Chinese circle?" she asks. I nod. "Of course," my mother says with a laugh. "We're not *that* backward."

"I'm sorry. I guess I am a snob."

"You're not, honey. Just finish what you were saying."

"Okay, well, you cannot have light without darkness, right?" I ask.

My mother keeps sewing, her fingers working effortlessly in spite of the pain I know she must feel, and she finishes my thought for me. "You can't know hunger without fullness, or peace in the absence of war. That's why there's heaven and hell, God and Satan both."

"Exactly," I say. "You need something to compare everything else to, in order to . . ."

She finishes for me, ". . . appreciate it."

"Right."

Mom says, "And, let me guess. Growing up with all this tacky stuff that your mom thinks is beautiful, you learned to recognize real beauty when you finally saw it, real design? Is that what this is about? Is that what Maggie thinks is being snobby? That you took my search for beauty to a whole new place?"

I shake my head vehemently. "No, mom. That's not what I'm saying at all. In fact, I think I'm saying the opposite. All these years, when I was studying and everything, I think that maybe I was living in reaction to a childhood of— I don't know, to a humble upbringing I guess. I mean, we were comfortable, but like you said, everything we had was used, and none of it matched. So when I saw all that Italian design, and the, I don't know, I guess the artistry of good design, I really appreciated it. So, yes, that's true, what you said, but not now. That was maybe true of me last year, or, shoot, like last week. But now, God! I don't know if I can even figure out how to articulate this, because it's just a feeling I have, it's just something so new, Mom."

My mother stops sewing to look at me with a peaceful smile, as though she has been leading me to this point. "May I try to figure out what you're trying to say?"

"Yes, please do. I'm inarticulate right now."

$\mathcal{I}$ think that you're saying that you might have thought, at one time, that great design meant you wouldn't have to worry about family problems anymore."

"Probably. I think so, but there's more."

My mother opens her mouth to speak, but stops herself, and nods in a gesture for me to continue.

"It's just that, I'm really embarrassed to say this. There's been beauty all around me, since I was a child, and I didn't see it."

"You didn't have anything to compare it to," she says, with a wicked smile, "except for all the beautiful Hollywood sets on the TV."

"Exactly. I've spent the last ten years hanging around with wealthy people and famous designers, only to realize, all these years later, that most of them—well, most of the clients but not all of the designers—most of them have no appreciation for what they have."

"Because they have nothing to compare it to."

"That's it. That's right. They have never had lives like ours, and don't know how to appreciate what they have, but Mom, this is the bigger point. Now that I've *had* that life, and seen how those people have all the same problems as everyone else, I realize I finally have something to compare this to."

"This?"

"Home, you and dad. This room. That tablecloth you're working on. Your kitchen, with all its crazy little knickknacks."

"You used to complain about it being tacky."

"I know, and I'm sorry for that, Mom. It's— It's actually wonderful. It's beautiful, because it's from the heart. It is you. Your home is completely yours, and no one else's. No one else could live here. It is yours."

We sit in silence for a moment, and my mother seems unable to lift her eyes to meet mine. I believe she's working hard not to cry.

"I realize, and it is so embarrassing, Mom, to say this. To have taken so long to see it. But there are many kinds of beauty in design, and you have to be open to circumstance, and choices, and warmth. Home should be a place of warmth. I don't think I've designed a warm home in eight years of my career. It has been all about form and function, and nothing about home, or community. I am embarrassed about that now."

A tear rolls down my mother's cheek, but she does not dignify it by wiping it away. "And what, exactly, do you think made you realize this?" she asks.

I think about the answer, even though I don't want to admit it.

"Dinner with Balthazar," I say. "Some pictures he took."

My mother smiles again. "I told you he was handsome," she says.

"This isn't about how he looks," I protest.

"And handsome isn't always about how someone looks, either, Christina. Sometimes it's about how someone sees, and the gift of sight they can give to others."

"Or insight," I offer.

"Or insight," she agrees.

I look at my mother and it is almost as if I am seeing her for the first time—the woman she has always been, the human being. She looks like me, and probably has every talent that I have, every ability, and yet she sacrificed her need for fine things and beauty in order to devote her life to me and my father, to care for us, opting to find beauty in small ways, to create a little life of great beauty with whatever she had available to her.

"I am so, so sorry," I tell her.

"No need for that. I knew it was only a matter of time, and that you'd come around when you were ready." She looks at her watch. "Now, you better hurry to that monkey camp. You're going to be late."

"I really don't want to go," I say. "I really don't like this guy at all. I like the other two, but not this one."

"That's what you thought about Balthazar," she reminds me.

"Sometimes you have to just open yourself up to hear what another person is saying, sweetheart. Sometimes you learn just by allowing yourself to go into a situation thinking that maybe, just maybe, it isn't what you thought it would be. There is something we can learn from every person we come in contact with. There is something for you to gain from this Melchior and his monkeys."

I realize, with another jolt of surprise, that my mother is right—and she is much, much wiser than I ever knew before.

This can mean only one thing: I have been a snob, after all.

I meet Melchior in his office, which is bigger than I expected, and more tastefully appointed. The sky is blazingly bright blue, a shocking winter sky that you only find in the desert.

The office is in your regular square adobe New Mexico building, but situated at the edge of a small cliff, and with windows looking out over the open mesa from the fourth floor. Melchior is dressed in jeans and a rugby-type shirt, and looks very strong and handsome—handsomer than I remember thinking he had looked on either of the previous occasions when I saw him. I swallow the urge to compliment him, and do what any Rules Girl would do—smile in a friendly, but not overly friendly, way.

He drops a couple of hand weights when I appear in the doorway, and comes to hug me as I enter the room. He smells of coconut sunscreen and hot coffee, and his body is warm from whatever he was doing with the weights.

"How are you, Christy?" he asks, and it seems as though he is actually stopping to listen to the answer, something I don't recall him doing last time, either. We engage in a bit of small talk as I take in the scene.

Melchior has gone for a serene feeling here, with whites and beiges, a blue carpet, and shelves of books broken up by the occasional seashell or piece of coral. He has framed photographs of desert landscapes in black and white, peaceful, beautiful. Whoever took the shots has an unusual eye, and a depth of spirit that can be found in only a handful of landscape photographers, Ansel Adams of course being at the top of the list.

Melchior is at a white sofa now, adjusting the contents of a large duffel bag open atop it, as I wander the room looking at the artwork and especially these photos.

"Who is this wonderful photographer?" I ask him, thinking I might like to use this artist in some of my own design.

Melchior looks surprised. "Balthazar, actually," he says.

"Balthazar?" I choke, incredulous.

"Yes, my cousin Balthazar," he says, as though I might know any other or might have forgotten this one.

I nod because it's too hard to try to think of something nice to say. Balthazar? I figured he'd only take pictures of people in the barrio so that he could try to make rich, uppity people like me feel like sellouts for trying to make more of our lives.

Melchior glances at me, and his gaze lingers for a moment. "Something wrong?" he asks.

"Huh? No."

"I'll be a minute, if you want to have a seat," he offers. "Make yourself at home. Can I get you a bottle of water? Coffee? We have a fully stocked kitchen here."

"No, thanks. I'm fine. I had Starbucks on the way up."

"Nice!" he says, and flashes me another power grin. Man, I like his smile.

I take the chair opposite the sofa and watch him. "So what exactly are you doing there?" I ask.

"Packing up our chimpanzee suits. They are clean animals, by their own standards, but we probably want to cover up around them. They like to touch and smear stuff."

"Eew?" I say.

He grins again. "Yeah, it's an awkward experience the first time. You'll be fine. This is why I didn't want you to wear anything too nice. We'll change downstairs. We have locker rooms here in the building."

I nod again and try to find something useful to do with my hands. Though I have met this man before, he is so much calmer and confident here—perhaps because it is his own environment and he is at ease—he feels like someone completely new. I could really get to like him, I realize.

"I meant to ask you if you were afraid of animals," he says as he zips up the bag at last. He turns to me with an impish look on his face that I find irresistible. "Seems a gross oversight to invite a lady to socialize with chimpanzees with me without knowing if she will fear them."

"I didn't realize we were socializing. Isn't it a little cold for that?"

"With the paper suit and your clothes underneath, you should be fine." He puffs his chest up, proudly. "Plus there's heat in the chimpanzees' house."

"They have a house?"

"A shelter, more like a cave, but it's rigged with lights and heat. I want them to be comfortable. This is obviously not their native habitat, and I've tried to make the most of what we've got."

"Sounds nice," I say stupidly.

He seems to laugh at me now, but in a nice way, like he finds my flaws cute.

"May I assume from this that you're not afraid of large mammals?" he asks.

"Only if they're recently paroled or terrorists."

Melchior cracks a wry smile and looks at me as though he might be reassessing me, too. "Good one, Miss de la Cruz. You have quite the sense of humor."

"Well, you know, some people just have a gift for the humor."

He laughs out loud at this, and then, after heaving the duffel bag onto the floor—with very little effort and a whole lot of biceps—he sits down on the sofa across from me and laces his fingers together in his lap. He inhales deeply, and blows out with his eyes closed, as though calming himself down.

"Listen," he says, "Christy. I just wanted to apologize to you, for our last date."

I sit up just a little straighter and pretend to look confused. This is time to practice The Rules some more, so that I don't blow it with Balthazar or Caspar later.

"Oh?" I say, blinking madly. "Why's that?"

"For how I acted on our first date. I— I know I went on and

on about my parents, and—" He stops to smack himself on the forehead and growl angrily at himself. "God, I always *do* that. I'm so stupid, stupid, stupid. I think sometimes I overshare. Sorry about that. Anyway."

I cut him off with an easygoing wave of the hand, a fine bit of acting on my part, considering how horrified I am by his Dr. Jekyll turn of mood. "It's okay. Don't worry about it."

Melchior tugs at his hair as though trying to lift himself up off the sofa. "No, I do worry about it. I act like a jackass half the time. Lots of girls have complained about it."

Why are there "lots" of them? I wonder. Is this man some sort of geek womanizer? I smile serenely, and reveal nothing. I remind myself that until there is a ring on your finger, you are a free agent and so is he. There is no room in a Rules Girl's life for jealousy, because she has so much to live for other than any one man.

He goes on, "It just comes out sometimes when I'm really nervous. I like you quite a lot, and have been nervous around you. I thought about it and I realized I shouldn't have done that to you. I should have made more of an effort. I have a tendency at times to be self-centered. My therapist—"

He gives me a worried look now.

"I hope that doesn't freak you out," he says.

"Everybody goes to therapy," I offer. "No biggie."

"I know, but sometimes—well, you never know with Mexican girls."

I blink some more because I worry that if I respond to this obnoxious comment I might say something I regret. One? I'm Mexican American, not Mexican. Two, any woman in America who has seen at least one episode of *Oprah* knows that therapy is not a bad thing, but whatever.

Melchior clarifies his statement: "The traditional ones, anyway. I'm not so insipid as to think any of us are predictable for belonging to an invented ethnic category. I didn't mean that. Sorry. But I can't tell you how many Mexican girls—well, women. I know. I shouldn't say *girls*. I see how you're looking at me."

"Me?"

"You. Please stop looking at me like you hate me."

"I'm not doing that," I say, while inside I am astounded by how well this whole Rules thing is working. This beautiful, intelligent, confident man is falling apart before me because he can't get through to me. It is magic.

"Yes, you are. You hate me."

"I don't hate you. Please finish what you were saying." I smile as patiently and confidently as I can, and wait.

This man is unstable, and incredibly insecure, I think. I congratulate myself for being enough on the ball to pretend I might not want him, instead of waiting for him to reject me, which would have been my pattern in the past. People can change.

He watches me a long moment as though trying to detect a lie, before continuing his rant against Mexicans.

"Anyway, the traditional girls—women, and the men, too, actually, you know how they are sometimes. They think that by going to therapy you're admitting that you're completely certifiably insane."

Which might be true in your case, I think, unkindly.

"I hear you," I say, because I do hear him. My ears are working nicely. I might not agree with him, but I hear his voice and he is talking. I mentally pat myself of the back for my diplomacy, and realize that in the past I might have taken this moment to argue with this man. In my old quest for control, I realize with a shock, I was always losing control because I came on too strong. The new me gains control by relinquishing the need for it, by letting people be who and what they are, by being full and complete on my own.

"I've gone for years, and my therapist says I have narcissistic tendencies—"

"When he can get a word in edgewise," I joke, lamely.

Melchior just blinks at me, rather like a monkey, before laughing out loud.

She. My therapist is a woman. She thinks I have narcissistic tendencies, but I don't think that's necessarily true. I mean, I don't seem that selfish, do I?"

I smile and shrug unhelpfully. "Don't know you that well. Can't say."

"If I'm a little concerned with my own stuff, it's just that—that I honed self-love as a survival skill when my parents—"

I can't help it this time, and a small guffaw escapes me. *Self-love*, think my inner Beavis and Butt Head. *Funny.*

Melchior seems to be trying to decide whether I've laughed or sneezed. "So, well, anyway. Enough of that. The point was . . ." He hesitates. "I suppose the point was all about me. Sorry—and I was doing it again, wasn't I?"

"Sort of."

"The point was that I'm sorry I'm self-absorbed and that I made such a bad first impression on you."

"Please don't worry so much," I tell him. "Let's just try to have fun."

Melchior's head is bowed and he seems to be peeking at me from beneath his eyebrows now. "Can I have another shot?"

"Look, this is just a silly thing we're doing to appease my cousin Maggie, who thinks every woman should be married with kids like she is, and I figure I'm making some new friends and seeing things I wouldn't have seen otherwise. I don't want you to think of it as 'a chance,' per se. It's not like that, at least not at this point. Let's go nice and slow." I say all of this even as my mind is imagining wild and amazing sex with this man. I remind myself that the best way to get to that point is to let him think he's leading me there.

Melchior is crestfallen. "Oh. It's not?"

Score!

"Let's just enjoy our time together and stop overthinking everything," I suggest, contrary to every impulse in my body.

"Right." He beams. "But I like what I've seen so far. I should tell you, you look beautiful today."

"Thanks," I say. "You look nice, too."

Melchior is one of those men who, if you were at a pizza place and he walked in with some other woman, chuckling and happy as he ordered a slice or two, you'd wonder how other women got such gorgeous men and you didn't. And, to my delight, he's nervous about me. Very nervous.

"But you're right, of course. I mean, let's not get ahead of ourselves," he says. "I admire a woman who likes to take things nice and slow, because, honestly, so many of you guys are ready to move in on the second date, it's a bit scary."

"So let's go see these chimpanzees of yours," I suggest, with a casual glance at my watch, designed to unnerve him even a little more.

"Shall we go then?" he asks. "Right, right. Sorry. I'm babbling. Are you bored? I hope I'm not boring you."

"I'm fine," I say.

And it is true.

And so it is that Melchior and I leave the office and walk through a maze of corridors and down several flights of stairs to find the locker rooms. He explains how to put the suit on, hands it over along with a padlock and key, and in I go. I'm the only woman in the place, and it is every bit as nice as the locker room of the upscale gym I frequent. Melchior has made himself quite a nice little chimp center here. In spite of all my self-control, I find my mind wandering to a fantasy where I'm married to Melchior and come here often. I don't know how I feel about it, honestly. Being married to the Chimp Prince. We'll see.

Leaving my things behind in the locker, ensconced in a large piece of awkward, thick, slightly damp-feeling paper, I step into the fluorescence of the corridor to wait for Melchior.

He appears moments later, and let me just say that if ever there was a man intended to wear form-fitting paper clothing, it is he. The body? Breathtaking. I work very hard not to show how much I like what I see. Perhaps, I think, I could have a night or two with him, no strings attached? No, no, no. It would only end in rejection and disappointment. Never mind.

He guides me through some more hallways, and finally we emerge into a parking lot. There's Becky, one of only three vehicles in sight. The contraption looks every bit as ridiculous now as it did on our first date.

"It's just a short drive," he tells me.

Mercifully, he doesn't blast me with hideous rock music this time. In relative silence, we drive down the hill and along a faint twist of road to a secluded dirt parking area in a sage grove. We ditch Becky there, and I follow a jovially whistling Melchior through a parting of the shrubbery, down a narrow sandy path to a fenced area that he accesses with a key card.

Beyond the fence is an isolated strip of scrubland, with what appear to be fake trees with long ropes, for climbing. There's also a building of some sort, like the kind you see at zoos, where the animals can take shelter. The space is open to the sky, but with very high walls topped with barbed wire. It is like a zoo enclosure, but larger.

"Wow," I say. "Impressive."

"The lab of Dr. Reyes, world-famous chimpanzee linguist."

I wait to see if he intends any irony in this self-puffery. He doesn't. I realize, with another shock, that even as gorgeous and successful as this man is, I might not actually like him all that much. I mean, there's nothing particularly wrong with him, but I think his self-aggrandizement would be exhausting. Amazing! I can't believe I'm actually forming an opinion that might lead me to reject a man, whereas in the past I might have just worried about my own ego and whether or not I could get him.

"Doctor, eh?"

"Me, I'm Dr. Reyes," he says with a look of disappointment. "I have a Ph.D. It's not the same as a medical doctor, but I can call myself *doctor*."

"I know. I understand."

"I'm Dr. Reyes," he repeats.

"I realize that," I say, holding back a laugh. "And let me guess: You are also the chimpanzee linguist."

He misses the humor in my tone. "Correct."

Melchior turns away from me now and fiddles with the lock. The scent of wild animal crap is overwhelming, and I realize I just don't have the stomach for it. It is new and sort of exciting, but it is not, in the end, for me. I am proud of myself for understanding this. The Chimp Whisperer, however, seems absolutely entranced.

He opens the gate, takes me to a small decrepit wooden house at one end of the enclosure, and unlocks it. I can hear strange animal noises in the distance, in a stand of trees, and I feel incredibly nervous and uncomfortable. Melchior observes me for a quick moment.

"Don't worry," he says. "You're safe. They're actually kinder than most people are."

Inside, the house has just two rooms. The front one is another office, decorated with Mexican rugs and complete with a little living room set and a bunch of computer and video equipment, plus other electronic gadgetry that I don't understand in the least. The back room is a rudimentary kitchen. He informs me that there is an outhouse behind the structure.

"A person could live here," I say. If a person were not averse to, say, bugs and cold and sand and chimpanzee hoots.

"I practically do," he tells me with a winning smile. "I spend at least three nights a week here. It has helped me to bond with my family."

"Ah," say I.

Then he brags about how the house is completely off the grid, runs on its own solar energy, and how he has a composting toilet, which frankly is more information about Melchior than I needed to know, but I do appreciate his enthusiasm for the planet's health and longevity. I just wish this type of enthusiasm smelled better.

Melchior hauls a couple of pairs of rawhide gloves and metal face masks out of the closet, and gives me a set, along with some big rubber boots to go over my shoes. He goes to a large refrigerator in the corner of the office. He takes out a large plastic freezer bag of what appears to be old banana bits and dumps them into a bucket. He mixes in what I think is tree bark and live ants. The smell is not endearing, but I can handle it.

He says we're ready, and off we go, out the door and through the scrub, the large treelike structures in the center of the enclosure. I hear calls and whinnies and other strange noises.

Melchior blows into a long narrow silver whistle that I associate with dog shows, and tells me to watch the trees. He points, and here come three large animals. Chimps. They are cute, and hideous, and much bigger than I had imagined they might be. Being an idiot, I immediately find my mind gone to horror films. I am certain I will be eaten by enormous chimps. Quickly, because my parents didn't raise a total fool, I realize it will probably be okay.

"Come on," says Melchior as he begins to lope toward the animals in imitation of their strange gait. They are waiting for him at the base of one of the structures. He makes a weird noise or two for them, then calls over his now-hunched shoulder to me, "I want you to meet my family."

Gingerly, I follow him. His family? Did he say that without even a droplet of irony? I suddenly pity the chimps. I am quite sure that without the cage and the forced starvation, they would not come to Melchior and his rotten bananas at the sound of his whistle. They would be off galavanting about somewhere in the jungle. I bet they hate being here as much as I do. I bet they need therapy. Can chimps bite? Their teeth look to be made of dirty wood. I wonder. Will they like me? Will I fall down? Will they attack me? Do The Rules work on other primates, or just men?

elchior goes among the chimps and begins to stoop and scratch and stomp around, and to make some noises that they look at him like they pity him for. They lift their big-eared heads and make little chattering noises at him, as though in greeting, pulling back their big lips to reveal enormous gums. He begins to toss food to the dirt near their feet. They stoop to grab it up, and I feel terribly sorry for them now. I stand back, with my arms crossed over my chest, and wish to be anywhere else but here.

"Don't worry, they're fine! Come on." Melchior waves me over with a smile. He is totally animated, alive here like he is nowhere else. This man loves his work.

I walk out a little farther, and soon smell the dirty, frigid air blowing past me as the chimps, curious, begin to circle around me. They smell positively rancid. One does a little jump, flapping its lips at me. Another does something that seems like a cruel laugh with a somersault. Screw you, too, I think.

"He's flirting," says Melchior.

"Ha-ha," I say.

"I'm serious. Chimpanzee society is formed around male bonds, and I'm the alpha male here. The other males are flirting, but in jest. They know you're my female."

"Right. Whatever you say, doctor."

"They have very complex societies. They are very, very intelligent. They use tools."

As soon as he says this, one of the chimps takes a poo from its own butt, sniffs it, and hurls it at Melchior.

"Is that a tool?" I ask.

"That, believe it or not, is a greeting."

"Ah. Just like at a rave."

"They use tools for gathering and preparing food, for fixing their dwellings."

"Must be hard for them to get to the Home Depot, no?" I joke.

He glares at me. "They use dried, crushed leaves to soak up drinking water."

"Oh."

"Things like that. They have language and empathy," he says, pouty and furious with me, still squatting and dancing around.

"That's *not* so hard without a Home Depot nearby," I offer, trying—and failing, apparently—to be funny. He watches the animals for a moment, with a growing look of confusion.

"They *like* you," says Melchior. "Though I'm not sure why, given the way you're acting."

"Perhaps they have a sense of humor?" I suggest.

"That's not it," he says, deadly serious.

The chimpanzees waddle closer to me now.

"Wow!" I say, and there is nothing faked about my excitement—or the terror that accompanies it. I know it sounds strange to be terrified of meeting chimps, but this is only how it will sound to those who have never been next to a chimp in the cold, dark desert at mealtime. I have never been this close to chimps, which is why I used to think they were cute and harmless. I have never had them notice me in any way, and I realize at this moment that this was the way life should have been. Life was better when chimps were oblivious of my existence.

They begin to circle me now, fast and close and exuberant, jumping around and looking an awful lot like they'd like to touch me—until, yep, there it is. They're touching me. Pawing at me. Hooting and whooping at me. I hold my elbows to the side, as high as they will go, and my hands over my chest and neck, preparing for my destruction.

"Omigod, omigod," I say. I hate this.

"They're just curious," says Melchior. "You don't need to be afraid. They're my friends, and I mean that."

"I thought they were your family. That one there sort of looks like you."

He stares me down. "They trust me. Just relax. They're good at picking up on body language. I don't want you to insult them."

"Well, what am I supposed to say to them, and how do I say it?"

"Just relax. Don't be afraid. Humans are not the only intelligent life on earth."

It is a salient point. I take it to heart. But I still don't want to be here.

I take a deep breath, exhale, and try to seem like I do this every day. A bit of chimp fingernail clips me, and I shriek. Melchior frowns at me.

"Please don't do that, they have very sensitive hearing."

"Sorry, I just had this crazy idea that I was going to die by monkey."

The frown becomes a full-blown glare now. "Chimpanzees," he hisses at me, "are not monkeys, and they are far more humane than human beings. You need to take that back."

I stare at him in disbelief. "What? You mean like when kids take things back?"

"Take it back," whines Melchior, and no, he's not joking.

"What?"

"Apologize to them."

I stare at him in disbelief. "To the chimps."

He glowers at me as though I would be stupid for not understanding the obvious, which is, clearly, that this man wants me to apologize to his animals.

"Sorry, chimpanzees," I say to them. They stare blankly at me. "I'm a putz."

"You didn't mean that," he whines. "That came out insincere."

When they were handing out humor, they forgot to give this guy a dose.

"Do it again," he demands.

"Sorry, no. One apology to chimps per day is enough for me."

"Just like the rest of humanity," he spits, about me, to the water. "And they say I'm the one who's self-centered!"

He is fuming now, and I begin to worry for my safety. I back up, maybe five feet, away from him and toward the house/shack thingy. Melchior makes weird noises to call his family back to him, and continues dumping food at them as he tells them how sorry he is for my bad behavior. When he's given all the food away, he hurls the bucket back toward the shack with astonishing power, in an arc that was probably chosen for its ability to scare me into thinking he might have been throwing it at my head.

Two hours later, he returns from socializing, and we go back to change out of the paper suits.

"I'm sorry," he says. "I didn't realize that much time had passed. I just forget about time when I'm with them. I really love them, but I know, it's not an excuse. I shouldn't have left you out in the cold. I'm very sorry."

"I hear you," I say, because I do. I hear every word.

It is nearly Christmas, and this means tamales.

I sit next to Maggie in the line of de la Cruz women (and other associated women related to us by marriage, etc.) in the middle of her mother's family room. Two large folding tables have been set up in a long row, draped with white plastic tablecloths. On top of the table are bowls filled with everything needed to make tamales.

Our mothers sit in their own folding chairs on the opposite side of the table from us. The four of us are the fillers, entrusted with stuffing spiced pork and chicken into the masa. At the end of the table to my right are the masa masters of the universe, my great-*tía* Peggy and her sister-in-law Dolores, who hate each other the rest of the year, but put aside their differences in the name of small corn dumplings, as we all should.

Since I was a child, this has been a holiday tradition, all the women in the family getting together and bundling up packages of pure Christmas yumminess. In the past, Maggie and I have mostly just listened to the stories and *chismes* (a.k.a. gossip), but this year, apparently, I *am* the *chisme*.

I get another text from Melchior. He's been blowing up my phone ever since the chimp date, apologizing nonstop, begging forgiveness for simply being who he is. I feel sorry for him, and know exactly how he feels. I am happy to report I no longer feel that way about myself, though. I'm learning to be happy in my own imperfect skin.

"Tell us more about this Monkey Whisperer," says Tía Peggy. Her glasses perch on the end of her nose, and for some reason I feel like crying and laughing at the same time because it is so absurd to hear her say the words. She's clever. Most of the women in my family are bright, I realize now. I'm not proud of my sudden realization that I have basically underestimated them most of my life, in my quest to find what I thought was the better life I saw in beautiful homes on television or in movies.

"Is he cute like *este mojadito bendito*, El Dog Whisperer?" asks

Tía Dolores, who is about a thousand years old and appears to have left her teeth at home. Maggie and I exchange a look. My mother lets out a whistle, the kind of catcall you might expect from a construction worker. I stare at her in shock.

"What?" she asks me. "I'm old, but I'm not dead yet."

Maggie's mother, to my horror, high-fives my mom.

"You think Cesar's hot, Tía?" Maggie asks her. "You think Cesar'd be good for a little boom-boom-pow?" Maggie does a weird little hip thrust that makes me even less comfortable than I was a moment before.

The ladies titter and smile secretly to themselves.

Tía Dolores—who looks like a very old tiny monkey herself, in Sears slacks and a Christmas sweater—shrugs and purses her lips, as though she had many options of men to bed, and might take Cesar in a pinch, as a favor to somebody.

"*Sabes*, he's *okay*," she says nonchalantly, sort of growling out the "okay" in a sing-songy way that I associate with Mexican humor, and we all giggle. "His shoes are too fancy for my taste. I like me a man with man's shoes, *que no?*"

"Give him some cowboy boots and he's *el mero mero de los perros*," jokes Maggie. The ladies laugh again. One of them says something in Spanish that I don't understand. Maggie, who didn't used to speak it, either, but who learned it from Rosetta Stone, translates for me.

"She says Cesar used to have man's shoes, before he went all Hollywood on us."

"She still don't talk Spanish?" Peggy asks my mother, pointedly.

"*Es que no quiere*," says my mother with a shrug.

"She says you don't want to," translates Maggie.

"I understood that much."

Peggy clicks her tongue and the others shake their heads.

"It's never too late," my mother suggests to me.

"Hey, you're the one who never taught me."

The ladies glare at me to let me know I should not disrespect my mother.

I smile awkwardly because I know the older ladies are annoyed by my lack of Spanish. I am struck with a pang of jealousy. Maggie was always better at navigating the world of de la Cruz ladies than I was. I was always the outcast, the one who might bring up Chaucer or Dickens at the wrong moment, and get met with blank stares. Maggie has the *mexicana* humor down pat. I should add, too, that old Mexican and Mexican American ladies have a *great* sense of humor, self-deprecating. And when the men aren't around?

They're downright raunchy.

There's so much men don't really understand about women, I think. And it's all perfectly good and fine that way.

ues, tell us about the monkey boy," says my great-aunt Gladys, a fit little old woman with a dyed black bob, who is wrapping finished tamales in corn husks at the other end of the table. She makes Melchior sound like some sort of freak superhero, which, from what I can tell, is only about halfway right. "Does he wear fancy shoes, or man's shoes?"

"He prefers rubber boots," I say.

"Rubbers?" asks Tía Dolores with a gleam in her eye.

Gladys wrinkles her nose. "Oh no, I don't know about a man in no rubbers. You can't feel nothing."

"I thought he seemed nice enough," my mother says, in a tone that indicates she thinks I am far too picky about men and will therefore end up single forever. "The good guys will wear rubbers, *sabes*. Don't trust one who won't."

"Rubber *boots*," shouts Maggie, doing her arms as if she were pulling on boots. "For walking in monkey shit."

The women laugh hysterically at this, and I'd be lying if I didn't say I joined in.

I proceed to tell them all about the date from hell with Melchior and his chimps, about how I had to wait there on the porch of that little shack for a good hour or more before he came back covered with chimp droppings and smears of noxious rotten fruit, still furious with me for not respecting his family.

"He sounds like he's not right in the head," says Tía Dolores.

"She makes all her men sound like they're not right in the head," says my mother.

"In this case, it's true," I say.

"You have to give men *time*," my mother says. She looks at the other ladies for sympathy, and adds, "She never gives them time, unless they're gay and gringos."

Maggie stands up now, wiping her hands on a dish towel. "I'm sorry, everyone, but I have to take the little ones from the neighbor and go pick up my oldest son from his friend's house. I'll be back in a while with them, if that's okay with you."

"Bring them, of course," says Tía Dolores, the de facto matriarch.

Maggie gives me a hug and whispers in my ear, "You gonna be okay with them?"

I nod, offended. Why wouldn't I be? She winks at me, grabs her purse and keys from under the table, makes the rounds hugging everyone, and then leaves.

Tía Gladys picks the conversation up right where we left it, unfortunately for me, saying, "They act like idiots the first few dates, most of them. Especially with a girl as pretty as you are."

"Give him another chance," suggests Maggie's mother, who always seems to talk more when Maggie's not around.

"What?" I cry. "No. No, thank you."

Tía Dolores shakes her head at me and says, "*Al mal paso, darle prisa.*"

I look to my mother for help, but it's Dolores herself who translates, in a shout.

"It means *get it over with.*"

Everyone laughs at me as though they know a secret.

"Oh."

"He's good-looking," says my mother to the ladies. "And he

has him a very good job. He's a researcher with the university, chimpanzee. He's a *doctor*."

"He's a monkey doctor?" asks Peggy.

"Like at the animal hospital?" says Dolores.

"I like animal doctors, very gentle people," says Gladys. She scowls at me. "You can't just walk away from an animal doctor like that. I think a man like that would be a very good father."

"If he could mate with a chimpanzee, sure," I say.

Everyone stares at me, dumbfounded and possibly a tad bit horrified.

"He's not a veterinarian," I explain to my aunties. "He's a professor of mammalian biology."

They look somewhat less impressed now.

"And he's just completely in love with himself and his work."

"But," says my mother, "that's because his mom and dad died in a car crash when he was a little kid, and he had to raise himself."

There is nothing anyone could have said to this particular group of women that would draw more pity than this. They all "awww" and "ooooh" about it, fretting over the child Melchior must certainly have been at one time.

"He was raised by his aunt and uncle," I say. "It's not like he was little Oliver Twist in button shoes begging for gruel or something."

Blank stares.

He *had* a family," I clarify. "He didn't live in an orphanage."

Tía Gladys stares me down, then looks at my mother. "Has she always been this cruel? I don't remember her this cruel."

"Not always," says my mother.

"You agree with that?" I ask my mom, in astonishment. "That I'm cruel? How can you *say* that, Mom?"

"Well," my mother says with a shrug. "It is a little unkind to say a boy whose parents died had family. I'm sorry, honey, but they're right."

"But he did! It's not like he lived on the streets or something."

"What a shame," Tía Dolores tells my mother, of me.

"You should give him another chance," says Peggy. "It sounds like he was just trying to show you his passion, for these chimps he loves so much, and you didn't even stay in the desert out there."

"I don't like being in the desert out there."

Tía Dolores leans across the table toward me now. "Let me tell you something," she says, pointing a masa-encrusted fork in my general direction. "Every woman here who has been married will tell you, all of us at some point end up standing in that desert we don't like."

No one seems to understand what she has just said, even though she sits back as though she has made some profound point.

"*Tía?*" asks my mother. "Can you explain that a little?"

Tía Dolores sighs deeply and stares at the ceiling before continuing.

"Every woman, if she is married to a man, will have to eventually do something with him that he loves and she isn't in the mood for."

Gasps around the table.

"That's not actually legal anymore, *tía*," I say.

Tía Dolores looks confused, then the look passes and one of extreme amusement takes its place.

"*Cochina!*" she says to me, which, if I'm not mistaken, means "pig." "I'm not talking about sex. But that's true, too, if you really love your husband you might end up doing it sometimes when you don't feel like it."

"But you almost always end up getting into it by the end," clarifies Tía Peggy.

"Maybe you do," says Dolores, critically. "But I can't imagine you ever not being into it, either."

"Look who's talking," says Peggy defensively.

Maggie's mother is blushing, and giggling, and my own mother is egging her on with funny faces. The shiest ones are always the biggest freaks, in my book.

Dolores finishes her thought. "Women and men both have to agree to do things that they don't like when they're married because the other person in the marriage likes it. My husband hates to shop for women's clothes, as an example," she says.

"Then why does he wear them all the time?" asks Peggy, still fuming from the earlier insult.

Dolores pauses to take a breath, but pretends Peggy hasn't spoken. "But he goes with me to the JCPenney and he sits there while I try on blouses. Why? Why does he do that? He could stay home watching television. I don't make him go with me. He goes with me because he loves me, and that's what you do when you love someone."

My mother chimes in now. "You sacrifice."

ou sacrifice," repeats Dolores, looking directly at me. "I don't like to watch football every Monday night. I don't understand football, and I don't like it, but I watch it with him because he likes my company. I make us hamburgers and I get him the beer he likes, and even though I don't like beer, I have a beer with him and watch the game because it's something he used to do with his two best friends, but then they got old and died, and our sons moved away, and I think, what is the big deal if I drink a little beer and watch a little football if it makes my husband happy? That's a small price to pay."

"I'm not married to Melchior," I say.

"And you never will be if you keep expecting everything to be about you, you, you all the time," says my mother.

"Well, good! Because you know what? I don't *want* to marry Melchior. I would rather be alone than marry Melchior! I don't want to have to go in the chimp desert."

"*Egoísta*," says Peggy.

"*Malcriada*," says Dolores.

"Don't blame me," says my mother. "She did not used to be this way. She used to be a very sweet girl. You 'member. She was in the Girl Scouts *y todo*."

"Stop it!" I cry. "I like my life just fine as it is. I don't have to have a man in my life to be complete, okay? I know that's what everyone in this room thinks, but I don't think like that. I'm okay on my own. You should all be okay with that, too, instead of acting like I'm useless unless I have a husband. Okay?"

I feel tears in my eyes.

"Don't cry in the tamales," says Tía Dolores, her eyes trained on the masa in her hands. There is not a hint of pity in her voice, but there is a dash of amusement.

"There's high blood pressure in the family," jokes Gladys. "No extra salt."

A few grins break out.

A tear rolls down my cheek. No one notices, or if they do, they don't care. I wipe it on my shoulder.

"She'll learn," says Tía Peggy. "All women do, eventually."

"Men, too," chimes in my mother, who, frankly, seems to have turned against me.

"Some do it the hard way," sighs Dolores.

"It's like they say in Mexico," says Peggy, "you can't make someone think with someone else's brain."

I look around the table. My little speech didn't move any-one. Nobody here feels sorry for me. I haven't changed anyone's mind, either. They don't respect what I do, or if they do, they're not about to admit it here. Everyone is busy working, as the women in my family have done for generations, maybe even for thousands of years, making tamales.

We remain this way for another twenty minutes or so, until the call comes from Cesar, and Maggie's mother, smiling as she answers the call, listens with growing horror on her face. By the time she hangs up, her face has drained of blood and her hands are trembling.

"What's the matter?" my mother cries, and runs to her side.

Maggie's mother turns to the rest of us and says, in a small, weak voice, "Maggie's been in an accident. Someone chased by the police ran the red light, smashed right into her car. All three boys were in the car. They're all at Lovelace hospital, downtown."

Lovelace hospital downtown is the doorway between heaven and earth most frequently used by members of the de la Cruz family. It is where I was born. It is where my grandmother died with me in the room. And it is where I am at the moment, in the emergency room waiting area with the rest of my family.

To my enormous annoyance, the TV hanging in the corner has been tuned to cable news, to a special about how Mexican immigrants are destroying the nation. To my eyes, everyone in the waiting room is Mexican or Mexican American, and none of us are, at the moment, ruining America.

I sit fuming for a moment, but finally grow a pair and get up,

stand on a nearby chair, and turn the mess of lies off. To my surprise, a small applause breaks out. If I weren't so wrung out and
terrified at the moment, I might curtsy like a wise ass. As it is, I
simply return to my seat.

Here is what we know.

Maggie and her three boys were all injured pretty seriously
in the crash—Maggie has two broken legs and a broken collar
bone, and the two younger boys have a lot of cuts and bruises.
Thankfully, the pregnant Claudia was home talking on the phone
with Rascal, her boyfriend, and had refused to come with her
mom earlier.

None were injured as badly as her oldest son, Quinten, the
recently outed gay kid, who was in the front passenger seat and
took the brunt of the direct hit from the oncoming speeding car.
Quinten, horrifyingly, was impaled with a piece of the door,
right through the middle.

The metal missed his organs, incredibly. We were told it was
a miracle that he survived, and that he is unconscious and lost
a lot of blood but will likely pull through if it is replaced.
The family was asked to come to the hospital to donate blood
because there was a shortage of the type he needed, and here
we all are, being tested to see if we are matches. To my pleasant
surprise, most of the extended family we've contacted have
come, in spite of Quinten's being gay. That's the thing about
Mexican families; you can count on them with your life, even
when they disagree with you or think you are going to hell.
They are intolerant in a time-honored biblical sense, yet loyal.
Blood, as they say, is thicker than water.

I was unfortunately not a match for Quinten, but a couple
of my uncles were. I know this because they returned to the

waiting room escorted by a nurse with a red clown nose on her face and pink Holly Hobbie cheeks painted on, her red hair pleated in braids on either side; she explained to us that she worked in the pediatric wing of the hospital, which is where they had Quinten now, and dressed this way to cheer up sick kids. I wanted to ask her how terrifying children helped them get well, but that didn't seem like the right time for it.

I see a worried, hurried Balthazar come rushing through the doors into the waiting area. He scans the room, and zips to Maggie's mother, leans down to her, embraces her, and talks to her in a low voice. He glances over at me, but doesn't smile or acknowledge me—not for bad manners, but because he appears to be in a panic. I watch him hurry to the check-in station, and then the clown-faced nurse comes and whisks him off. He is already rolling up the sleeves on his shirt, ready to be pricked and tested for blood type.

I resume my seat with the other members of the family. My mother links her arm in mine and we just sit there, frozen, in shock. Maggie's mother is crying softly—silently, actually. Her sisters and aunts sit with her, comforting her in their quiet way.

"Balthazar was here," my mother tells me.

"I saw him."

"He's not even family, but he came."

"I realize that," I say, as the awareness that in the past ten minutes this man has faced the two biggest fears in his life to save my nephew's life sinks in.

"He's an artist like you are," she reminds me.

"I know. Mom, please, now's not the time to sell me on a man."

"All right," she says. "You're right. But I'm just saying, he's a good man."

I think about this, and in spite of myself I realize she is right. I nod. "I know."

"He doesn't have the money the other ones do, it's true," my mother says, "but money doesn't make you happy."

"You're right."

"Sense of duty, and family, that's what makes you happy."

"It's like they say in Mexico," says my aunt Gladys, who, as usual, has been eavesdropping while pretending to knit. "It is easier for a camel to get through the eye of a needle than it is for a rich man to get into heaven."

"That's the Bible, actually," I tell her. "They say it everywhere, *tía*."

She stares me down, before hitting me with her comeback. "Yeah? Well, in Mexico they *believe* it. Not like here."

"They don't have insurance," says my mother.

"But they both work," I say, in shock.

"The companies keep their thirty-five hours low so they don't have to pay insurance."

"That blows," I say.

"Yes, it does," says my aunt Gladys. "It blows."

I look up at the now-silent television, and realize, again, that the women in my family are smarter than I am, in ways I have taken far too long to understand. Then, in a gesture so foreign to me that I'm almost not even sure it is me doing it, I get up, walk over to Maggie's mother, and I wrap my arms around her.

"I love you, *tía*," I tell her. I feel her sobbing increase in my embrace. "And I know that everything is going to be fine."

I go back to my seat and see that my mother is praying. Everyone in the family joins her with bowed heads, holding hands and reciting the rosary quietly.

A few minutes later, Balthazar returns, looking woozy, on the arm of the clown nurse. The nurse holds what appear to be smelling salts under his nose. He is pale, and clutches a kid's box of apple juice in one hand and a package of graham crackers in the other. The crook of his arm, still exposed with the sleeve rolled up, is bandaged tightly. He walks unsteadily to Maggie's mother, assures the clown that he's okay, kneels in front of my aunt, and shares the good news.

"I'm a match," he tells her with a weak smile. "I gave as much as I could."

"Thank God," says Maggie's mother. She clutches for him and holds him for a long moment.

"It's going to be okay," he tells her. "No worries, okay? God's watching over them."

When the embrace ends, Balthazar stands shakily, and looks around for an empty seat. There is one next to me. He glances at me, worriedly, as though I might refuse to let him sit near me. I scoot a bit away from it to let him know it's his if he wants it. I smile at him, and he blinks in a dazed confusion but begins to stagger over.

When he gingerly takes the seat, I reach for his hand, give it a squeeze, look him directly in the eye. "Thank you, Balthazar. You're—you're a good guy. I'm so sorry—for everything."

On the other side of me, my mother is beaming at me. I don't have to look at her to know—after decades of the opposite expression on her face, I can pretty much *feel* it.

"Does this mean we'll have a second date?" he asks, cynically.

My mother leans across my lap and answers for me.

"Yes," she says, patting my knee the way she did when I was a child. "It does."

I smile at him again, and say, "As long as we don't go to the circus or the Red Cross. You look terrible."

Balthazar laughs out loud.

"A damn *clown*," he says, shaking his head. "Can you believe it? They sent a damn *clown* to take my blood."

"Did she perform for you?"

"She talked in this weird clown-kid voice," he says with a shudder. "She had *puppets*."

"The horror," I say.

"Seriously. She did a ventriloquist act, where she was jabbing me with a needle and simultaneously voicing a puppet sitting on a chair. It was like my deepest nightmare."

"Good thing you passed out, then," I offer.

"Yeah, right?"

We chuckle, and I gather courage to compliment this man once more.

"You're very brave," I say.

Balthazar smirks and shakes his head in disagreement, his eyes leaving my own for the moment, to focus on the floor.

"It ain't about *brave*," he says softly, though his smile tells me he enjoyed the compliment. He looks me in the eye again, taps himself melodramatically on the chest in a way that reminds me of all the old men in my family when they've had a bit too much to drink and start reminiscing about the Old Country, and says, "As usual, you missed the point. It's about *this*."

Of course, I know what he means by "this," and it is love, or his heart, or something sappy and meaningful like that. But because I'm not good with that particular emotion, and because I am *quite* good at being a smart-ass, and because I am deeply offended by his use of "as usual" in describing me doing a stupid thing, particularly in emotionally difficult situations, I answer like the idiot I was, am, and perhaps always shall be.

"Your *pecs*? That was my first guess! I *knew* it was all about your pecs."

He leans closer, and whispers in my ear. "I don't want to be getting all up in your business or anything, but I think it'd be great if you could maybe help Maggie out with the bills from this thing, when they come due. It's going to be hella expensive, man."

I stare at him for a moment.

"Hey," he says. "I'm not saying you're rich or nothin' like that. And for what it's worth, I plan to help 'em out, too. With whatever I got. It was just a suggestion." He pats my hand patiently and, I believe, patronizingly. "Just a suggestion, girl, relax. I'm not gonna hurt you again."

I snatch my hand out from under his, all his past mistreatment of me flooding back in a panic of adrenaline.

I look at him a long moment, and say, "You're right. You're not going to hurt me again. I won't let you."

We move Christmas dinner to Maggie's house, because— let's be honest here—a woman with casts on both legs just can't get around like she used to. Or at all, really. I know. I shouldn't joke about it, but that's what we do in the de la Cruz family, when something is tragic or too terrible to bear. We joke about it. Unless, you know, it is really, really tragic, like death, in which case we basically just don't talk about it at all.

Maggie is, at the moment, propped up against some pillows in her bed, demanding that I draw a "hot cowboy" on her cast.

I sit on a folding chair next to the bed. The door to the room is open, and I can hear my mother and the other ladies laughing about something as they prepare the food in the cold, bare-bones kitchen. The men are all gathered in the family room watching a college football game. The formal dining room of the house is finally being used for something other than storing kids' bikes, with red candles and the old china set that our great-grandmother left to Maggie.

"Make him all macho, with big strong arms," she says of the cowboy she intends for me to draw.

"I can't do that," I tell her. My phone buzzes with another text, this time from Balthazar, apologizing for lecturing me at the hospital. Amazing, I think. As soon as you stop arguing with them and just leave them be, they seem to be able to realize on their own just how ridiculous they've been. I delete the message and, per The Rules, don't text back right away.

"You used to be able to draw anything," she reminds me.

"No, I mean I can do it, for a price. There's an extra fee for hot cowboys."

"No hot cowboys," says Cesar, from the doorway, where he's just popped his head in. He's got a couple of dirty plates in his hands, from having just been to Quinten's room with grub. I do a double take when I look at him, because he's wearing an apron. "Or if you do, model them on this." He sticks his *panza* out like it might excite us. We laugh, which isn't nice, but is somehow comforting.

"Nice apron," I say.

"Hot," says Maggie. "I never thought I'd think he looked so hot in an apron, but it's been nice having Cesar wait on me hand and foot." To him, she says, "You should serve me more often."

Cesar winks at her. "You should have car accidents more often," he jokes.

"How's Quinten?" I ask.

"Doing better," Cesar tells me. "He's in there playing video games."

Maggie rolls her eyes lovingly. "We gave him his present early. I can't believe how expensive those video game things are."

"Yeah," I say, even though I have no idea how much such things cost. They are foreign to my world, which is all about—well, all about me, basically. I'm starting to think this is not such a good thing. I realize, with a sick feeling, that I probably should have gotten him a video game for Christmas instead of a book. Oh, well.

"What are you two waiting for?" asks Maggie, in mock annoyance. "Get me in that chair already."

By "that chair" she means the wheelchair that has been jerry-rigged to accommodate her casts. Cesar sets the dirty dishes down on the dresser. I'm guessing they contained *pan dulce* from the looks of the crumbs. Then, he and I hoist Maggie from the bed to the chair. I help her to the dresser, and fix her hair a bit. She takes the hand mirror and does her makeup, puts on some earrings shaped like Christmas tree ornaments, and I wheel her out into the family room.

As we pass the entry table, I feel my wallet calling out to me from inside my purse. Don't be stingy, it tells me—but there is a part of me that can't stand the idea that I have to pay for the things my cousin could have had, if she'd made better decisions.

The scent of fresh tamales, pinto beans, red chile, and homemade tortillas wafts in from the kitchen. The house is packed with people, from babies to the elderly. Everyone greets Maggie casually, as though there were nothing wrong with her being in a wheelchair. We would not want to make her feel badly about it, now would we?

"Over there," she tells me, pointing to a corner of the room with an empty wing chair in it. "Let's talk."

I wheel her over. Cesar enters the kitchen with the dishes, to teasing catcalls from all the women there. He sticks a hip out to one side and puts his hand behind his head, modeling for them. Everyone finds this hilarious.

"So when's the next date?" asks Maggie.

"What?" I stare at her in shock. This is the farthest thing from my mind.

"You still have, what, five dates left?"

"Maggie," I say. "Come on. I'm not going to keep doing that, not with you like this."

Maggie stares me down now. "Uhm, okay. I'm housebound now, and the only thing I really have to look forward to is living vicariously through you, and you're going to cancel on me?"

"Maggie! I thought I might stick around here and help you out."

She shoots me a crazed look. "Cesar is taking time off work to wait on me. I love it. I know this sounds weird, Christy, but I feel like we needed this accident to happen so that we could grow, as a family."

"What?"

"It's hard to explain. But since the accident, I don't know. It's like we all had what really matters underlined for us with a big red Magic Marker."

"Are you serious?"

"Yes. Like, Cesar." She lowers her voice. "He's talking about going back to school to study to be a lawyer, girl, and he wants to have more time with us even when I'm out of the casts. And we both had this long talk about how, you know, how everything with Quinten— how we don't want any of that to get in the way of us loving him. He's fine the way he is."

"Cesar said that?"

Maggie nods. "He did. We both did. Thinking about life without him around made us both realize that we love Quinten just the way he is, and we don't really give a shit what the Pope thinks. Cesar thinks the Pope must be gay to hate gay people so much."

I say nothing, because I'm speechless.

So what I'm saying, Christy, is we're making progress here as a family, and I don't need you coming in and messing everything up."

"Excuse me?"

"Don't come in here making Cesar think he's off the hook with the housework and all that. I think he's finally starting to understand how hard it is, what I do all day."

"Right."

"Plus, you can't get all weepy and go into mourning if we all survived."

"I guess."

"You have to do this for me, as my Christmas present," she says. "You can't bag out on it."

"What is the big deal?" I ask. "Plus, I don't think I can stand another date with Melchior."

"Just give him one more chance."

"He's an insufferable bore."

"I understand. But it's amusing for me to hear the stories."

"I am pleased to know my suffering brings you pleasure."

"Plus, I might have put a little money down on it."

"On what?" I cry. "On who I'm going to pick?"

She nods. "Not a lot, but, you know, a few of us have little wagers going."

"A few of who?"

Maggie looks around the room, with her eyebrows raised suggestively. I look at my ancient uncles and the children who play with LEGOs at their feet, and feel betrayed at every turn.

"Ridiculous," I say. "My own family is gambling on my love life now?"

"Pretty much. Yep."

"My *mom*?" I ask, cringing.

Maggie nods gingerly with a wince.

"I don't believe this."

She gives me a pouty face now, and blinks her eyes rapidly.

"Who'd you put money on?" I ask her.

"I can't tell you that, that would be cheating," she says.

"I feel very dirty right now."

"Me, too," she says, happily. "Isn't it fun?"

"No Melchior," I say. "Caspar, yes. I can see him again. And Balthazar. But not Melchior."

"You have to see them all," she whines, "or the bets won't be valid."

"You put a lot down on this?"

"Maybe."

"You have an illness, you know that?"

"Maybe so. But you're my favorite enabler."

She pouts in my direction some more.

"Fine," I spit. "Just stop looking at me like that. With your legs in casts, and that look on your face, it's almost too pathetic to stand."

Maggie lights up, happy once more. "I knew I could count on you."

I get up and head to the kitchen for another cup of strong coffee.

It is only five o'clock, and I have another seven hours before the start of midnight mass.

So, here I am, in the sixth pew back in the nave at San Felipe de Neri Catholic church in Old Town Albuquerque. I am not big on the whole church thing, but I'm not so obnoxious as to deny that this is a beautiful old church, as churches go, with three steeples, in the *penitente* tradition. For more than three hundred years it has stood in the heart of this city. If you have to pick a church to sit in, in the middle of the night, this would be my first choice—though it would still be a distant second place to, say, staying home and sleeping. Peer pressure is a powerful thing, however, especially when your peers are your mom and dad, and you have been coming to this church since you were born.

We're on the left side of the nave, as is customary for our family. We started this tradition because my long-dead maternal grandfather was hard of hearing in his left ear, and we have continued it for no particular reason except that around here people pretty much stay where they've always been. There are churches closer to our home neighborhood, and our family will on occasion use them if we are rushed. But this is the church my mother grew up in, as did her father, and his parents before him.

I'm sandwiched between my mother and father now, with members of the extended family all around. There would be no escape, even if I wanted it, and so I might as well just relax and try to get something positive out of this experience.

My mind travels back to when I was a child, forced to this very mass, and how my mom used to let me bring my favorite pillow, with the Barbie pillowcase, so that I could curl up and sleep on the pew next to her.

When I suggested earlier that I do this tonight, my mother swatted me with a dish towel and told me to stop being so *traviesa*, which sounds an awful lot like *travesty* but actually means "naughty" or something like that.

All this is a way of saying I am asleep yet upright, lapsed yet in church, single yet feeling very hopeful about Caspar thanks to the wisdom of The Rules, doubting of God yet somewhat convinced he can see me here and knows, as did Santa Claus, that I haven't actually been a good girl this year. I hope that God, like Santa, is able to overlook my imperfections. Something tells me he is.

It is just a little before midnight, and I'm in that jumpy zone that is a mix of extreme exhaustion, far too much caffeine, and weariness of one's own family members. My mother, who counts allergies among the many ills that haunt her body, keeps clearing her throat in a way that makes me want to run away or strangle her.

Neither of these are wholesome thoughts under the best of

circumstances, and are positively revolting in the context of Church. I can't help it, though. The gross phlegmy burble is one of those noises that has alway bothered me but that, in small doses, can be tolerated. When stuck next to it, with no escape, in the middle of a too-warm church that smells of bready, pious breath, in the middle of the night, when I'd rather be sleeping, however? Annoying. Suffocating.

I am a bad Catholic, but like a good Catholic, I feel guilty about it.

I gaze at the altar and say a small, silent prayer for patience, and that I might stay awake and find some sort of enlightenment. I thank the Virgin for having sent me three men at precisely the time I needed them. I feel a chill run through me that tells me there is, in fact, something bigger out there. Zach was an atheist, but I now realize that the most unwavering among us, the least accepting of spiritual diversity, are the atheists, who take God's absence on pure faith.

I take a deep breath, and release it. I know all the reasons I have to suspect the Catholic Church of not being perfect—the lack of women priests, the stance against birth control, etc.; yet I cannot explain the odd, holy feeling I get inside churches, and this church in particular. I should find it comforting rather than creepy, but there are some things beyond our control. Creepy is actually not quite the right word. It's more a sense of enormity, something far beyond my reach, and an overwhelming wash of love that pours over me. I'm so used to expecting rejection and failure in love that Church unnerves me. There is never a shortage of love here.

It is not unusual for me to shed a tear at some point during the Mass whenever I'm here, and I'm never sure why—am I happy? Sad? Filled with regrets? I don't know. I cannot focus on the creepy tears long enough to sort them all out, because I suppose I realize somewhere deep down inside that if I were to do such a thing, I would probably have to make changes in my life, and I sort of actually really like my life the way it is.

I don't know if it is my overactive imagination, or whether there truly is a spiritual presence here, or if God himself/herself is communing with me right this minute. What I do know is that I feel goose bumps rise on the flesh of my arms, and I feel a pressure deep below my sternum, and I don't know what to make of it. I love this church even as I resent it in a thousand little ways, and I feel that in its own grand, beautiful way, it loves and judges me back.

This is where I was baptized, and where I held my first communion. It is where my grandfather's funeral was held. It is probably where I'll get married if anyone ever bothers to ask me to do such a thing, and by anyone, yes, I am presently hoping it would be someone a lot like Caspar. Zach did not want a church wedding, and in those days whatever Zach wanted was okay by me. Now? I realize that I very much want a church wedding next time.

What was I talking about? Oh, yes. The church. Sorry, a bit sleepy here. The church is a special place for me, and no matter how many beautiful and artistic spaces I have been in, none have ever compared in power to this place. Creepy, like I said.

I glance down the pew, to the end nearest to the wall, and see Maggie there, in her wheelchair, with Cesar seated at her side and the three boys next to them. Claudia and Rascal are in the pew in front of us.

Maggie and Cesar hold hands and look at one another with respect and humor. I have seen her in a lot of relationships, but never in one where the man looked at her like this. I do believe her injuries have been a test for Cesar, and he has passed it, beautifully. I do believe I've been wrong about him.

And if I've been wrong about Cesar, what else might I have been wrong about?

One of the biggest issues I used to have with the Church's teachings had always been suffering. If there were a God, why did he cause suffering, or allow it? Looking at Maggie now, however, I have a mild epiphany. Sometimes, I think, God allows us hardships and challenges not because he is angry with us or believes us worth punishing, but rather because he knows human nature and realizes that this is the only way we're going to ever learn whatever it is we need to learn.

Then again, there might be no God, and I scare myself sitting here even having thoughts like this. But of course there is a God, because how else can you explain the three men appearing just after I've prayed for them?

I haven't worked this all out yet, as you can see, but then again neither had Mother Theresa, if you believe her private diaries. She was filled with doubt, even at the end of her life, which is pretty damn scary if you think about it. If Mother Theresa did not have all the answers, then how the heck am I supposed to have any?

A deeper hush falls over the crowd as the service begins. It's sort of like that part at the movies when the lights get low and the talking popcorn container walks out onto the screen next to the soda with legs and high heels to remind you to turn off your cell phone, except that in the Catholic version there are calesthenics.

We kneel, stand, sit, and sing as required by tradition. Why the Catholic Church has to be a cardiovascular workout, I have no idea. Up, down, up, down, even the little old men and women with their dowager's humps, up and down like extras from a Richard Simmons video.

Oh, but that's not all. We also close our eyes, bow our heads, and, most of all, we listen to the words said by the young priest, who is new here and whose energy is dazzling in spite of my inherent mistrust of men in gowns and other such people.

This man? He cares about the folks gathered here—either that or he is a very good actor—even if he is talking about how we must all obey, obey, obey and believe, believe, believe without proof, proof, proof.

Still, I can appreciate hard work when I see it, and he's clearly put a lot of thought into his homily, which, even though it sounds like something to do with grits is actually a fancy Catholic word for *lecture*.

As always when I visit this church, the words he has picked seem to have been hand-picked just to make me feel like a selfish sinner whose cynicism taints everything in life and who is therefore still single and childless because, really, who in their right mind could love a woman like me?

Today is no exception.

Proof: The reading is from Isaiah, about walking from the darkness into the light, about realizing that joy comes to people when they share what they have, not when they believe they need more, and more.

Guess I shouldn't have bought myself those extra Christmas presents (hey, the jewelry was on sale on the Tiffany Web site, what do you expect from me?) when I was supposed to be shopping for my relatives, but you know, at least I managed to get stuff for other people, too.

Is the priest looking right at me? Can he read my mind? Ugh. Why, oh, why do I feel so dirty? Oh, well. I knew there was a reason I stopped going to church, and maybe I'll just stop listening now, and get on with it already, will ya? La la la, can't hear you. So on and so forth, blah blah blah, yadda yadda yadda, amen.

And then, as though it was planted in my mind from somewhere else, I have a complete feeling and thought, and a vision of Balthazar donating blood to a clown nurse, and I am filled with the knowledge of a thing that I know I must do.

I have to give money where it is needed and stop being so selfish.

I have to give money to Maggie.

Sometimes, I realize, God brings men into your life—but it might not be for the reasons you hoped they'd come.

The Virgin of Guadalupe has brought me men, but not for the reason I had intended. She is clever like that.

She brings men and other people and sometimes animals and situations to save us from ourselves, to deliver us gifts of insight that we, for whatever reason, have lacked. If we listen, we can hear the message.

If we don't, we're me the way I was yesterday.

It is the day after Christmas, and Caspar—who, I should add, sent me a beautiful candle set from Neiman Marcus for Christmas (with four delicious truffles tucked into the luxurious crepe paper) even though I sent him nothing (this is A-OK according to The Rules, by the way)—has asked me to plan for an overnight date tonight, which has made me instantly suspicious that he is planning to break the "friends-only" code of the dating game.

Being a reasonable and imaginative woman, I am very secretly hopeful that this is indeed the case.

Being a respectable woman who realizes the possibilities of being regarded as a whore among my own family members should I do something out of line, I pretend I am not flooded with images from the covers of the romance novels lining my mother's bookshelf—me, in a bustier or German beer frau's frock, bent helplessly backward in the powerful embrace of Caspar, who is inexplicably dressed like a matador. Or: Caspar standing behind me, silhouetted by the full moon as a wolf howls on the hillside in the distance, burly arms wrapped around me in such a way as to barely hold up my gauzy nothing of a purple top that, having a mind of its own, keeps slipping down to reveal my full, heaving bosom.

Ah, yes. It could be a lovely overnight trip, if things went right.

He's told me to pack comfortable, casual clothes, however. Nothing whatsoever about a gauzy flowy top, and something about a substantial winter jacket and warm socks. He tells me to be ready at 4 P.M.; I hang up the phone with him, and instantly field questions from my mother, who is visiting.

"And? So?" she asks, peering up at me over the tops of her reading glasses. "What did Balthazar say?"

"Caspar," I scold. "I'm smiling because it was Caspar. If it had been Balthazar you would see an altogether different sort of expression. It would look like this." I pantomime slitting my own wrists.

"Enough." My mother makes the sign of the cross on her chest, just like she does at every intersection when she's driving. "It is not funny to joke about suicide."

"That's what Melchior would say. He doesn't think I'm funny."

"Neither do I, with jokes like that."

"I just know what I like and what I don't like, and as it happens, I don't like humorless men who find me snobby."

My mother appears to be biting her lip for a moment, a habit of hers. She does this to literally keep herself from saying something she will regret. After a bit, she sighs deeply and rephrases her initial question.

"What did Caspar say?"

I tell her the basic details, omitting the part where I'm excited about the possibilities of me and Caspar naked and rolling to-gether, and exaggerating the part where I'm concerned that the whole overnight arrangement might, in fact, be inappropriate.

"I think I should check with Maggie," I say.

My mother pooh-poohs this idea with a wave. "Maggie schmaggie," she says. "You know the rules, and you trust each other to live up to your promises. You get a separate room, if there's a hotel. It doesn't concern Maggie. Maggie has no room to judge you."

Unsure about how this little diatribe on the part of my mother makes me feel—does she support me? does she find me a hopeless slut?—I excuse myself to go pack.

I realize I have no condoms, and realize I might actually want some, so I tell my mother I've started my period (untrue, as I am ovulating) and excuse myself for a quick trip to the drug-store; this is no easy feat because my mother, still pleased with my newfound generosity, has offered to go for me.

"It's been so long since I bought tampons, it'd make me feel like a girl again," she jokes.

"No, that's okay, I also need some gum," I say.

"*Pues*, and I can't buy you gum?"

"Mom, I'd really just rather buy my own tampons and gum, okay?"

She looks intently at me, and shakes her head. "You just be careful," she says. "I'm glad I did not raise a dummy."

At the drugstore now. Because I don't like to be caught buying condoms and nothing more, I load up on hand cream, body wash, tampons (for show, in case Mom snoops), O magazine, and a few other items I hope will lessen the humiliation factor of having a box of Trojans up in the mix.

I avoid direct eye contact with the cashier because I am lame like that, and then I scurry back to the car after tossing the receipt in the outside trash can (but not before ripping it to shreds because you never know when my mother might check the garbage outside the Walgreens). I hide the condoms deep in the darkest recesses of my handbag, and return to the house.

A few hours and a meticulous shower (I even shaved) later, Caspar comes to the front door of the apartment (The Rules say it's okay to let the man into the living room, but nowhere else, on date two) looking like he just stepped out of the pages of an REI catalog, all fresh-faced, pink-cheeked, grinningly healthy, and wearing jeans and a T-shirt with a long-sleeved button-down open over it. His hair is as it has been before, gelled into place in a strategic mess of goodness. He might have just come from a hike, or a horseback ride, or fishing. He oozes confidence, competence, kindness, and pleasantness, and he looks like he might taste like testosterone ice cream. He smells like fresh-baked cookies. He feels, crazily, like home.

"Here, let me get that for you," he says after greeting me and my mother with hugs, of my suitcase.

"Ay, *qué* polite," muses my mother. She gives me an approving glance and wishes us a good time.

"You be a good boy," she directs him. "I don't want to hear about any funny business."

"No funny business," says Caspar, with a laugh.

"Even if there were, you'd never hear about it," I remind her.

"I don't want to have to send her dad out after you," my mother jokes. "Even though she's already practically ready for the retirement home, and we're thinking she's on her last eggs, we have our family reputation to think about."

Caspar laughs some more, and I hang my head in embarrassment.

"She's joking," I assure him.

"I'll uphold your good name, Mrs. de la Cruz," he calls out to her. "No worries."

He hauls my suitcase to the trunk, and as he heaves it up and in, he jokes about it weighing a lot. It's just a night away, he tells me.

"Yeah, but I'm a girl," I remind him.

His eyes flit up and down my body, quickly and discreetly, as my mother is now leaning over my balcony, observing us.

"You don't need to remind me," says Caspar under his breath, with a seductive smile. "I'm already in pain because of it."

I wave at my mother, and she waves back, and into the BMW

I go. I rather think I deserve this BMW. It is just right. When I bought my Mercedes, I wasn't sure whether I should get a Beemer instead. They're quite comparable.

I think it would be nice to share a life with a man with a BMW, as a woman with a Mercedes. Shallow, sure. But what is life without a little shallowness? Communism, that's what. Green fatigues and gray apartments. Ah, yes, a BMW to go with my Mercedes, and a Caspar to go with me. It would be just, just, just right.

For what it's worth, The Rules acknowledge that women are stupidly crazy about fantasizing in this exact manner about the men they date, but they are also clear about the need for restraint in telling said men any of it. I keep it to myself and do what I can to appear pleasant, mysterious, and only mildly excited.

Caspar gets in, starts the car, and dispenses with the whole secretive pretense of the past date.

"I'll just tell you, because it's sort of cheesy to have you sitting there defenseless and wondering whether I'm taking you to do something horrible."

"Like play Catch the Poo with chimps," I suggest.

"Melchy!" cries Caspar. "How'd that go for ya?"

"I don't like chimpanzees after all, it seems, and I don't like men who choose hairy, stinking, feces-throwing mammals over their dates."

"Then Melchior Reyes ain't your man," says Caspar.

I consider agreeing, but realize it would be much more effective to say this instead: "Oh, I don't know. He's sort of fascinating."

Caspar's triumphant expression fades into a look of faint worry.

Bingo.

"He's a great guy, don't get me wrong. I love my cousin, and I have an incredible amount of respect for him and all the work he's doing. Did you know he's thought of as like, the number one guy in the world for what he does, decoding chimpanzee language and society?"

"No."

"Yeah, well, he is. And he's got no shortage of hot biology babes hoping to land him, either."

"Good," I say, and I mean it. "That's exactly what he needs."

"I agree. You're too terrestrial for Melchy."

"Oh, I don't know. I might be a biology babe. You don't really know me very well yet."

"So," he says, with that change in volume and posture that generally indicates a change of topic. "Being terrestrial and all, I am hoping that you will also like the idea of getting away to Chama for a night."

"Taos? Like, the place with the train?" My mind goes back to when I was a child and my parents took us up into Chama, a little town in the mountains famous for the Cumbres & Toltec Railroad, which is basically a train that chugs along sheer cliffs and beautiful scenery.

"Ah," he says sagely. "So you haven't been to Chama since you were a kid, I take it?"

"How did you know?"

"Because children go to Chama for the train, whereas adults such as ourselves go to Chama for the beautiful scenery and the excellent wineries."

I try to control my mind upon hearing this gorgeous man refer to us as adults. Consenting adults, I want to blurt. I want to bite his cheek. But I am a strong woman, with upstanding morals. Sort of.

They have wineries there now?" I ask lamely, because from what he's just said, this much is evident.

"Oh, the best. You like that kind of thing?"

I nod enthusiastically because, in fact, wineries and scenery are two of my favorite things, along with how this man looks, smells, and thinks. He is pleased, I am pleased, and we spend the next two hours' drive talking about everything under the sun, and, to my amazement, we agree on just about all of it.

As Caspar pulls his beautiful car off the road and into the parking lot of The Lodge at Chama, a rustic lodge where he has reserved a cabin, I am fighting back cynical thoughts such as "this is too good to be true," and "it will never last," and "he must be a serial killer because this is too perfect." Something, somehow, has to go wrong. That's how it has always been with me, and how it shall thus ever be, so decreed by the powers of love and cupid and all his cherubic little friends. Except, I reason, that I do in fact have the power to change things.

Rules Girls don't think like this, I remind myself; neither do real Catholics, who trust in God's plans.

He parks the car, looks at me as I wrestle with my own fretting mind, and asks me if I'm okay. That transparent, eh? Oh, well.

"Sure," I say, all fakery and self-flagellation. "Why wouldn't I be?"

"You look a little spooked," he says. "You cool with the woods and all this?"

"Totally cool."

"You don't seem cool."

"That is because I myself, as a human being, am entirely un-cool," I try to joke.

"We don't have to stay here if it's not your thing," he assures me. "I mean, usually, when I'm actually dating someone, we come to a consensus about what we're going to spend our time to-gether doing. This whole dictator thing is new to me."

I laugh. "It's okay."

"If you hate Chama speak now. If it isn't your thing."

"It's my thing. That's not it. Don't worry."

"Ah, so there is an *it*, though."

"What?"

"You said 'that's not it,' which, to me, implies that there is, in fact, an 'it' that is bothering you. Come on, Christy. We're friends here. You can tell me if something's bothering you."

Unable to control myself, I stuff The Rules where the sun don't shine and stupidly blurt, "Nothing's *bothering* me, okay? Except that you're, I don't know, too good to be true or something. I'm scared. You and I get along way too well for this to be real."

"We get along great," he says.

"Too great. You, you seem like you've been studying the 'Christy's Perfect Guy Handbook' or something."

Caspar looks taken aback for a moment, but only a moment, before smiling uncomfortably, and I realize that I'm probably going to scare him away before this is all over.

Even though we seem perfectly well-suited to one another, I do have a singular gift for blowing it with good men, meaning that if there is a foot anywhere nearby, I am guaranteed to find a way to shove it into my mouth.

"You just think I'm great because you haven't gotten to know me yet," he jokes as he opens his door and starts to step out of the car.

"Maybe," I say.

"No fear." He leans back into the car for a moment. But I can tell that I've already blown the independent woman mystique. Caspar is colder now. He seems bored. "Okay? Let's go see our cabin."

And he's out the door, and the door is shut. Maybe it's just my imagination now, but I can almost already feel him pulling away. This is what I do. I wish I didn't. But I know what I am, and what I am is an idiot.

"Sure," I say sullenly, convinced that by this time tomorrow he will dump me before we even have a chance for date three. "Let's go."

Caspar has rented an actual cabin, which is like a sweet little gingerbread log cabin of a house, dark brown outside, with white trim, and completely perfect, surrounded by forest and fallen leaves and oh-so-wintery and cozy.

Inside, the litle house is decorated in a style that I think of as "Midwestern mom," all pink and blue bedspreads and mismatched furniture, cheerful but sort of Lutheran in its sparseness and lack of drama. It is, nonetheless, utterly charming and perfect for what it is—a log cabin in the woods.

There is a small bedroom, which Caspar assures me is mine, all mine, and a living room with a wood-burning stove, sofa, and a comfy white wing chair and ottoman at its side. There is a sunroom, with a glass-top table and four wrought-iron chairs, and views of nature beyond. The living area is spartan, with decorations limited mostly to the odd basket of dried flowers nailed to the wall.

"I'm sure your designer's eye is finding fault," he says as he watches me looking around the living area, "but go easy on 'em. They're just a little rural lodge."

"I think it's great," I tell him truthfully.

"I'll camp out on the sofa here, if that's okay with you. If you'd rather, I can get my own room."

"Uh, no," I say, but I do not finish the thought out loud, which is to say that I do not say that I would like to figure out some way to get this man onto my bed, naked, by, say, midnight.

Caspar peeks at his watch, which I immediately assume means he's tired of me.

"Looks like it's about dinnertime," he says, proving my assumptions wrong, again. "We can stay here—I understand they have a pretty good chef and a decent dining room—or we can head into Chama for something a little bit fancier. Up to you, m'lady."

"Hey, I'm no lady."

"Right. You're more of a broad."

"Broad. I like that."

"So," he says, hopping onto the sofa with his hands perched behind his head. "What do you think? Stay in, or go out?"

"Seeing as I haven't been here since I was, like, nine years old, I'm probably the wrong broad to ask. I wouldn't want to be responsible for ruining our evening. Unless, of course, you think it's already ruined." I mean for this last part to come out as a joke, but it comes out sort of pessimistic and pathetic instead.

"Hey, now," says Caspar. "Nothing's ruined yet."

"Ah, that means there's still time."

He laughs at me, but seems confused at the same time. "Okay, well, I'm no big expert on this town, either. I looked everything up online. Frommer's basically says there are two restaurants worth going to in town, and neither of them is all that fancy. But I figure we'll do fancy tomorrow, at the wineries."

"Fancy and drunk."

"Depends on how you hold your wine," he quips.

"I'm a lightweight."

He just sits there grinning at me for a moment, as though he's trying to decide just what, exactly, is wrong with me and why, exactly, he used to think he dug me. I could make a nice long list for him, but I'll wait.

"Let's go to town, then," he says. "You like Italian?"

"*Andiamo!*" I say, practicing a bit of the Italian I have picked up on my few excursions to Italy in search of furniture for various clients.

"*Sei pazza*" says Caspar in response. Of course he knows more Italian than I do, I think. Not even my little Italian can impress this man.

I'm sunk.

hat does that mean?" I ask.

"It means 'you're crazy,'" he says.

"Gee, thanks."

"No, it's good!" He gets up and comes to wrap an arm around me, to better control me when the other hand comes around to give me a nuggie. "My mom's Italian. I don't know if you knew that."

"I knew she was white."

Caspar nuggies me even harder now. "White. That doesn't mean anything. It's vague. She's one hundred percent Italian."

"Please stop doing that," I say, as my scalp begins to burn.

He releases me. "Sorry. It's just, I was looking for a good excuse to touch you, in a brotherly, friendly way so that we wouldn't break any rules."

"Oh?" I adjust my hair a bit and try to look normal again.

"You're a little bit irresistible for me," he explains.

"Yeah," I joke, "especially when you screw my hair up and make me look like some kind of sock puppet."

"You look cute."

"I look a mess," I say, as I adjust myself a bit more with the help of a mirror. I look at him through it, which is a little less daunting for some reason than it might be to actually look directly at him. "For the record, next time you're overcome with an urge to touch me, just do it. Don't bully me like I'm your high school nemesis."

"Right. That's Balthazar's job," he says, and I laugh out loud.

"Not sure I want to be touched by Balthazar," I say.

"He's a good-looking guy."

"True. But he hates me," I say. Caspar looks worried, so I look away from him. Too much work trying to figure that look out.

"He's probably just having some issues because of his financial situation," says Caspar. "I wouldn't take it personally. I'm sure it has nothing to do with you."

I turn away from the mirror and walk back toward the little living area, where Caspar stands near the front door.

"What kind of financial issues?" I ask.

"I shouldn't be talking about it," he says.

"Too late."

I reach for my jacket, which is on a nearby armchair, and Caspar immediately jumps to get it for me. He holds it up in invitation for me to shimmy into it.

"Let's just say he had a little tax problem that I helped him clear up. You know how artists can be."

I slide my arm into one of the sleeves of my jacket and try not to notice how cookielike this man smells, or how warm and close he is, or how he has enough money to help out his less-fortunate jerk of a cousin.

"That was nice of you," I say as I slip my second arm into the jacket.

"Thank you," says Caspar. I have finished putting on the jacket, but he has not let go of it. In fact, he has moved in from behind, just like the men on the covers of so many romance novels, and has wrapped his arms around my own arms, and placed his mouth ever so close to my ear.

"You smell good," he tells me, in a whisper. My body goes electric and goose bumpy, and I'm frozen, salivating a little more than I was a moment before.

"Thanks," I manage weakly.

His lips move closer and brush ever so slightly across my cheek, and against my better judgment, I lean back slightly, into him. He meets my pressure with equal pressure of his own, and presses his lips against my cheek harder now, in a little kiss. I groan. I don't mean to do it, but I do it. I turn my head a little, and his kiss moves closer to my mouth, but still on my cheek.

"We can't," I protest, in a soft voice.

"I know," he says, kissing me again, this time a little closer to the lips, just at the edge of my mouth. "We're not."

"No, we have to— Stop, stop."

"You told me to just touch you next time," he whispers. "This is next time."

"Beats a nuggie," I say. I feel him smile.

My eyes close, and I hold my breath. His hands gently turn my body to face him, and he plants a little delicate kiss on my lips. It burns me straight through with liquid electricity.

"We have to stop," I say.

"So stop me."

He grins and kisses me again. This time his lips part, as do mine, and our tongues seek each other out. He is an excellent kisser, and soon enough I am leaning harder into him, and he is pushing me back, and I am walking backward, toward the bedroom, and then we're over the threshold, and we've pretty much forgotten about dinner, and rules, and everything but each other. The clothes come off, and I forget them, too. And there we are, moving together, thrashing around. He's good, but seems like he's performing for himself. He can't seem to look me in the eye.

Oh, well. Doesn't matter. It feels good. That's all that matters right now.

These things happen. It's just that they're usually happening to someone else, which is never fair and always annoying. I'd feel bad about the whole thing if I wasn't so damn happy at the moment. I'd regret breaking the rules of this whole dating game, I'd chastise myself for going too fast, even, perhaps, if I wasn't busy thinking: *It's about freakin' time.*

The next thought I have is: The Rules don't effing *work*.

I sit in the bland family room at Maggie's house, on a reclining chair, and watch her as she points and clicks the remote at the massive TV in the corner. Like most homes around here, my cousin's has one of the biggest TVs you can get at Costco. This is a sign, to her, that she's made it; it is also one of the main reasons I have been reluctant to give her money over the years, because when it comes to frivolous stuff, Maggie always finds a way to get it.

She settles on a daytime talk show, and lowers the volume so that we can talk with the background noise on. Why not just turn it off? Because that would be crazy. You don't spend a month's pay on a TV only to have it turned off.

"So, you look like you're hiding something," she tells me as she scoops some dry-roasted peanuts out of a glass bowl on the end table and drops them into her mouth. She eyes me suspiciously. She can tell, of course, that something happened between me and Caspar.

"I'm not hiding anything," I lie.

Maggie stares me down for another minute or two. "You went away for a night with the guy," she clarifies, "but nothing happened?"

"He had his own room," I lie again.

Maggie continues to stare at me and I have the disconcerting sense that she can actually see right through me to the dark rotten pit of my soul where lying comes from.

"I see," she says, confirming my suspicion that she has X-ray vision. Her voice is doubtful.

"How are you feeling?" I ask, to change the subject.

"You already asked me that when you came in," she reminds me.

"I know, but since then. How are you feeling now?"

"That was only ten minutes ago."

"I know, but a lot can change in ten minutes," I offer weakly.

"Yes," she says, "like you can sleep with a man against the rules of the game, and The Rules of your book."

"It would be sad if it only lasted that long," I suggest.

Maggie's eyes narrow. "Was it good?" she asks.

I balk. "Was what good?"

She continues to look at me with those slit eyes, a gleam of humor in them.

"Please stop looking at me like a Nazi interrogator," I say.

"You swear nothing happened?"

"No, I mean, stuff happened. We went hiking in the snow with these little tennis-racket shoes—snow-shoeing. Which sucks, by the way. Uhm, and we went around tasting wine. We sat on the enclosed porch and watched winter birds darting in to get seeds from the feeder."

"You *bird*-watched." She says this in a way that suggests she would have found it more believable if I'd told her I'd been, say, shooting wolves from a helicopter with Sarah Palin.

"Right." I sip from the can of Diet Coke I got myself from the fridge a few minutes before, and try to seem casual.

Maggie laughs out loud at me. "Birds," she says derisively.

"What?" I ask. "Is it so hard to believe that I might enjoy watching a bird or two? They, you know, they flit around. You watch them."

Maggie's booming laugh fills the room.

"Lots of birds in the forest," I suggest weakly.

"Wine tasting, huh? So you were probably wasted."

"Oh," I add, "and pie. We had apple pie."

"With wine."

"Well, no. Not at the same time. And, no, we weren't wasted. You don't guzzle the wine. You take a little sip here, a little sip there."

"I see." She keeps staring as though trying to find something hidden in my gaze.

"How are the boys?" I ask. "And Claudia?"

"You asked me that already. What's wrong, Christy? Are you forgetting things? Maybe you're distracted."

"I'm not distracted."

"You look distracted."

"What's Cesar up to today?" I ask.

Maggie shakes her head at me. "You can't tell anyone," she says.

"Why, is Cesar doing something top secret?"

Maggie leans toward me with her eyes widening for emphasis. "No, Christy. I mean, you can't tell anyone you slept with Caspar."

"But," I stammer. I can feel my cheeks flaming red.

"Seriously, I'll be out all the money I put on it."

"Excuse me?"

"Some of the people, they were betting you'd sleep with one of them. Me, I was like, no way. Christy is a respectable girl. She's all into that stupid book that white girls need to remind them how to act like Latinas."

"I am a respectable girl. And I'm not a white girl."

"But you slept with him."

"Wait a minute," I say. "Who bet that I'd sleep around? Someone in the family?"

"*Pues*, of course," she says, as though this were obvious—which I suppose it is. Who else would be in on this whole bet thing but my own family members?

"Who?" I cry. "Who thinks I'm a slut? My mom? Dad?"

Maggie makes as though she had a key in her fingers and uses it to lock her mouth. "Not telling," she says.

"Great." I down what's left of the soda, and belch softly into my hand. "Just great. I'm glad I can be a source of amusement and revenue for all of you."

"I won't tell anyone. This has to be our little secret. You have to tell that man not to go flapping his lips, either."

"There's nothing to tell," I insist.

"If he tells them, or if they find out, the bets are off."

"Heavens," I say sarcastically. "We wouldn't want that to happen."

"Just tell me the truth," she says. "Was it good?"

"I don't know what you mean." I cannot hold her gaze; I look away.

"Girl, I have known you since you were born. I knew you when you got your first training bra, and I knew the instant you got your first kiss, and—"

I stop her. "Enough. You don't need to go through all my firsts."

"So, was it good?" she asks again.

I give up, and nod. "Yeah. It was good," I say. "Excellent chemistry."

Maggie smiles a little, but it doesn't entirely mask her disappointment. "You know, I really thought you had it in you to wait."

"It's been a long time, Maggie, and Caspar—I don't know. He's pretty great. In every way."

"Okay," she says. She looks very nervous, and a little worried. It hits me why.

"Oh, no," I say. "You didn't bet on him, did you?"

"I can't tell you, or I forfeit. I'm not Martha Stewart. No insider trading deal here."

"Who did you think it'd be?" I ask.

"It's not over yet," she says.

"Yes, it is," I say. "It pretty much is."

"But you have to go on the rest of the dates."

"I know. And I will. But I'm pretty much leaning toward this guy. He's perfect."

Maggie's eyes narrow so violently now that they are nearly closed. "Just remember, there's no such thing as perfect, okay? And whatever you do, don't sleep with the other ones. Please.

Get your power tools out again, make the lights flicker all over town. Do whatever you have to do so you act like a real lady next time."

"Sure," I tell her. "I'll keep that in mind."

New Year's Eve is upon us, and with it a looming discomfort about what happened with Caspar, from whom I have heard not a peep since we tussled in the bed together, other than the awkward next day's drive back to Albuquerque, when he clearly seemed less interested in me than before.

I can only discuss this with Crystal Gutierrez, my doctor friend with the flirty husband, and Loida Acosta and Molly Sanchez, the other two women in our small group of friends. Maggie would not boost me up and encourage me the way these professional women do. Maggie would, unfortunately, tell me the truth.

We're having a late girls-only New Year's dinner (read: drinking) party at Crystal's sprawling North Valley adobe home, a one-story remodel with 3,700 square feet. It sits on two acres of perfectly manicured land, gardens here, lawns for the kids there, and a grove of cottonwoods behind the beautiful inground pool, covered now for the winter but loads of fun in the summer.

I met Crystal seven years ago, when she and Fred hired me to decorate with them, and through her I met Loida, a graphic designer, and Molly, an investment banker. They are all Latina, like me, but they grew up in the Northeast Heights instead of the South Valley, and all went to St. Pius X High School, where

I take it they were popular together and have remained friends ever since.

Crystal is about my height, very pale in the way of many Hispanic women in this area, with dark hair, a natural unibrow that she waxes, and bright red lipstick that makes her look like a witch. She's gotten sort of baggy in the belly and legs from having had children; she is a bit bottom-heavy but still pretty, with her short brown bob and lopsided smile. I might describe her more lovingly if I did not resent the way she seems to believe she has the perfect life when everyone else knows she doesn't.

Loida is very tall, and very thin, with beautiful, smooth pink-brown skin; she wears her dark hair long, straightened, and then curled prettily at the ends; she has white veneers on her teeth and youthful clothes, and always looks very well put-together. Loida is married to a police detective who, it turns out, had to work tonight. She has two grown children from her first marriage, both away at Ivy League colleges, though she herself looks young enough to fit in with their classmates.

Molly stands barely five feet tall, but is strong and elegant in dress and manners, with dark brown skin made darker by the fact that she dyes her shoulder-length bob blond; she's originally from the Bay Area but moved to New Mexico in middle school; she's a marathon runner, athletic, and measured in her thoughts, and seems to have as much trouble as I do with men. Like me, she is divorced. Like me, she has had bad luck dating men around this city.

Given that I was an outcast who did not have very many friends other than my cousin growing up, and given that I went to public school and focused only on getting good grades so I could move away, I don't have a group of friends like this. I am grateful to have been adopted by this one, however. I also feel a pang of envy whenever they talk about growing up middle class, in the white part of town. I do believe that if I'd had their opportunities, I might have had many more friends.

Unlike most clients, Crystal has great taste and actually helped a lot, participating in the making of her own home. The result is a muted neutral mix of Tuscan and New Mexico pueblo styles— big, solid quality furniture and soft, glowing light. It is a home at once nurturing and comfortable, and exquisite.

It is nine at night, and I sit at the twelve-person dining table, between Crystal and Loida, picking at my plate of homemade pasta. Crystal tells us that in her free time (when she's not being a cardiologist and the perfect mother to two perfect children, volunteering at church, or participating in the lasBMW book club) she has been taking cooking classes at the Whole Foods on Academy. She has made fettuccine with cream sauce and walnuts, but I can't get my mouth to open and close right. Really, the food is excellent, but my appetite is nonexistent thanks to the fact that Caspar has not called or texted, *not once*, and it has been four days since we did the deed. Like a good Rules Girl (who screwed up, literally) I have refused to call or text him, letting him make the next move. So far, there is no motion at all.

"Come on, you have to eat," says Molly.

"I'm sorry, I just don't feel well."

Fred decided—mercifully—to spend New Year's hunting elk with his buddies in Wyoming, and so tonight it's just the girls.

They all know my sob story. There are several sob stories in the room tonight, as we all sit and talk about men. Somehow, this seems to be the main activity when we get together. Being happily married, or so they think, Loida and Crystal share stories of losers past. Molly and I have fresh wounds to lick.

"Maybe he's been busy," suggests Crystal, who has a patient, superior air toward those of us here who have man problems. I assume this is because she thinks she has the most perfect husband who ever lived, a sentiment she blasts to all of us on Facebook all the time. None of her profile photos are of her alone; they're all of her and Fred. Fred's Facebook page, meanwhile, is all Fred, no pictures of her. She apparently either hasn't noticed, or doesn't see a problem with it.

"Maybe," I say.

Loida, who says she used a version of The Rules to snare her detective husband (after having escaped an abusive first marriage), shakes her head. "It's not that he's busy. It's that you slept with him. I'm sorry if that hurts your feelings, honey, but these men are different from us."

"You guys can't really believe that," says Molly. She is trying to be independent, but I can see the terror in her eyes as the reality of male difference slowly sinks in.

"I swear by it," says Loida. "Anyway, Christy, aren't there the other two?"

I nod, somberly. "Balthazar has turned out okay, but he's got no money."

"Forget him," says Molly.

Crystal shrugs. "You make enough for two," she tells me.

"But I don't want to support a grown man," I say.

"I think that's fair," says Loida.

"What about the other one? Melchior?" asks Molly.

"He's okay, but a little weird and into himself."

"And that's different from all men how?" asks Molly.

"He texts me all the time," I say. "He's dead set on being my man, I think."

"See?" says Loida. "That's because he's the one you like the least. The trick is to make them all feel like that."

"That's crap," says Molly.

"Time-tested crap," I say. "I think it's pretty true. That means I totally blew it with the best one, by letting my hormones take over."

"Probably so," says Loida.

"What about you, Crystal?" asks Molly. "Do you think The Rules work? Is that why this guy hasn't called her yet?"

Crystal is up from her seat with a look of smug empathy on her face, filling people's champagne flutes.

"It's hard to say without knowing him. It's the holidays, people get busy." She rubs my shoulder lightly. "I think you should try to give it some time and stop thinking so hard about it."

Molly hounds Crystal a little more. "But, okay, in your case, did you sleep with Fred right away when you started dating?"

Crystal shakes her head. "I was a virgin when I met him, actually. I waited until our wedding night."

We all express alarm at this.

"I was a good girl, that's how I was raised," Crystal jokes. "Don't let that fool you, though. Fred and I are very experimental now."

Yeah, I think, especially Fred.

"I want to text him so badly," I whine, whipping my smart phone out of the pocket of my long gray cardigan.

As if they are one being, my friends roar in unison: "Don't!"

"But I want to."

Molly stares me down. "You can't. You can't give that man the satisfaction of knowing that you're thinking about him."

"I thought you didn't buy into The Rules," I tell Molly.

"I don't. But I also think you should make him wait and miss you."

"That's The Rules!" I tell her.

Molly shrugs. "I've never read the book."

"You should," I tell her. "I'll let you borrow it."

"Yeah, you probably shouldn't call him," says Crystal. "Just let him come after you, if that's what he wants. Otherwise, you just set yourself up for rejection."

Loida nods. "That's right. Just pretend he's not there, act like you don't like him at all. That's what men want."

"What is wrong with them?" I cry. "Why do they want us only when we don't want them?"

Loida laughs and shakes her head. "That's easy," she says. "They are designed for the thrill of the hunt."

Molly adds, "Plus, in this society, everything is about quality and expense. The harder it is to buy something, the more we like it."

"Exactly," says Loida. "Make them work for you, that way they appreciate you more."

"But doesn't that mean they'll always lose interest, eventually, if you ever actually come to love them and cherish them and belong to them? I mean, don't you basically have to treat them like shit for the rest of their lives to keep them interested in you?"

Crystal takes her seat, folds her hands neatly on her lap, and says, smugly, "No, not necessarily. There are good men out there. Trust me, I found one."

"Oh, God," I groan. "We're all doomed."

Crystal looks at me funny, like a dog that thinks it might have heard a whistle but can't decide to bark yet or not. "Sorry?" she asks.

"Nothing," I say. "I'm glad for you." It sounds sarcastic. "I really am."

"Don't be jealous, sweetie," Crystal tells me. "Your time will come. Just be patient and ladylike."

I feel like telling her the truth about her "great" husband, but Molly stops me by clearing her throat quite loudly. We discussed whether or not to tell her, and decided that she was so drunk off the Great Hubby Kool-Aid that the only outcome would be that she stopped being friends with us, blamed us, or thought we were lying out of jealousy.

Molly, who is the only one here who knows that Fred hit on me (and, she says, has hit on her, too), seizes the moment to change the subject.

"Crystal, this pasta is incredible," she says. "Can you show me how to make it sometime?"

Crystal gloats for a moment, content and proud as a mama hen looking out at her brood, at ease in her beautiful house, married to the best guy on earth, convinced that all is right and wonderful in her world.

"Of course," she says. "Anytime." Then, to me she says, "Chin up, Christy! Positive thoughts!"

I positively think she's positively delusional.

Balthazar has asked me to meet him at a bar in the Nob Hill neighborhood for a drink, as our second date. I warned him that this might qualify him to be disqualified from the contest, to which he replied, cheerily, "*Ni modo,*" which translates nicely as "oh well," and not so nicely as "I could give a flying (bleep)."

I agreed to meet him because Maggie told me that I had to see the date through to the end, just to make sure he didn't have anything wonderful stashed up his sleeve. I'm feeling so icky about sleeping with Caspar (who still hasn't called or texted, by the way) that I just really want to stay home with a pint of Chunky Monkey and forget the whole thing.

"That doesn't sound like a Rules Girl to me," says Maggie, on the phone for the requisite predate pep talk I've come to rely on.

"No, I guess not."

"A Rules Girl gets out there, brushes a tear aside so she doesn't smear her mascara, and faces life filled with hope and optimism."

"I guess. But what if Caspar told Balthazar about my little indiscretion?"

"Then you go with the flow," says Maggie. "Just be yourself. Who knows? Maybe the man of your dreams will be sitting next to Balthazar at the bar. Right?"

"Surely you don't mean that. About me being myself."

"Actually, yeah. I do. You're good just the way you are."

I hang up and put on a Rules Girl outfit. For what it's worth, the book recommends that women dress like "women," which means in dresses and heels, with low-cut blouses, but not skanky. This is harder to pull off than you might think, especially when it is the first week of January in Albuquerque, and the mercury is hovering near the twenty-degree mark.

I opt for black woolen leggings, with black Uggs, and a flattering black cowl-neck sweater dress that is tight enough to reveal curves but not so tight as to suggest I am the easy type. Even though I am. Or was. Damn it! Why did I have to go and sleep with that guy? It was clearly against The Rules and now it's making me miserable. See, that's what superfeminists like my friend Molly don't understand about The Rules. They're there to protect us, not to diminish us.

Anyway.

I fix my hair, curling it in the right spots, straightening it in others, and I do my makeup—going a little extra heavy on the eyes for a smoky nighttime bar look. I realize this is the first halfway normal date I've been on in a very long time, and I am happy, for the moment, to know that it will not involve chimpanzees, or rabid squirrels, or watching frozen birds slowly starve.

I spritz myself with a bit of expensive perfume, do a last-minute check of the loft, set the alarm, and fly the coop.

I arrive at the trendy, modern, upscale restaurant and bar first, and stake my claim to a far end of the bar, where I can people-watch and see Balthazar come in. I try to channel my inner Diamond Self, that wench Cassandra, to sit confidently, and to smile coyly at any attractive eligible men in the room. This is all so contrary to my nature I almost can't stand it, but I'm told it will all get easier, with time.

Ten minutes later, Balthazar arrives in a brown leather jacket and jeans, looking gorgeous as always, his black nerd glasses only adding to his smart-boy mystique. I can't help it. I'm a sucker for intelligent-looking men with broad shoulders and meaty arms. He scans the room, sees me, and waves with a small smile, making his way through the room. I notice a few women watching him, and giving me the once-over when they realize he's come to meet me. Small victory, feels good.

I stand, and give him a tepid hug. He plants a kiss on my cheek, European style, and we take our stools. The usual small talk ensues—how are you, fine and you, good good, how was your day, great been here long, no, good, nice place, you look good, how's your cousin doing and the kids, everyone's on the mend, excellent, what are you having, etc.

The bartender is one of those human stork women with a tummy flat as uncooked lasagne noodles, who tend to find employment in these places. Her belly shows, even though it is January, and she's got an edgy tattoo encircling her navel, giving her the look of someone who might have just been shot in the gut with a rifle. Everything above her neck is stuck through with sharp pieces of metal, and her earlobes have holes in them that have been stretched to contain black metal circles the diameter of large coins. I try not to stare at her, because she's obviously dying for negative attention and I don't appreciate public cries for help that force me to react to people I don't care about. I also try hard not to make any kind of nauseated expression as she takes my order for a cosmopolitan, because she'd like that, too. She smirks at the passé nature of my drink of choice, and I decide I shall not give her a tip. Then I remember that Rules Girls don't pay for their own drinks. Even better. I shall not give her a cent.

Balthazar orders some kind of fancy German beer I've never heard of, and a plate of gourmet nachos.

We wait for the drinks, chitchat a bit. I notice, again, how incredibly bright and straight his smile is, and all the old emotions from high school come flooding back through me. He is the cutest boy in school, the most popular, the most everything, all over again.

The drinks come, and the nachos, which I shouldn't eat but under pressure from my companion do.

We down it all, order more, and then, as the rock music gets louder, the crowd gets thicker, and the lights grow dimmer, we begin to talk.

So, this date is mundane," I tell him, shouting a little to be heard over the crowd, as people tend to do in bars.

"You think?"

"Maggie might disqualify you."

Balthazar shrugs as though he couldn't care less, and my heart falls, but only for a moment because he follows the gesture by saying, "Maggie couldn't keep me away from you, no matter how hard she tried."

The falling heart lurches upward again, and explodes into butterflies. I am suddenly at a complete loss for words, because this is the first time Balthazar has expressed interest in me without criticizing me, or judging me, or teasing me, in some way.

I want to ask him if that means he likes seeing me, or if it means he wants to see me again, but that seems clingy and anti–Rules Girl. I take a moment to think, and ask myself what a Rules Girl would say. Then it hits me.

"Maggie could stop anyone, if she wanted to. She's a tough woman."

"Oh, no doubt," says Balthazar. "But even the toughest of people would have a hard time stopping me from going after something if I really wanted it."

"Is that right?" I ask, flirty. He winks.

"Fact," he says.

I try to conceal my smile, and busy myself looking around the room.

"I'll be right back," he says, standing up. "Bathroom break."

"Cool," I say.

"Don't take off," he jokes. "We have some serious talking left to do."

"Okay," I say.

I watch him walk away, but divert my eyes when he looks back to smile at me before turning down the hall to the men's room. My heart is beating so fast it feels like it will explode. Balthazar Reyes is on a date with me, and he's flirting. Flirting! With me? It doesn't make any sense.

In a panic, I text Loida to ask her what to do. She does not text back right away, so I just set the phone next to my bag on the bar. Balthazar returns a couple of minutes later, totally relaxed and at home with this place, with me, with himself.

I ask him about his teaching, and he is telling me about a couple of his most talented kids, when my phone dings to let me know I have a text. Maybe it's because I'm a little sloppy from the drinks, but I stupidly pick it up and see Loida's name, and press to retrieve the message. Balthazar, who was still talking, seems taken aback, though not terribly irritated, by my rude behavior.

"Must be important," he says, craning his neck to see the screen on my smart phone.

JUST FOLLOW THE RULES. BE A RULES GIRL AND HE'LL LUV U. YOU CAN'T LOSE.

By the time I realize Balthazar has read the words, he's already chuckling to himself and giving me the strangest look I have ever seen on a man's face—part flattered, part amused, part shocked.

"No!" I cry, stuffing the phone into my purse. "You did *not* just see that."

"The rules?" he asks, incredulous. "Like, The Rules everyone was talking about back in the nineties? That old-fashioned anti-feminist crap?"

"No!" I lie.

He is still chuckling and shaking his head. "Wow," he says. "Women, man. I feel sort of sorry for you guys."

I look at him unkindly now.

"Seriously," he says. "I remember my sister was all into that shit once. It was all she talked about. She and all her desperate friends. You know, a chick would be cheated on by some homeless cokehead dropout motherfucker, and the chick would be all, like, 'It's my fault, I was too forward,' and I was always, like, 'What the fuck, man? You got involved with a loser, that's your only fault in this.' Women think everything is either their fault, or in their control. It's all about fear of rejection, right? The Rules. They promise you'll never suffer if you act like a 1950s housewife. Fucking hilarious if it weren't so sad. I tried to tell her it was bogus from the start."

"But it's *not* bogus," I protest. "It really works."

"You think if you'd followed The Rules your gay ex-husband would like pussy?" he asks, his crass mouth lubricated by the alcohol.

"He's not gay," I blurt.

"Sorry?"

I tell Balthazar about seeing him with the pink-sweats big-boobs woman, and he listens with a look of concern on his face.

"That guy just needs his ass kicked," he says. "What a douche-bag."

"Yes, but maybe if I'd followed The Rules, and gotten implants, and made myself better for him, he wouldn't have left me."

"Omigod," he says. "You are not seriously saying this, are you, woman? Are you insane?"

"Maybe."

"You have a beautiful body. You're an amazing person. You are funny as shit, and you're gorgeous and talented."

"Thank you."

"I'm sorry to tell you this, but your husband was a dick."

"And not even that big," I say, holding my thumb and pointer two inches apart.

The chuckle becomes a full-on belly laugh now, and he orders another beer with a hand gesture to the barmaid. "You want another?" he asks me.

"Probably shouldn't, but what the hell. My cover's blown anyway." I drop my head into my hands, but only for a brief moment.

He smiles at me like I am the cutest and most pitiful puppy at the pet store.

"You chicks give all your power away," he tells me.

"What?"

"Women. You guys lap up these books that are supposed to have all these secrets about how to get and keep men. But there's a really big secret no one seems to have bothered to tell you yet."

"Which is?"

Balthazar gets his new beer and takes a drink before answering, dabbing his mouth with a cocktail napkin first.

"Men are people, just like women."

"Well, duh."

"And," he says, "you didn't let me finish."

"Finish."

"And—being people, we are individuals, and being individuals, some of us are cool and communicative, and some of us are shallow pricks."

"Which side do you fall on?" I ask, full of my old usual smart-assery.

"I'd like to think I'm the cool and communicative type," he says. "Meaning, please listen to what I'm saying, okay? Meaning that I don't like mindfuck head games, and I don't have time for chicks who play them."

"Oh."

"When my sister used The Rules, she used to get men hooked pretty quick, but it never lasted because sooner or later, if you end up in a relationship with some schmo, you're going to end up slipping up and acting like yourself. And if he fell for you because you were working overtime not to act like yourself, then you're fucked."

"Yeah. I know."

"You sure?"

"Maybe."

Balthazar reaches toward me now, and musses my hair. I retaliate by shoving him on the arm, but, being made of granite, he hardly moves.

"You're a dork," he tells me.

"No, you are," I say.

"You were always a dork," he says.

"And you were always . . ." I stop myself from saying that he was always a jerk, which is what a Rules Girl might have said. I focus to see what it is I'm really feeling, and then I say it. "And you were always the guy who was way too good for me."

I feel a tear form in each eye, and one by one, they roll down my cheeks. Balthazar loses the lighthearted attitude now, and looks at me with tremendous compassion and understanding in his eyes. He uses his pointer to stop the tears, wipes them on the cocktail napkin, and looks at me again.

"Christy," he says, moving in closer, so close now that my heart begins to race again. I work very hard to stop crying, and try to stop myself from wanting to fall into his arms and melt.

"Christy," he repeats, with a supreme confidence in his eyes. "I was never too good for you. You were too good for me. Okay? Let's get that straight. I was an idiot to you, and I regret it like crazy now, and it's not just because you're thinner now. I regret it because I hurt you, and knowing you now, and being able to see that vulnerability still in your eyes, and now, knowing that you're trying to take the advice of a couple of crazy bitches in New York about how to make men love you— Damn it! It pisses me off."

He moves in closer still, and his eyes move from my eyes to my lips. He licks his own just a little, and then I feel his large, strong hand on the back of my neck, pulling me in toward him. And then Balthazar kisses me, gently, and with incredible kindness, and it is wonderful, and he is kind, and perhaps he is right about The Rules, but given the way men act, I doubt it. If I sleep with him, he'll never call me again. That's how they are, it's true, I swear it!

I will kiss him, yes, I will kiss him here at this bar, half-drunk and ecstatic, but I will not sleep with this man. You hear me, self?

I. Will. Not. Sleep. With. Him. Yet. I don't think. But, God, he smells so good! Argh! What is wrong with me?

With great effort, I push him away, knowing in the back of my mind that this is the only way to draw him nearer. I remind myself that I have toys at home that won't hurt me when they neglect to call me tomorrow.

"I can't," I say.

He does not look hurt, as I would, or devastated, as I would, or rejected. He doesn't even look confused. True to The Rules, he looks like he's just been challenged to a game he knows he'll win. He looks . . . alive with excitement.

"Sorry," he says. "You're right. I shouldn't have done that."

With even more effort and pain, I look at my watch, smile demurely as the book tells me to, and tell him that I really, really have to get going home.

"So much to do tomorrow," I say mysteriously, trying to set him on edge. "Have to get some rest."

He looks impressed that I have a life. He also looks like he's lost a lot of his earlier confidence, and replaced it with verve.

"Sure, no problem," he says, and I swear to you that I can see the wheels turning in his head as he plots his next move to snare me. "Here. Let me help you with your coat."

Maggie is propped up in her bed with the television on, popping Cheez Doodles into her mouth three at a time. Cesar is at work and the kids are doing their own things. I sit at the edge of the bed, distractedly watching *Oprah* and trying to carry on a conversation with my cousin.

"So," she says through a mouthful of orange powder. "You just left him hanging?"

"Yep," I say, beaming. Whereas it was painful to do at the time, my rejection of Balthazar feels like a badge of honor to me now. I feel stronger because of it.

"And?" she asks, her eyes on the TV but her ears on me.

"And he's texted me six times since then. I didn't answer the first three, and it was like he got sort of frantic and kept texting, just to see if I was there. He didn't ask me what was wrong, exactly, but he kept asking me other things, like how was my day. He put smiley faces everywhere in the text."

Maggie continues to munch and gives me a look of approval, telling me that men like to feel like they're in charge, like they did all the hard work.

"They're like dogs," she says. "Dogs see you have the treat, and you both pretty much know you want to give it to them, because there's no way you're going to eat that treat all by yourself. . . ."

"Not unless you're really, really flexible," I add.

Maggie laughs. "Exactly. The dog knows that's his treat, but he wants you to tell him to do something for it. He is conditioned to work for his reward. If you give dogs treats without making them work for them, they basically just feel cheated and bored and they start to hate you and then they turn into those dogs you hear about whose masters died and were all alone and spent three days dead in the armchair and then the dog started to eat their feet."

"God, Maggie."

"I'm just sayin'." Maggie grabs the remote and flips through the channels for a minute, then goes back to *Oprah*.

"Yeah, I know. I think you're right."

She asks me about Caspar and Melchior. I tell her what I know, which is that Melchior is blowing up my phone about as much as Balthazar now, but Caspar has been silent.

"Give me the phone," she says.

"What? My phone?"

"Your phone."

"Why?"

She looks at me like she's going to kill me, so I do as she's asked. She finds Caspar's number in my address book, and calls it from her land line, using the cordless phone she keeps in her lap with the junk food.

"What the heck are you doing?" I demand.

"Shh."

"But Maggie!"

She holds up a hand to silence me, and I listen in horror to her half of the conversation.

"Caspar. It's Maggie, Christy's cousin. Listen, Christy's been real busy and I worry she's going to flake out on the last dates with everyone, so I'm just playing Julie the Cruise Director here, and setting up her social calendar. Do you have a third date planned out yet?"

Silence, as she listens and says uh-huh and rolls her eyes and wheels her hand as if she wishes he would just get on with it already.

"Well, that's fine," she says, finally. "Christy is super-busy, and I think that will work just fine. I'll let her know. Thanks."

She presses the phone off and drops it on the bed once more.

"Well?" I ask. "What did he say?"

"Saturday night, Santa Fe, he's taking you to an art opening."

I point out that The Rules says in long-distance relationships, if the man is actually interested in you, he will come to your city and not request things be the other way around.

"Yeah," she says, disinterestedly. "So now we really know where he stands."

"I don't want to go on a date like that!" I say.

"Why not? You had a *marriage* like that."

I consider what she's said and realize how true it is. I was always bending over backward for Zach. I always went to his place, his city, to his family's house for the holidays. It was never about Zach coming to me.

"I just don't think I should go."

"I do," she says, shortly.

"Why? Because you have a bet on it?"

She shakes her head, then thinks better of it and nods. "Well, yes and no. But, trust me, there's a good reason you should go."

"Tell me."

She considers it before letting me down.

"Nah. I think you have to see it on your own. But I also think I need to call my bookie, so if you don't mind, scoot scoot."

Caspar picks me up in his usual fashion, meaning he looks like a slightly meatier version of Colin Farrell with a gleaming BMW. There was a time when these things would have flipped me for a loop, but today I just don't feel much like going out with a guy I screwed and never heard from again. It is creepy and embarrassing in the worst of ways. How to find dignity under such circumstances?

I spent the morning reading a suspense novel on my sofa, which probably has not helped ease the creep factor. I feel paranoid now. Everyone is out to get me. Horrors await.

I decide to go casual and not try too hard, because let's face it, Caspar thinks I'm a whore and we have no future now that I broke The Rules. I opt for jeans that aren't fresh or even clean. They have whipped cream on them from where I wiped it when a bit of my hot cocoa dribbled onto my hand. Hey, I'm not perfect. I don't try to be. Caspar's not worth clean jeans. I don't feel like doing laundry. I don't feel like much except hibernating. Anyway, I've paired the jeans with a black sweater and black boots. Voilà, basic, boring. Fine.

I see him on the sidewalk and he is looking at his watch and tapping his toe. Great. He's already got somewhere else to go. I hate him. I love him. I hate him. And why is this always the way it ends up?

He looks up as I come out the door of my building and smiles.

"Hi," I say, speaking first, because, hell, I might as well break all The Rules now.

"Hello!" He is cheerful all out of proportion to the disaster of us. He hugs me, and plants a warm kiss on my cheek. He tells me I look great, which I know can't be true because I've wiped all my hair back in a ponytail and only dabbed a bit of blush on my cheeks.

"Nice to see you," I lie.

"You ready for our obligatory third date, a.k.a your big break?" he asks me cryptically as he escorts me on his elbow to the car waiting at the curb in front of the building.

"Ready as I'll ever be," I say cleverly, because what he said doesn't mean much to me.

Fifteen minutes later, we arrive at something called Ricardo's House of Destruction, in Valencia County. Caspar is giddy about it. I have never heard of the place, which delights him because he seems to be under the illusion that I will like it and he will be the one to introduce me to it.

"Oh, it's great," he says. "After some time here, you'll feel very relaxed."

He parks, and I help him haul large shopping bags full of what appear to be old dishes into the place. I can't help notice how much the dishes remind me of the ones my mother has collected over the years. I am struck with the urge to fill my cabinets with them. Recycle chic, I think. Someone needs to make recycling old unmatched plates cool, and that someone should be me. Who better?

"What is this?" I ask him, as we enter the front door.

"You'll see," he says impishly.

Turns out that Ricardo's House of Destruction is exactly what it sounds like, a place you go to unleash your inner Gallagher—hopefully minus the mullet perm and pattern baldness, but whatever, this *is* Valencia County and such things have never gone out of fashion here.

So here's the point: You bring stuff to Ricardo's, and they give you an empty room in which to smash it to smithereens. They also give you a black rubber jumpsuit, gloves, goggles of the type worn by welders, and, if you forgot to wear some, closed-toe shoes. Caspar, for some unexplainable reason, thinks this is all going to be a form of high entertainment.

The building itself is a nondescript warehouse, decorated in a style I can only describe as "checkered Vans antiseptic," with black-and-white checkerboard walls, interspersed with the occasional yellow or red tile. The floors are dark blue. It is creepy and claustrophobic, like a hospital ward designed by Amy Winehouse.

I don't feel like smashing anything, much less something that I know several members of my family would find a perfectly good use for.

"The shards are donated to struggling artists, to make mosaics," the girl behind the front counter assures me through her smacking of bubble gum. Her sickly sweet pink breath permeates the place. Her pimples need popping.

"It's all for art, baby!" exclaims Caspar, as he pays an obscene amount of money for the opportunity to break perfectly good stuff.

Raised rich, I think.

Clueless.

e take our helmets and goggles, and find our room. Caspar has brought his iPod, and the room has a jack for it.

"They totally let you blast your tunes," he says. He grins like this is the best thing ever, which it is not. Soon, Mexican speed metal is blasting through the speakers hidden in the ceiling, and Caspar is bouncing around on his toes like a boxer warming up.

"I don't really want to do this," I shout. He nods and grins in a way that tells me he did not understand or hear me, so I repeat myself, louder and in closer range.

"Oh, come on! It'll be fun. Get your aggressions out."

"I don't think I have any aggressions."

"Whatever. Everyone has aggressions."

"Nope. Not me."

"That's because you hang out with hippies; they smoke aggression out of you. Watch. It's easy."

Caspar takes out a pale yellow plate and hurls it against the wall like a Frisbee, while I stand as far from him as I can, terrified a shard will pierce me.

"God, that felt good!" he roars in a voice best described as Professional Wrestler. He pumps his fists in the air. "You have to try it!"

"No, thanks."

Caspar's shoulders sag for a brief moment, before he goes back to the bag for another plate. I watch him demolish six plates this way, and can't help wondering about all the families in Barrio East San Jose who are struggling to make ends meet. What might they do with all these plates?

I wonder if the old me, the me I was, say, two months ago, might make of this smashing. I probably would have found it ironic and interesting. Right now, however, I just find it wasteful and indulgent.

"You're really not going to do any of this?" he asks me.

I shake my head. "I'm no good at smashing stuff," I say lamely. "I'm more into building things."

At this moment, Caspar's cell phone rings. He asks me to excuse him a moment, turns off the iPod, and answers the call. He smiles and gestures with his hands as he speaks to whoever it is on the other line, as though they might magically be able to see him and—more tellingly—as though I were not there at all.

"Yeah," he shouts into the phone. "That's exactly what I meant. The kid is talented, but he's green. The family is totally naive. Dude, that rocks for us. You know it. They'll basically take whatever we give 'em and be happy to get it."

I listen in horror. Caspar is clearly plotting to take advantage of someone. At the same time he is gleefully smashing stuff people somewhere might need. He doesn't look handsome to me anymore. He looks ugly, even if he could be a model.

I realize, with a jolt of insight, that it wouldn't matter if I'd played by The Rules or not; I might not actually have liked this man at all, once I actually got to know him.

Light bulb, ping!

Opera. That's right," he says. "The boy sings opera. I'm thinking Disney and PBS both, dude. Like a kid version of Bocelli, you feel me? He's going to be a gold mine. I think we can easily take thirty percent, and they won't know the difference. Just, you know, make it look right for me. That's all. Okay, I'm kind of in the middle of something here. Catch you later."

He hangs up, and smiles at me.

"Not even one little cup?" he asks. He reaches into the bag and produces a coffee mug, bright red with a black cat silhouette, in perfectly usable condition. "Chicks usually dig this place."

"Were you talking about Jacob?" I ask him.

"Who?" he says, looking surprised and—let's be honest here—caught.

"Jacob Lewis. The kid who sang at Switchblade Mouff's house in Santa Fe."

"No," he lies.

"You have some other kid opera singer you just signed?" I ask.

Caspar hurls the coffee mug against the floor and grins as it explodes. "Crap," he says, with an awkward smile.

"Crap?"

"I forgot you were with me on that one."

"Really." I say this not as a question, but as a statement.

"Okay, you caught me," he says, with a gleam in his eyes. He digs through the bag and holds out a small plate. "You caught me being an agent. Care to smash?"

"What are you doing? Planning to take thirty percent, when you told the kid and his family you'd take, what was it? Ten? I mean, it's none of my business, but that seems a little sleazy, doesn't it?"

Casper pushes the hair out of his eyes and shrugs at me, like a little boy. This, I realize, is his biggest weapon. He looks sweet and harmless, and he talks a good game, he makes you think he actually cares, but deep down he is the kind of man who gets off on destroying things.

"That kid," he tells me, in a vicious sort of voice, "is going to make millions. He is going to make millions because of *me*. I, in other words, am going to make millions *for* that kid, and it's going to take a shitload of work on my part."

"You told him ten percent, and he believed you. His family trusts you."

"They will never know the difference," he says. "The paperwork will reflect ten percent."

"That's not legal."

"It is if there's no paper trail."

"How can you do that?"

"Ancient Hollywood secret."

"That's disgusting."

"No, my dear. That's *agenting*. They're going to have more money than they will know what to do with. You should quit worrying about those people."

"And so will you, you'll have more money than you could use."

"Right." He grins at me. "Everyone's happy. See? It's not neuroscience, Christy. It's entertainment. Jesus."

"I'm not happy."

"Okay. Everyone's happy, except Christy de la Cruz."

"I want to go home," I say.

"But we just started. We've got bags of dishes to go."

"*You* just started," I say. "Me? I'm done."

"But we still have another date tonight," he says.

"No, I don't think we do."

"Listen," he says, following me out the door of the smash room, down the hall, and out of the disgusting establishment altogether. "I promised Maggie I'd take you to this other place later tonight— get all our dates over in one day. We have to go."

"Just take me home, please," I say.

Caspar doesn't speak again until we're back on the freeway, headed north to Albuquerque once more.

"Listen," he says with a deep sigh. "I'm sorry you heard that conversation, and I'm even sorrier you figured out what it was about. But you have to understand the nature of my business. I'm an agent. I'm not a priest. I'm not a guidance counselor. I'm one step lower on the food chain than a lawyer. Lawyers eat us the way flies eat shit."

I say nothing, because I don't feel like arguing and I don't like his imagery.

"I'm in entertainment. It's a cutthroat business, and if you aren't looking out for yourself, you die. No one else is looking out for you. That's the nature of the business."

"Nice," I say sarcastically.

"No, it's not. It's *not* nice, and I'm the first person to admit that. And now that you seem to be pretty much done with me anyway, I'll just tell you a couple of other things. I'm an agent because I'm a liar. I've always *been* a liar. It is a useful survival skill to have, and I actually enjoy lying. Now I lie for a living."

"And you're proud of this?"

Caspar smiles at me in an unnervingly innocent sort of way. He continues, "I've never had a lifelong friend, the way other people do. I forget about people almost as soon as I've met them. I have an uncanny ability to put people in boxes and close the boxes and forget. I don't really care that much about people, Christy, and I never have. I like money, and I like me, and I'm okay with that because that's how it is and in spite of all my efforts to be otherwise, this is what I am. It's how I came into this world. I wish it were different, but it's not."

Caspar skips my exit, and instead gets off at Central Avenue and heads east, away from downtown.

"Where are you going?" I say, with some discernible fear in my voice now.

"I have something to show you." He has a filthy smile.

don't think that's a good idea. I want to go home," I say.

"Don't worry. I won't hurt you." He laughs at me. "Please. I'm a scumbag and an agent, but I'm not a psychotic murderer. Stop looking at me like that."

"Where are you taking me?" I ask, my heart pounding now.

"Like I was saying, I've never been a guy who cared about

anything, not like Melchior, who's got social-skill problems, but if you get to know him and have patience for his weirdness, is actually a pretty decent guy at heart. Melchy actually gives a shit about something."

Caspar sounds angry now, annoyed with himself. It scares me.

"Me? I don't. I don't really care, but that's okay, because I've become very rich that way."

"In money only," I say.

"True. In money only. And you know what? That's enough for me."

"That's why you never called me after I slept with you."

He looks at me without feeling. "Yeah, hey, sorry about that. Look, for a guy like me, and I'm going to be totally upfront with you about this, it's all about the chase."

"For all men," I grumble.

"Not so," he says. "Really. Women think that, but that shit's not true. There are good men out there. Cowardly lions and brainless scarecrows."

"And you're the heartless tin man?" I ask.

"Good armor," he tells me.

"I guess."

He continues. "I thought maybe I could be better, you know, make myself better with enough money, good enough for a girl like you, because—and this is not a lie now—you're pretty great. But now that I'm out in the open, I might as well just come clean and tell the truth, the whole truth, and nothing but the truth, which is basically that I'm a scoundrel. I hoped to do better with you, but in the end I gave you the same Caspar treatment they all get. And you deserve better than a scoundrel."

He drives faster.

"Where are we going?" I ask him.

"You'll see."

"No, I don't want any more surprises."

Caspar takes a deep breath and smiles, and I swear to God it looks like he's sad, like he's about to cry, like he is full of regrets in spite of the words he's just said. I decide the best course of action right now is to remain quiet.

We take Central south to Rio Grande, then take that north to Mountain. Soon, we are at the Albuquerque Museum of Art. He parks next to Tiguex Park and gets out, motioning for me to follow. I do.

"You remember when I told you Balthazar was struggling?" he asks.

I nod as we walk toward the gorgeous museum.

"I lied."

"Sorry?"

He gives me that little boy look again, and actually sort of giggles.

"Yep. Ever since we were kids, that prick was all about doing the right thing, you know? And me, I wanted to make money. He was always telling me that money didn't matter, and I always felt like, you know, that was the one thing I'd have over him, you know, if he was going to be all high and mighty about morals and whatever, then at least I'd be the one with the most money and toys, and the one with the most toys wins."

I stare at him, frozen.

"I want to show you one of his sculptures, Christy."

"What? Why?"

"Because you're right. I'm scum. I realize that. But I'm not actually heartless. I like to think I am, and I talk like I am, but I do recognize that what I'm doing is wrong. There is a conscience somewhere in here. I feel like I at least owe you the truth about Balthazar, because it's obvious to me that he's the guy you need to end up with, not me and not Melchy."

"What?"

"It's been obvious since day one, but I didn't— I don't like to lose, and I was pretty committed to kicking his ass in this contest, mostly because he beat me at wrestling when we were kids."

I can't think of anything to say.

"That, and also because you're way too nice a girl for me."

"You *think?*" I deadpan.

"I need a shallow bimbo type, someone who will be impressed by tacky parties with rap stars. Someone stupid enough not to realize that the conversation I'm having on the phone in front of her is about taking advantage of an eleven-year-old boy with incredible talent."

"Yeah, then pretty much, I'm not your girl."

"I realize that. But I also realize that I helped poison you against Balthazar because I wanted to win, and I wanted to win only because I wanted to screw with Balthazar, not because I necessarily wanted to end up with you, per se."

"Wow."

"Sorry if that hurts, but it's the truth. This is why I'm a liar, by the way. Whenever I'm honest with people I just end up with new enemies. Anyway, lying about Zar. That was stupid and wrong, and I figure I can manage to do at least one right thing every year, or so, especially around Christmas."

"Where is this sculpture?"

"See, that's the thing I hate most about Zar, man. He got this massive commission from the city, to do a huge installation here in front of the museum, right outside the museum, and he never even told you about it."

"He what?"

"I bet he never told you about it."

"No, he didn't."

"See, if it were me, that sculpture would be on my business cards, I'd be pushing it up in your face every five minutes, like, look at this! I beat out a thousand other assholes to have the chance to be considered one of the top sculptors in the nation."

I am now very curious.

"It's right around this corner," Caspar tells me.

I go with him. We find the sculpture, and it is breathtaking, a huge bronze woman's face, made of thick straps of metal woven together and bent and molded to make a realistic head eleven feet high. It looks like the wind is blowing the woman's hair back. The plate at the base of the sculpture says it is the head of Metis, the Greek goddess eaten by Zeus when he realized he'd impregnated her with a goddess even more powerful than himself—Athena, who was born from his head anyway. It was commissioned in celebration of International Women's Day. A feminist sculpture, by a man I have gotten all wrong.

"They paid him a million bucks for this one," says Caspar. "He has five more, same price range, all over the country. All in the past three years. You might say he's the new darling of the sculpture world. He has told no one, really, except us in his family, and he asked us not to brag about it to anyone. He gives most of his money away. Socialist fucker."

I am struck dumb. I can't think of anything to say.

"*He* deserves you," Caspar tells me, with a grin.

"It's pretty noble of you to say that," I tell him.

Caspar shrugs this off. "Please. Don't overestimate me," he says. "Women only find themselves heartbroken whenever they do that."

"I bet."

"I'm still a schmuck."

"True."

"But I should tell you, the date I had planned for us tonight? It was going to be a visit to a gallery in Santa Fe that has an opening of Balthazar's photography. I wanted to either do that, so you'd think he was hot shit, or to take you to his studio for you to see him at work. All sweaty and manly and creative. I felt like at least I owed you that."

I walk another loop around the sculpture, and feel the same sense of the divine in Balthazar's work that I feel in church. Inspired.

"So, you still want to go?" he asks.

I look him dead in the eye and say, clearly, "No, thanks."

"What? I figure you'd like to see old Zar after all this."

"I would," I tell him honestly. "But, no offense, I'd rather see him without you around."

Caspar laughs at this, unhurt as is probably the norm for his type. "Touché," he says. "But what about the gambling cousin?"

"Maggie?"

"The one and only. Word on the street is she's got some serious dough riding on this endeavor."

"How did you know about that?"

"I like a little gamble myself," he says.

"You bet on this?"

"She wouldn't let me. Said it was unethical."

I cannot stop myself from laughing out loud now.

"She'll lose it all if we bail early," he says.

"Do what you do best, and tell her a lie," I say. "Let's tell her we had the best third date ever."

Caspar laughs even louder now, but not so loud that it drowns out the renewed ringing of his cell phone.

"Careful, there, Christy. You keep talking like that, I'm not going to want to let you get away," he says, with utmost apparent sincerity, before turning away from me and taking the call in a loud, exuberant voice, joking around and asking tenderly about the spouse and kid of the next unsuspecting sap he's about to rob blind.

"Don't worry," I mutter with a smile, my finger trailing across Balthazar's bronze. "That decision, counter to the wisdom of desperate single women who write dating books, is not yours alone to make, and, really, I'm just not that into you."

Caspar leaves me at my condo, and contrary to everything they teach you in The Rules, I rush to get my car from the parking garage with the sole intention of surprising Balthazar later in the day, at his photo opening.

I drive to the Uptown mall, get myself a new outfit at Anthropologie. I try to step a bit out of my work mind-set, and opt for a breezy short, full navy blue velvet skirt, with a black sheer long-sleeved top, tight, worn with a belted winter-white jacket with bright geometric patterns on it. I pair this with brown leggings and ankle boots. I top it with a new emerald necklace, large and chunky. Then I hit the M.A.C store for some new makeup.

I go home, shower, get dressed up and fixed up, and then, in the late afternoon, with my copy of The Rules stuffed angrily into my underwear drawer and Julieta Venegas blasting on the iPod, I drive to Santa Fe, thinking about how wrong I've been about The Rules, and wondering about what else I might have been wrong about.

I realize today is January 6, Three Kings Day, and laugh out loud. My Three Kings have brought me gifts, too, I realize, but thankfully they do not involve frankincense, which might have smelled good to people two thousand years ago, but pales in comparison to my favorite Jo Malone candles now.

No, no, I think as I watch the vast, sparse landscape of a winter desert slip past me under a darkening sky.

Melchior reminded me about the value of passion in your life and career, and made me rethink the fact that I gave up my more artistic dreams of painted silk clothing to chase money in interior design for people who don't appreciate it. Perhaps this year I will start to get back into my silk painting. And, yes, Melchior has made me think twice about my inconsistent recycling practices. It really is a very small planet, and we really won't be able to inhabit it much longer if we continue to live the way we have. All the other issues that matter to us won't matter at all if the biggest issue facing us as a species—climate change—is not solved, and quickly.

Caspar made me realize that, yes, I can tend to rush into thinking I like a man, even before I actually know him. My own insecurity and fears of being alone have propelled me to think of myself as the one for sale, and the man as the buyer, when in fact I am also free to decide whether or not I like a man. I am also guilty, I realize (thank you, Caspar) of putting my designer's eye to work when I meet men. Rather than accepting them as they are, I begin to massage here, fix there, tidy up this part and redo that, until in my mind's eye the man is perfect—even though he has not changed one bit. I have realized that my powerful artist's imagination must be reined in completely when dating men, and that they must be seen exactly as they are, no more and no less. Caspar, if I had gotten to know him, if I had waited, say, the three dates required by The Rules (I'll hand this one to them, anyway)—I would have realized that he wasn't the right guy for me. Or, for that matter, for any woman who walks upright and has a pulse.

What I'm not clear on yet is what I have to learn from Balthazar, though it is starting to come through.

The gallery is on Water Street, adobe like all things Santa Fe, and seems elegant as I drive past. The windows are large, the rooms inside well-lighted and crowded with people in fancy clothes, holding glasses of wine as is required at such events. I'm a few minutes late, so I have to park a good eight blocks away, on a side street, and crunch my way through hardened, dirty snow to backtrack.

By the time I step into the gallery, my feet are nearly frozen through. The open room is welcoming and warm, and as I thaw on the outside I realize that a part of me is thawing on the inside, too. This is what I was born for, this place and these people, this environment. It is home for me. Caspar, as horrible as he is, knew this. He saw this in me. He realized something I had refused to see.

I hand my dark red overcoat to the coat check girl in the front hallway, and wander over to the bar that has been set up in the corner of the large room. I scan the room quickly for Balthazar, but cannot find him. I order a glass of red wine, and begin to walk slowly along the edge of the room, looking at the magnificent framed black-and-white photos, some of them small as a postcard, others large as the side of a refrigerator. They are not, as I had somehow assumed, all of barrio life. Rather, the show appears to be a pop culture reworking of classic Greek mythology.

In one photograph, entitled *Theseus,* an arrogant-looking Barack Obama is shown in relief against a white column of the White House, addressing a crowd of reporters whose faces appear sullen and suspicious. From my imperfect recollection of Greek mythology, Theseus was a king who was thought to help the poor, and was well-loved for a time, but who was eventually proved to be more of the same, and eventually reviled. It is a gutsy statement in a liberal town like this, and I wonder what Balthazar's thoughts on the man are.

In another photo, an uncharacteristically makeup-free Missy

Elliott smiles sweetly—a look I have never seen on her—as she talks to two awed little girls she seems to have just run into on the street. Her eyes are focused on the girls, intelligent, happy, soft, unguarded. The title? *Calliope*, the Greek muse of epic poetry. The photo gives me goose bumps, I'm not sure why—probably because there is something very naked and raw about a woman without her makeup and attitude, a peek inside the soul of this very scripted public person.

In yet another photo, ACLU president Anthony Romero is shown posing in a white robe, holding a golden goblet, staring straight into the camera with a dozen rifle butts pointed directly at him, a small grin playing across his face. Caption: *Epicurus*. I am confused by the image.

My thoughts are interrupted by the sound of feedback from a microphone. I turn to face the noise, and find a small clearing has been made at the far end of the room. A woman with frizzy blond hair and the colorful shawl worn by so many arts matrons in Santa Fe takes the mike and introduces Balthazar, informing the crowd that he was recently chosen by *Smithsonian* magazine as one of the twenty rising stars of contemporary art in the nation. She says he has been called the visual Tom Wolfe.

I feel my cheeks burn because of all the unkind thoughts I'd had of him over the past three weeks, and because I had assumed, due to his humility and lack of bragging, that he was a loser.

Then, there he is. Dressed all in black, with his black glasses and—adorable!—a black fedora hat with a white ribbon around it. He takes the microphone from the woman, gives her a hug, smiles to the thunder of applause, looks out across the room with a sheepish smile I have never seen on his face. Then, his eyes find me, and the smile momentarily disappears, replaced by a moment of registered surprise.

To my relief, he smiles again, only bigger, and waves at me, happy to see me here.

ack of fear," Balthazar tells me, as we stand looking at the photo of Anthony Romero.

"I don't get it," I say.

"Well," he gulps down a bit of his beer, his eyes alight with the pleasure that comes only with sharing the work of your heart and soul with someone who cares. "People think Epicurus was all about pleasure, but that's not actually the case. They mistake hedonism with epicurianism."

"So what is Epicurus about, then?"

"Epicurus was about keeping yourself comfortable so that you could conquer your fears."

"Ah," I say. I look at the photo again. I feel Balthazar watching me. I try to look intelligent.

"See, in the past few years, no one has been more fearless, in my opinion, than this guy. He's taken on every scumbag trying to take away our basic rights, and he's done it calmly, through the law, and he's never looked away. Everyone else was tempted to look away, tempted by money, sex, pleasure, violence, whatever got them off, we had a Washington full of hedonists, and here was this guy, the first openly gay head of the ACLU, and the first Latino, staring down the monster, standing up for everything that is truly American, on our behalf. It's like he held the Constitution in his hands, and through the sheer force and will of his spirit, kept them from destroying it altogether. I give him mad props, man."

I look at the photo anew, and feel a sense of shame for not knowing any of this. I do know, however, that the light and shadow, the expression, the exposure, everything is just right. I look at Balthazar and tell him the only thing that makes sense and is true.

"It's beautiful."

After I spent time following Balthazar around the room as he shakes hands and hands out business cards, he takes me to a quiet corner of the gallery and sits on a *banco* with me to ask me why I've come.

I tell him the truth, and I mean the whole truth, about Caspar, and my revelations. He listens calmly, his eyes moving between the floor and my own eyes, nodding his understanding in a way that does not seem to judge me at all. When I have finished telling him about the lessons I believe I've gained from having dated his cousins, he blinks once, slowly, and exhales.

"And me?" he asks. "What lesson have you taken from me?"

I shake my head. "This is where I'm not sure. But I think there's more than one."

He smiles. "That's nice. I like that."

"One, humility," I say.

His brows jump up a tiny bit. "Go on," he says.

"I mean, here you are, a major star, and you never let on. You knew I thought you were some struggling high school teacher, and yet . . ."

He interrupts me. "I am a struggling high school teacher."

"You're a high school teacher, sure, but you're hardly struggling. Caspar showed me your sculpture at the museum, and he told me how much you got for it."

Balthazar laughs. "Of course he did, that shithead."

"So you can't exactly say you're struggling."

"Sure I can," he tells me matter-of-factly. "Who's to say that financial is the only kind of struggle?"

I consider this. "Most Americans," I say.

He nods, but says, "That's the tragedy of the place, don't you think?"

I consider most of my clients, who are financially golden, but struggling to keep some sort of humanity.

I smile at Balthazar.

He smiles back, touches my arm gently, and says, "Which is not to say there aren't people struggling financially, right? Some of them quite close to you, as I recall."

And then it hits me. The lesson I have learned—or am learning at this very moment—from this man, this king, this kindred spirit.

I'm struck with a sudden, urgent sense that I have to leave this place, that, as much as I enjoy art and Balthazar himself, this is not where I am meant to be this night. There will be other nights, many of them spent with him; I know it.

"I'm sorry," I tell him. "I just remembered something. I'm going to have to go."

"Okay," he says, confident and unperturbed. "Thanks for coming. Call me."

I smile and hug him, and say, meaning every non-Rules word of it, "I will. Soon."

It is raining hard outside now, a cold, harsh downpour. I run from the curb to Maggie's front door, and bang because I know the doorbell doesn't work.

Claudia answers the door, big enough to pop, her face droopy and sad and shy. She is due any moment now. She wears a thin SpongeBob nightgown, a little girl's sleeper, and my heart breaks to see her like this. What, I wonder, must she feel right now? Fear? Shame? I look her in the eye, something I realize I have essentially avoided doing since I learned of the pregnancy and was over-whelmed with disappointment and bitterness for her.

"How are you?" I ask her.

She shrugs and starts to turn away from me, a girl so used to rejection she assumes insincerity from me. I stop her with a gentle hand to her shoulder, and take her hand in mine.

"No," I say. "Look at me, sweetie. I mean it. How are you?"

Claudia looks up at me, timid and isolated, in her own pri-vate hell. I smooth a piece of hair back from her eyes and smile at her, love pouring from me in a way I have never felt. It feels good, caring, allowing myself to care. It feels good remembering that my cousin and her family are not much different from me after all. No, wait. They aren't different from me. At all.

"It's going to be alright," I tell her. "I promise you, everything is going to be fine."

"Yeah," she says, a little confused maybe, taken aback by the new expression on my face. I don't think I've ever looked at this girl this way. I hug her, and she comes out of it looking stunned.

I find Maggie, Cesar, and the kids all piled onto the second-hand sofa and lopsided easy chairs in their living room, watching a crime show on television. The light is on overhead, an old fixture whose glow is harsh white and too bright, not soothing at all and all wrong for a family home. I will redo this house for them, at my own expense, I think. I will make it a home. The scent of fried corn tortillas and beef is in the air. On the floor, two dented pots from the kitchen, to catch the fast, hard drips from the leaky ceiling. Everyone is bundled in a jacket or blanket, the heat being off or at a very low setting, to save money.

"Christy!" says Maggie, in shock. She makes as though to get up from the couch, casts and all, and I wave her back down.

"No, don't get up. I'm fine."

"Everything all right?" she asks. She looks frightened, and worried about me, because, of course, I would never have just stopped by in the evening before unless, you know, I needed something urgently, for myself.

"I'm fine, everything's fine. I just stopped by, I, uhm, I wanted to say hello."

Maggie and Cesar share a look of disbelief.

"Yeah, whatever." Maggie starts to get up again. I try to stop her, but now Cesar is up and helping her into the wheelchair. Once seated in it, Maggie waves me to follow her into the bedroom.

"Okay, hold on," I say. Then I go, one by one, through my

three nephews, hugging them hard and long, and telling them how special they are and how proud I am of them and everything they have done and will do. The middle boy needs braces. Maggie had mentioned this a year ago, but he never got them. I need to do something about that, too.

They all stare at me in much the same puzzled way their sister did. I even hug Cesar, a guy I have never even really talked to or made eye contact with because I have assumed him below me and subhuman, if I am totally honest about it.

"Thank you," I tell him.

"For what?" he asks, his eyes wide with shock.

"For loving Maggie. For getting off the streets. For being a father to these kids. For being you, and a good man."

Cesar blinks hard a few times, and if I didn't know better I'd say he was fighting back tears. Then he laughs away his discomfort, a manly man, and says, "Yo, I don't know what you been smokin', but I bet it ain't legal."

I smile at him, overwhelmed with the new me, the me I found in Santa Fe tonight, the one who finally realized that the problem with being Mexican from the South Valley has never been, as I assumed for so long, that I was Mexican from the South Valley; it has been that racists, ethnocentrists, and classists have thought it was a problem and have tried to rob us of our humanity.

The solution has never been to *leave*; the solution has been to *love*.

Ten minutes later, after listening to my little speech about the three kings, and the lessons each gave me, and how I've realized thanks to Balthazar that I have more money than I need, and I really ought to share the rest, Maggie shakes her head back and forth, the way people do when something impossible has happened in front of their eyes.

"Who are you and what have you done to my selfish coco-cousin?" she asks.

I laugh. "It's me, I know it's hard to believe, but it is."

"No," Maggie says, her eyes spilling over with tears, the envelope sitting torn open in her lap. She holds the check in her shaking hand. It is for an amount double what she and Cesar make in a year. "You've gone stone crazy, heina."

"Maybe," I say, feeling light on my feet and happier than I can recall. "But that's yours now. I don't need it."

"Is it Monopoly money, then?" she asks, funny and annoying as ever.

"Deposit it and see. That's the only way to find out for sure."

She looks up at me, sniffling. "But why, *loca?*"

"Because you need it, and I don't, and I love you."

"But it's yours," she says, looking at the check again. "You earned it. That's what you always told me when I suggested you help your parents out. What's the thing you always say? Personal responsibility?"

"Right," I say. "But now I know I was only able to earn it because of you, and them. They're my next stop, by the way. I am personally responsible for you guys. I am sorry I failed to see it before."

"What are you talking about?"

"See, I am who I am because I have known you, and you have loved me, and you've loved me no matter what kind of a horrible bitch I've been. Without you, Maggie, I would not have gone on these dates, or gotten the knowledge they forced me to get about myself."

Maggie is sobbing now, and Cesar comes in to find out what the ruckus is about.

"What is she saying?" he asks Maggie, suspicious. "Did she offend you again?"

Maggie sniffles, and laughs while crying, shaking her head and apparently unable to speak. She hands Cesar the check. He stares at it, then at me.

"What is this for?" he asks me.

"Whatever you need it for," I say. "I'm thinking there are probably some medical bills left over from the accident, and you might want to patch up the roof, then there's tuition for both of you, and—wow, that reminds me. I have no kids of my own. I think I'll start four college funds for the little ragamuffins in the other room. Different money. No worries."

Cesar and Maggie stare at each other in astonishment, a mix of gratitude, disbelief, and shame on their faces. The moment, however, is broken by a terrified wail from the bathroom across the hall.

"Mom! Help me! I'm dying!" cries Claudia, frantic.

Cesar bolts out into the hall, Maggie follows, wheeling herself, and I trail them both, terrified, too.

"What is it?" cries Maggie to the shut bathroom door. "What's wrong?"

Claudia's voice comes from the other side. "Mom! Mom! I thought I was peeing, but it just kept coming out, all this water, and it won't stop, and now my stomach hurts! Mom! Help me! I'm dying! It won't stop coming out!"

Maggie relaxes a bit, rolls her eyes with a relieved smile, and tells Cesar to get the overnight bags ready.

"You're not dying, *hija*," she yells back. "You're having a baby."

We stare at each other now, Maggie and I, while everything changes into high, dramatic gear, with people running for bags, and waddling to the car. I grab my cousin's hand as I wheel her to the Impala through the cold, hard rain, and give it a squeeze. I am surprised to find that hers is trembling.

"You better make that five college funds, Miss freakin' Santa Claus," Maggie calls out to me with false bravado.

"Don't worry," I tell her, with a big hug around her neck and tears in my eyes, before we all head off to the hospital once more. "Seriously, I mean it. Don't worry anymore. It has taken me a while to realize I should have done this, and I've been distracted feeling lonely when I had you guys—my family—all along. But just know this: I've finally got your back.

"Valdes-Rodriguez really shines." —*Sunday Journal*

Amid the **tangle** of freeways and ingrained insecurity, three women try and crack the L.A. code to snare **love** and **success**.

Meet Ricky Biscayne, a **sexy** Latin singing **sensation**, and all the **women** who surround him . . . .

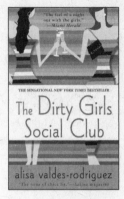

Six **unforgettable** women **dish, dine, whine,** and compare notes as they sort out the **bumpy** course of **life** and **love.**

The Dirty Girls are back, **saucier** and **sexier** than ever . . . but are they any **wiser?**

Why does every man who seems like they might be **the one,** turn out to be **somebody else's?**